The ROMAN MYSTERIES

BOOK XV

The Scribes from Alexandria

CAROLINE LAWRENCE

Orion
Children's Books

First published in Great Britain in 2008
by Orion Children's Books
First published in paperback in Great Britain in 2008
by Orion Children's Books
Reissued in 2012 by Orion Children's Books
a division of the Orion Publishing Group Ltd
Orion House
5 Upper St Martin's Lane
London WC2H 9EA

An Hachette UK company

7

ISBN 978 1 84255 605 4

Printed in Great Britain by Clays Ltd, St Ives plc

The Orion Publishing Group's policy is to use papers that are natural,
renewable and recyclable products made from wood grown in sustainable
forests. The logging and manufacturing processes are expected to
conform to the environmental regulations of the country of origin.

www.romanmysteries.com
www.orionbooks.co.uk

To Nan Rachel Peel
The Scribe from Long Island

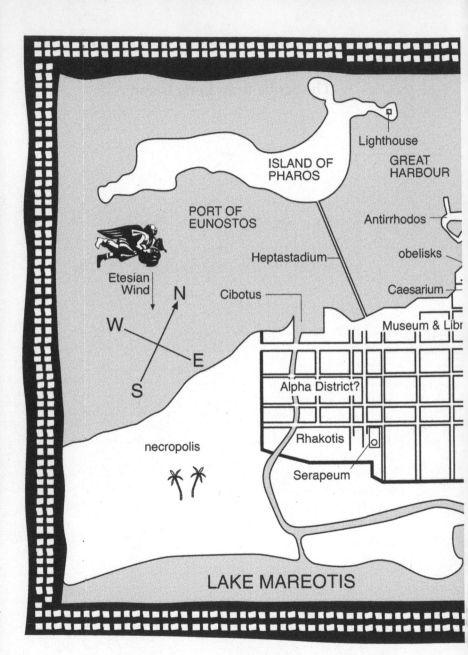

Lighthouse

ISLAND OF PHAROS

GREAT HARBOUR

PORT OF EUNOSTOS

Antirrhodos

Heptastadium

obelisks

Etesian Wind

Cibotus

Caesarium

N

W

E

S

Museum & Libr

Alpha District?

Rhakotis

necropolis

Serapeum

LAKE MAREOTIS

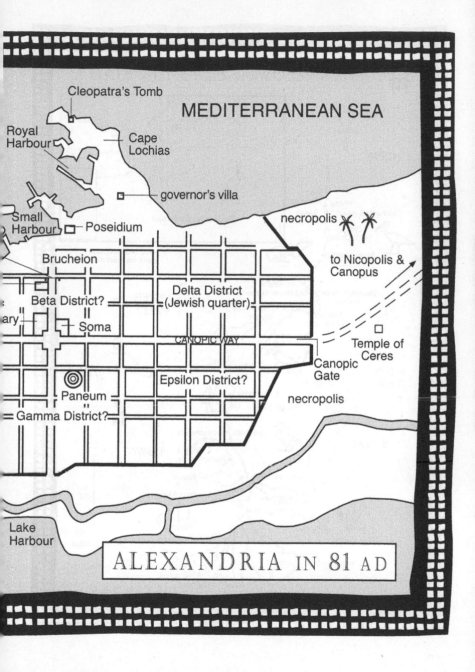

Cleopatra's Tomb

MEDITERRANEAN SEA

Royal Harbour

Cape Lochias

governor's villa

necropolis

Small Harbour

Poseidium

to Nicopolis & Canopus

Brucheion

Delta District (Jewish quarter)

Beta District?

Temple of Ceres

ary

Soma

CANOPIC WAY

Canopic Gate

Epsilon District?

necropolis

Paneum

Gamma District?

Lake Harbour

ALEXANDRIA IN 81 AD

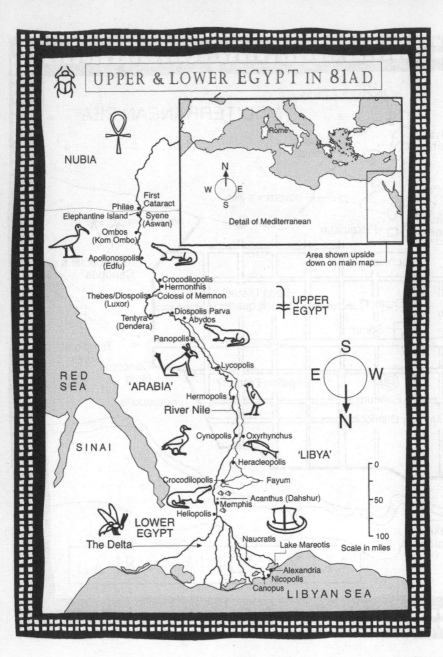

UPPER & LOWER EGYPT IN 81AD

NUBIA

First Cataract
Philae
Elephantine Island
Syene (Aswan)
Ombos (Kom Ombo)
Apollonospolis (Edfu)

Crocodilopolis
Hermonthis
Thebes/Diospolis (Luxor)
Colossi of Memnon
Tentyra (Dendera)
Diospolis Parva
Abydos
Panopolis
Lycopolis

'ARABIA'

Hermopolis

River Nile

Cynopolis
Oxyrhynchus
Heracleopolis

'LIBYA'

RED SEA

SINAI

Crocodilopolis
Fayum
Acanthus (Dahshur)
Memphis
Heliopolis

LOWER EGYPT

The Delta

Naucratis
Lake Mareotis
Alexandria
Nicopolis
Canopus

LIBYAN SEA

UPPER EGYPT

Rome

N
W — E
S

Detail of Mediterranean

Area shown upside down on main map

S
E — W
N

0
50
100
Scale in miles

LATIN ALPHABET IN HIEROGLYPHS

FLAVIA   NUBIA

A		H		O		V
B		I		P		W
C		J		Q		X
D		K		R		Y
E		L		S		Z
F		M		T		KH
G		N		U		SH

hieroglyphs drawn by Caroline

JONATHAN   LUPUS

This story takes place in ancient Roman times, so a few of the words may look strange.

If you don't know them, 'Aristo's Scroll' at the back of the book will tell you what they mean and how to pronounce them.

On the previous pages, you will find a map of Egypt as the Romans saw it and a map of Alexandria. There is also a handy page showing which hieroglyphs correspond with the letters in the alphabet.

SCROLL I

In the black storm-tossed waters of the Libyan Sea, a dark-skinned girl was treading water and fighting for breath.

For three days the sailors had struggled to keep the Roman merchant ship *Tyche* afloat. On the first day they had passed ropes under the ship to hold it together. On the second day they had thrown all the cargo overboard: the priceless elephant tooth, terebinth resin and exotic spices. On the third day the crew had jettisoned the ship's tackle and anything else not nailed down.

At dusk on the third day, a point of light appeared briefly on the southern horizon. It was too low to be a star, so they made for it. Presently it was veiled by a squall. Some time during the night the *Tyche* came to a violent, juddering standstill, and gave a resounding groan. There were a few moments of confusion, punctuated by shouts and screams on deck, where the girl had been huddling with her friends. Torches moved in the darkness but were extinguished as the ship began to break apart and sink.

The girl was tumbled along the deck into the cold black water. The sea heaved and plunged around her. For a moment the clouds parted, and moonlight showed the head of a person in the dark trough of a wave. When she tried to call out, bitter salt water filled her mouth. She clutched a floating spar as it passed, but it was not buoyant enough to support her.

The girl choked as salt water filled her mouth and nose again. She looked around desperately for something to hold on to. After a few moments she saw a large wooden box sliding down a glassy slope of water. From within she heard the roar of a lion, so she let it pass by. She watched it rise up, then plunge out of sight over the crest of a wave. A moment later the fast-moving clouds blotted out the moon and she could barely see in the cold, stinging wetness.

The girl was a strong swimmer, but weakened by three days of seasickness and cold, she knew she could not keep afloat much longer.

'Neptune!' she cried out. 'Help me, Neptune! If you save me . . .' she paused to cough out seawater. 'If you save me, I will give you my most precious possession.'

But even as Nubia uttered the words, she knew it was hopeless.

The next morning dawned misty and mild. The only signs of the previous night's storm were the stunted angry waves hissing up onto the shore.

One of these waves touched the bare foot of a fair-skinned girl lying on the beach. She had lost both sandals, her sky-blue tunic was damp, and her light brown hair unpinned and tangled.

Another wave foamed up around her feet. The girl opened her eyes and saw that she was still clinging to a huge wooden swan's neck ornament, the kind found on the sterns of many Roman merchant ships.

Flavia Gemina released the swan's neck, then pushed

herself up onto one elbow and looked around. The world was colourless, featureless, empty. Nothing but waves and sand and tatters of drifting fog. But at least she was alive. She had held on to the polished wooden swan's neck, and it had kept her afloat.

Flavia offered up a silent thanksgiving. *Thank you, Neptune. Thank you, Venus,* she prayed. *Thank you, Castor and Pollux. And thank you, too, Jupiter, who once took the form of a swan.*

Shakily, Flavia rose to her feet. Keeping the waves on her right, she moved unsteadily towards a vague shape further along the beach. As she came nearer, the object grew darker, more solid, and finally she saw that it was a wooden barrel, embedded at an angle in the sand. She gripped its rim and looked into it. Half a foot of seawater at its bottom, and a tiny fish swimming in it. She raised her eyes and saw another shape further along the shore. This proved to be a broken spar, still attached to a tangle of rope. She left it to investigate a large square object that resolved itself into a wooden box with small slits near the top: a beast-cage. The *Tyche* had been carrying goods from Africa to Rome, including two lions for the arena.

Heart thumping, Flavia moved cautiously towards the cage. It was broken and empty. Had the lion escaped? She examined the sand around the box, but there were no paw prints. Nor were there any further up the beach, beyond the smoothing effect of the waves. *Poor lion,* thought Flavia, staring out to sea. *You never made it to land.*

A noise made her turn her head. Above the hiss of the waves warbled the faint but unmistakable notes of a flute.

'Nubia!' she whispered through parched lips. And then louder: 'Nubia? Is that you?'

The flute ceased abruptly and there was the sound of laughter, muffled by the fog.

'Nubia!' cried Flavia. 'Jonathan! Lupus! Uncle Gaius! Where are you?'

Now she heard a woman's excited voice and she stumbled towards it.

Out of the mist emerged two figures, moving unsteadily towards Flavia.

When the couple saw her, they smiled and waved.

Flavia stopped, and stared in disbelief. The woman wore a golden shift and gilded sandals, and held a silver flute in her hand. She had straight black hair – cut Egyptian-style – and a golden snakehead diadem. Her eyes were lined with black kohl to make them look dramatically exotic, and despite her large nose and strong chin, she was captivating. The man was a Roman officer, but his leather cuirass was of the old-fashioned Republican kind. His curly dark hair was greying at the temples, and it was partly obscured by a garland of ivy leaves, like that worn by the god Dionysus.

They were not survivors from the shipwreck. She had never seen them before. And so it was impossible that Flavia should recognise the couple standing before her.

But she did.

'Cleopatra?' breathed Flavia. 'And Marcus Antonius?'

The woman laughed with delight and clapped her hands. Turning to her handsome companion, she said in Greek: 'What a clever girl! She recognised us.'

'But it can't be,' whispered Flavia. 'You died more than a hundred years ago.'

Suddenly, with a thrill of horror, Flavia noticed the

snake coiled around Cleopatra's arm and the two spots of blood on her neck. And she saw that Antonius's leather cuirass was split and that the tunic beneath it was soaked with blood where he had stabbed himself in the stomach.

The horrible realisation dawned on Flavia. She was not alive. She had not survived the shipwreck. She had drowned.

And now she was in the land of the dead.

The smiling faces of Anthony and Cleopatra began to shrink and speed away from her. She tried to reach out to them, but now they were gone, and everything was black.

SCROLL II

The scent of honeyed wine filled Flavia's head and the sweet, strong taste of it on her tongue made her cough. But it was good, so when the leather nozzle was pressed against her teeth again, she drank greedily.

She heard the woman's bubbling laugh and the man's slurred rebuke in Greek: 'Don't laugh. The poor girl's obviously survived a shipwreck. By the gods, I think I need a drink, too.'

Flavia opened her eyes to see Marcus Antonius sucking at the wineskin. A dribble of amber wine trickled from the corner of his mouth. Cleopatra leant forward to lick it. Antonius responded with a passionate kiss.

Flavia's head thumped back onto the sand.

'Silly man!' giggled Cleopatra. 'You've dropped her.'

Antonius cursed.

Flavia pushed herself up on her elbows and looked at them. 'Am I dead?' she asked in halting Greek. 'Is this the Underworld?'

Cleopatra giggled and Antonius said. 'No, dear girl. It's Canopus.' He took another swig from the wineskin.

'Oh!' cried Cleopatra. 'She thinks she's in Hades, because we're dressed up as dead people.' She turned to Flavia and pulled off her black wig, revealing frizzy brown hair pinned tightly in a bun. 'I'm not really Cleopatra,' she said. 'My name's Myrrhina. Thonis and I have just been to a party. We all had to dress up as famous dead people. They do love the dead here.'

Flavia blinked. 'Here? Where is here?'

'I told you: Canopus!' Myrrhina gave her bubbling laugh. 'Look!' She gestured behind her. The sun was burning off the mist and Flavia could see the red-tiled roofs of seaside villas, fringed by lofty palm trees.

'See that light?' Thonis was pointing towards a yellow star on the horizon.

Flavia nodded.

'That's the great Pharos,' he said. 'The lighthouse.'

Flavia rose unsteadily to her feet and stared at the couple. 'The great Pharos of Alexandria?' she said, and when they both nodded she gasped. 'Great Juno's peacock! I'm in Egypt!'

Thonis was wrapping his red cloak around Flavia when Myrrhina uttered a cry: the early morning mist was clearing and she had spotted something further up the beach.

Flavia followed her gaze and saw a small dark form lying on the sand. It was the naked body of a boy, curled up on his side, facing away from her.

'Lupus!' she cried. She let the cloak fall and stumbled towards him. 'Oh no! It's Lupus!'

'A wolf?' Thonis called after her, his voice still slurred with wine. 'Is it a wolf?'

'No!' cried Flavia over her shoulder. 'It's one of my friends. He was on the ship.'

When she reached the body she fell to her knees and reached out a trembling hand.

7

'Oh, praise Juno!' she sobbed. The boy's body was warm.

Lupus groaned and opened his eyes.

For a moment he blinked up at them, frowning.

'Cover him with your cloak!' cried Flavia, speaking Latin in her excitement. 'And give him some mulsum!' Thonis obviously understood Latin, for he knelt down and wrapped his scarlet cloak around the boy. Then he squirted a few drops of wine into his mouth. Lupus coughed and began to choke. 'No, let him do it himself!' said Flavia. 'He has no tongue and it might go down the wrong way.'

Thonis helped Lupus sit up and let him suck at the skin. After a few moments the boy grunted, put the wineskin on the sand, and pulled the cloak tightly around his body. He was shivering.

'Oh, Lupus!' cried Flavia, giving him a hug. 'Praise the gods you're alive! I think our ship must have hit a sand bar. It broke up so quickly. I was looking for you but it was dark and everyone was shouting and crying and suddenly the mast was falling straight towards me. So I jumped overboard. I found the wooden swan's head and held onto that.'

Lupus nodded and blinked groggily.

'Where was your ship bound for?' asked Thonis.

'Ostia,' said Flavia. 'The port of Rome. We were returning home from Mauretania Tingitana and had just passed through the Pillars of Hercules when a storm caught us and drove us here.'

'Ostia is a long way from Alexandria,' said Myrrhina.

'I know,' said Flavia, and turned to her friend. 'Lupus! We're in Egypt!'

Lupus stared up at her in wide-eyed amazement, then

frowned and wrote in the sand: WHERE ARE OTHERS? He raised his eyebrows questioningly at Flavia.

She shook her head. 'We haven't seen Jonathan or Nubia. Or Uncle Gaius. But if we survived there's a good chance they did, too.'

Lupus grunted, took another squirt of wine, then handed the skin up to Thonis with a nod of thanks.

Flavia stood up so that she could help Lupus to his feet, but the world suddenly tipped on its side.

'Ohe!' cried Thonis, catching her and setting her upright. '*Festina lente!* You've just survived a shipwreck.'

Myrrhina slipped a warm arm around Flavia's shoulders as Thonis helped Lupus to his feet.

'Lupus,' said Flavia. 'Meet Thonis and Myrrhina. They were at a fancy dress party at one of those big villas beyond the palm trees. They're going to help us.' She turned to the woman. 'You'll help us, won't you?' she said in Greek.

'Of course we will,' said Myrrhina.

Thonis added, 'We'll help you find your other friends and then I can take you into Alexandria. I live there. From there you can get a ship to Rome.'

'Oh thank you!' cried Flavia. 'My father's a sea captain and he might even be in Alexandria. He was due to sail there at the beginning of March. What day is it today?'

'The Nones of May,' said Thonis.

Lupus grunted and pointed further down the beach.

'Oh! Look!' cried Flavia. 'There's someone else! Is it Uncle Gaius?'

The four of them ran towards a man lying on the beach.

9

'Great Juno!' cried Flavia. 'It's the captain! His eyes are still open but ...'

Lupus nodded and drew the side of his hand across his neck.

'Oh!' whispered Flavia.

Myrrhina uttered a cry of dismay and buried her face in Thonis's shoulder. 'There's a little crab crawling in his beard!' came her muffled voice.

Flavia averted her eyes from the corpse, and as she did so, she saw another couple coming towards them from the direction of the villas.

The man wore only a stiff linen kilt and a jackal mask which completely covered his head and shoulders. The woman wore a curious outfit made of strips of white cloth, like a dead person's shroud, leaving only her dark eyes visible.

Lupus stared in disbelief and Flavia made the sign against evil.

'Don't be alarmed,' said Thonis, taking a suck from his wineskin. 'It's only Diomedes and Obelliana. They came to the party dressed as Anubis and a mummy.'

Like Thonis and Myrrhina, the couple had obviously been up all night drinking, for they staggered and giggled as they came to meet their friends.

'Oooh!' slurred the woman in swaddling clothes. 'Who are these?' She looked from Flavia to Lupus to the captain's body. Then her kohl-lined eyes widened in horror at the sight of the dead man, and she began to scream.

SCROLL III

An hour later, Lupus and Flavia stood watching the bodies of four men burn on a pyre of dried palm fronds. The man in the dog-headed mask had taken away the screaming woman and gone to get help. The rich hostess of the party – a woman named Isidora – had arrived with four muscular slaves. She was dressed as Queen Dido, with a tower of golden curls and a bloody stola. She had taken charge immediately, sending her slaves to search the beach. They had found the bodies of three crewmembers, in addition to the captain, and were still looking for other survivors.

As Lupus watched the blackening bodies shiver in the flames, he remembered another pyre on another beach, and the burning body of the man who had cut out his tongue. Then his eyes focussed on the figures standing on the other side of the pyre. Isidora was having a quiet discussion with Thonis and Myrrhina. She was shaking her head, as if to say: no hope.

Lupus felt a tap on his shoulder.

Turning, he saw a boy with dark curly hair and warm brown eyes smiling weakly at him. The boy was wheezing and holding a damp herb pouch under his nose.

Lupus's cloak fell to the sand as he threw his arms around his friend.

'Ohe!' said Jonathan. 'More than I want to see!' He grinned and bent to retrieve Lupus's cloak.

'Oh, Jonathan!' cried Flavia, and threw her arms around him. 'Praise the gods! You're alive! Have you seen Nubia? Or Uncle Gaius?'

Jonathan shook his head. 'I'm sorry,' he wheezed, 'I haven't seen either of them.' I woke up on the beach and I saw the smoke. He looked around. 'Where are we?'

'Canopus, a town in Egypt.'

Lupus nodded vigorously, pointed towards the south-east and grunted.

Flavia explained: 'See that star with the smudge above it, where Lupus is pointing? That's the fire and smoke from the lighthouse of Alexandria.'

'Master of the Universe!' Jonathan squinted towards the distant lighthouse, then turned back to them and lowered his voice. 'Who are those people?' he said. 'Actors? Mimes?'

Lupus imitated someone drinking from a wineskin and swayed on his feet, as if tipsy.

'They're revellers from a party at one of those villas,' whispered Flavia. 'Some of them are a bit drunk and they all speak Greek, but they've been kind to us. The couple dressed up as Anthony and Cleopatra found me, and the lady with blonde hair is Isidora, the hostess. They've been helping us look for bodies. You can see we found the captain and three crewmembers, including that nice Phoenician who always used to let Lupus win at dice.'

'Well, there's nobody back that way,' said Jonathan quietly. 'Only the dead body of one of the lions.'

'How did you survive?' asked Flavia.

'Barrel,' said Jonathan. 'I held on to a barrel of something. When it broke apart I thought I was dead. Then I felt the bottom of the sea under my feet and I managed to walk ashore.'

'I know,' said Flavia. 'I think it's very shallow for a long way out. That's why the ship was wrecked. It ran aground.'

'Who's this?' said Thonis in Latin, coming up to them with Myrrhina and Isidora close behind. Lupus noted that although his eyes were still bloodshot, his speech was no longer slurred.

'This is our friend Jonathan ben Mordecai,' said Flavia. 'He was with us on the *Tyche*.'

Thonis handed Jonathan his wine skin. 'Here, have some wine. It's from the vineyards of Lake Mareotis, and the finest in the region.' While Jonathan drank, Lupus heard Thonis whisper to Myrrhina in rapid Greek. 'The *Tyche* – "Good Fortune". Ironic, eh? But the gods have certainly favoured these three.'

Lupus did not let on that he understood Greek perfectly. Instead he turned to Flavia and imitated someone playing a flute.

Flavia nodded at him and turned to Thonis. 'We still need to find our friend Nubia. And my uncle.'

Lupus saw her eyes fill with tears, and he patted her on the back. But his attempt to comfort her did not have the desired effect: Flavia began to cry. Myrrhina took Flavia in her arms and whispered soothing words in Greek.

Thonis turned to the woman dressed as Queen Dido. 'Isidora,' he said. 'These children are exhausted. They need food and water and sleep. Can you help them?'

'Of course,' she said. 'Lampon and Pindarus went

home at dawn. I'll have another bed brought in and the children can stay in that room.'

Thonis turned back to Lupus and Jonathan. 'You children go with Isidora and get some food and rest. Don't worry about your missing friend or your uncle. Isidora's slaves are scouring the beach. If they survived, we'll find them.'

SCROLL IV

The next morning, Jonathan and his two friends found themselves riding along the coastal road in a two-horse chariot. They had given the beach a final search at dawn, but found no more survivors or bodies. Now Thonis was driving them into Alexandria.

'Great Juno's beard!' said Jonathan, gazing at the smudge of smoke on the blue horizon before them. 'Is that the Pharos? How far away is it?'

'About fifty stades,' said Thonis. He was dressed in the Greek fashion, in a cream tunic and blue chlamys. His curly hair was anointed with expensive oil of terebinth and Jonathan could smell its distinctive sweet turpentine scent.

'How far is fifty stades in miles?' asked Flavia, raising her voice to be heard above the clopping of the horses' hooves.

Lupus held up his left hand – fingers spread – and his right forefinger.

'You think six miles?' Jonathan asked him. Lupus nodded.

Thonis said over his shoulder. 'That's right. If you reckon eight stades to a mile.'

'The Pharos must be enormous if you can see its smoke six miles away,' said Jonathan.

Thonis chucked. 'It's five hundred feet tall. And it's not actually called the Pharos. That's the name—'

'—of the island on which it's built!' interrupted Flavia. 'I know that from Pliny's *Natural History*,' she added. 'And I also know that it's considered one of the Seven Sights of the world.'

'Ehem!' laughed Thonis. 'Well, well! You children are quite the little scholars, aren't you?' The beat of the horses' hooves quickened as he whipped them into a gallop.

Lupus whooped and punched his fist in the air.

'Enjoying your chariot ride?' said Thonis.

'We've been in a chariot before,' shouted Flavia over the clatter of hooves. 'In the Circus Maximus!'

'But we've never travelled in one,' added Jonathan. 'At home we usually catch a slow mule-cart into Rome.'

Thonis nodded and called over his shoulder. 'Here in Alexandria everybody who's anybody drives a chariot.'

'How do you make the wheels run so smoothly and quietly?' asked Jonathan.

'Look for yourself,' said Thonis. 'See the palm fibre padding, woven around the wooden wheel? Very tough and durable. The slaves only have to replace it every few weeks.'

'Is that Alexandria?' asked Flavia, pointing to a cluster of gleaming marble buildings coming up on their left.

'Nicopolis,' said Thonis, reining in the horses to a trot. 'It was there that Octavian forced Anthony to kill himself. Octavian called it Nicopolis after his victory. He hoped it would rival Alexandria. See the theatre? He built that and a stadium, and a fort big enough for two legions. Most of the Roman officials and merchants live there,' he added.

They passed the town of Nicopolis, and as they reached its further outskirts, Thonis pointed to a high-walled building behind a grove of palm trees. 'There! Do you see the Roman fort?'

Jonathan nodded. He could see the sentries on the walls. Above the rhythmic clop of the horses' hooves he thought he could hear the distinctive clank of a cohort of men performing manoeuvres inside.

The road curved away from the coast and took them south through shaggy palm groves. Jonathan caught glimpses of a city wall through gaps in the palms. Alexandria's town walls were built of massive hewn blocks of pale yellow limestone, with semi-circular towers every hundred and fifty feet. As in Ostia, tombs lined the road, but unlike those in Ostia, many were adorned with sphinxes and the strange coloured picture writing of the Egyptians.

'That's the Temple of Ceres,' said Thonis, gesturing towards a massive Graeco-Roman temple that lay outside the city walls. 'Wheat is Egypt's wealth, you know, so Ceres is an important goddess.'

'We know,' said Flavia. 'Ostia's granaries are full of Egyptian wheat and we worship Ceres, too.'

At last they came within sight of a massive arch in the city wall, flanked by Roman soldiers acting as guards. There were some carts and another chariot in front of them, waiting to enter the city.

'This is the Canopic Gate,' said Thonis as he slowed the horses to a walk. 'Entrance to the most beautiful city in the world.'

'Look at that tomb, Jonathan!' said Flavia pointing. They were moving slowly enough to read the inscription. 'The epitaph's in Hebrew, isn't it? Sh-moo-ell,' she read haltingly, then looked at Jonathan bright-eyed. 'Samuel! That means Samuel!'

'Yes,' said Jonathan. 'And that next one's in Greek. It's Jewish too. In fact, most of the tombs here seem to be Jewish.'

'There are more Jews here in Alexandria,' said Thonis, 'than there are in Rome. That's why there are so many Jewish graves here in this necropolis. The gate up ahead leads right into the Delta District, where most of the Jews live.'

They had reached the gate now and he reined in the horses as a guard clanked over to them.

'I am Thonis son of Sabbios,' said Thonis to the guard. 'A cloth merchant, with a workshop in the Gamma District and a warehouse in the Brucheion. These children have been shipwrecked. I'm taking them to see the authorities.'

The guard shook his head. 'How do I know these aren't slaves you want to sell at the market, trying to avoid the slave tax?'

'We're freeborn,' said Flavia. 'Look! Jonathan and I have imperial passes.' She pulled out a small ivory lozenge on a cord around her neck. Jonathan pulled his out, too.

The guard's eyes grew wide. 'I've never seen children wearing these,' he said, 'but they seem genuine.' He shrugged, gave a cursory glance into the back of the chariot, then waved them on.

'Where in the world did you get those?' asked Thonis, as he flicked his team into motion.

'We told you at Isidora's,' said Flavia. 'We were on a mission for the Emperor Titus. He gave them to us.'

Thonis looked over his shoulder at Lupus. 'Don't you have one?'

Lupus nodded, then pointed towards the sea and shrugged.

'He must have lost his in the shipwreck,' explained Flavia.

'Too bad,' said Thonis. 'They're worth a small fortune. Especially the ivory ones, like yours.'

'Don't we have to get out and walk now?' asked Jonathan, as they passed under the massive arch of the city gate.

'Whatever for?'

'In Rome they don't allow wheeled traffic during the hours of daylight.'

Thonis chuckled and pointed with his chin, 'That's because the streets of Rome are not one hundred feet wide.'

'Great Juno's beard!' exclaimed Jonathan, as they finally emerged from beneath the arch. 'It's amazing!'

'It's amazing!' Flavia echoed Jonathan's words as they passed through the arch of the Canopic gate. The broad, granite-paved boulevard was lined with lofty palm trees. In the centre was a narrow central barrier studded with obelisks, statues and sphinxes. 'I've never seen a street so wide,' cried Flavia. 'Or so long. You can see straight ahead for miles!'

'Three miles to be exact,' said Thonis proudly.

Lupus grunted and pointed at the dazzling white lighthouse rearing up ahead of them and to their right, its plume of smoke dark against the clear blue sky of mid-morning.

'Oooh!' they all breathed.

'And look at the buildings either side,' said Jonathan. 'And the colonnades that never seem to end.'

Flavia nodded. 'This big street reminds me of the Circus Maximus.'

'You're right,' agreed Jonathan. 'Look, they've even divided it into two lanes. So you've got your fast-moving chariots and horses in the central lane, closest to the barrier. Then you have your carts and camels and donkeys in the slow outside lane. And a pavement either side for pedestrians and sedan-chairs and litters.'

'What's that conical green hill rising above the roofs?' Flavia pointed towards the south. 'It looks like one of the turning posts of a racecourse, only fatter.'

'That's the Paneum,' said Thonis over his shoulder. 'It's a man-made hill and sanctuary to the god Pan. And this big street we're driving down is called the Canopic Way. See the double colonnade on either side? The most expensive shops in Alexandria are to be found along this boulevard. You can buy goods made of brass, copper, bronze, Corinthian bronze, iron, gold, silver, tin. And there are special markets for glass, ivory, tortoiseshell and rhinoceros horn. You can purchase wine, olive oil, sesame oil, honey, wheat, and perfume. My friend Lampon owns a papyrus factory down that side street.' He gestured to the left. 'You name it. We've got it.'

Flavia gazed at green canvas awnings casting emerald light over stalls full of coloured cones of spices and sacks of dry goods. Most of the pedestrians here were bearded with the skullcaps that marked them as Jewish. But she also saw clean-shaven, turban-wearing Egyptians, ebony-black Ethiopians, olive-skinned Greeks and even some red-bearded Gauls. There were women, too, walking in groups or pairs, most of them heavily veiled but one or two carrying parasols with their faces exposed in the Roman way. Men as well as women wore long loose tunics, like the one Isidora had given to Flavia.

Lupus grunted and pointed at a handsome youth in a short tunic the colour of papyrus. He was scooping up something with a wooden paddle and putting it in a hempen bag slung round his shoulder.

'What's he doing?' asked Flavia.

Lupus pointed to his bottom and held his nose.

'He's collecting dung?' said Jonathan.

Lupus nodded and grinned.

Thonis chuckled. 'Lupus is right,' he said. 'That's one of our official street-cleaners. The town council pays them a few coppers from public taxes and they supplement their income by selling dung to farmers and market gardeners outside the city.'

'Now that you mention it,' said Jonathan, 'the streets are very clean.'

'We also have our own vigiles,' said Thonis, 'though fires are rare in a city of marble like this. And then there are the men who maintain the fire on the Pharos. Even the scholars and scribes of the Great Library are paid from public taxes.'

'Speaking of the Great Library,' said Flavia, 'where is it?'

'You can't actually see it,' said Thonis. 'It's part of the Museum. The Museum is the centre of all knowledge in the world.' Suddenly Thonis cursed and reined in his team as a little boy in a grubby loincloth chased a black cat across the Canopic Way. The boy almost went under the hooves of their horses, but managed to scamper to safety, sweeping his cat under one arm and making a rude gesture at them with his other.

Lupus gestured back and Flavia laughed to see the two boys grinning at each other. The boy in the loincloth scrambled up onto a small granite sphinx on the central barrier and straddled it like a horse. He waved as the chariot moved forward again. Flavia turned to watch him.

'That boy's cat is wearing a jewelled collar,' she remarked. 'It's better dressed than he is.'

'It's probably not his cat,' said Thonis. 'Probably belongs to one of the temples in the Beta District up ahead,' he added.

'Maybe he's going to steal the jewels from the cat's collar,' said Jonathan.

'They'd execute him if he did,' said Thonis. 'Cats are sacred here in Egypt. The penalty for hurting one – or even robbing one – is death.'

Jonathan and Lupus exchanged looks of wide-eyed amazement but Flavia had caught sight of something up ahead: 'Oh!' she cried. 'What's that amazing building with the coloured columns and dome?'

'That is the Soma, where the mummified body of Alexander the Great lies in a sarcophagus made of granite and glass. They say when Octavian Augustus went to view it a hundred years ago he couldn't resist touching the nose.'

'What happened?' asked Jonathan.

'What do you think?' said Thonis with a laugh. 'He broke Alexander's nose. Would you like to see it?'

Lupus tugged Flavia's long tunic and nodded enthusiastically.

'Yes,' said Flavia. 'We would love to see the noseless and mummified corpse of Alexander the Great. But first—'

'I know, I know,' interrupted Thonis. 'You want to visit the harbour-master to see if your father is still here in port.'

'But even before that,' said Flavia. 'We must visit the temple of Neptune and thank him properly for saving us. I don't want to make the same mistake Menelaus made when he was here.'

'Ah, yes,' said Thonis, and quoted: *Although I was anxious to return, the gods kept me in Egypt because I failed to offer the proper sacrifice . . .*

SCROLL V

The Soma and the Museum marked the great cross-roads of Alexandria, and as they turned right towards the lighthouse and the harbour, a deliciously cool breeze touched Jonathan's face and ruffled his long, brown tunic.

'Feel that?' said Thonis over his shoulder. 'That's the Etesian Wind, the secret of this city's success. Alexander's architects planned the street grid so that half the streets face northwest, perfectly aligned to catch that wonderful zephyr that blows all summer. It keeps the city cool and fresh and free of pestilence.'

'It's lovely,' said Flavia, and Lupus nodded his agreement.

Jonathan nodded, too, but now he was gazing at the buildings and colonnades on either side. If anything, this street was more impressive than the Canopic Way.

'Is this street also a hundred feet wide?' he asked Thonis.

'Yes, it is.'

'And how tall are those obelisks?' he said, pointing towards the end of the boulevard, where two obelisks stood.

'About eighty or ninety feet high, I'd guess,' replied Thonis.

'They're just like the one in the Circus Maximus,' said Flavia. 'I wonder if they have those funny pictures on it.'

'Hieroglyphs,' said Thonis. 'Holy writing of the Egyptians.'

Jonathan was gazing at a marble theatre when he felt Lupus tug his tunic and heard Flavia gasp.

He turned to see a dazzling building come into view on their left, near the two obelisks.

'Master of the Universe,' he breathed. 'It's made of gold and silver.'

'That is the Caesarium,' said Thonis. 'A temple begun by Cleopatra in honour of Marcus Antonius, but finished by Octavian Augustus who then dedicated it to himself. Inside are hidden courtyards, colonnades, gardens and even a library.'

'*The* Library?' asked Flavia eagerly. 'The world-famous one?'

'No. I told you: that's in the Museum, back at the crossroads, near the Soma. The Museum is even bigger than the Caesarium. It also has hidden gardens and courtyards, but it's not gilded.'

As they passed between the twin obelisks at the end of the boulevard, Jonathan's jaw dropped. A massive harbour lay before them, with a hundred white sails against the sapphire-blue water.

'Look at that harbour!' he exclaimed. 'It's even bigger than the one at Portus or Rhodes.'

Thonis looked pleased. 'There are actually five sea harbours here. Eunostus and Cibotus to the west, and this eastern harbour: also called the Great Harbour.'

'You said five,' observed Jonathan.

'Yes. That small island straight ahead – the one shaped like a crescent moon – is called Antirrhodos. It's like a miniature Rhodes. The little harbour between it and us is the Small Harbour. And over there to the right is the Royal Harbour. In the old days you were only allowed to use it if you were a Ptolemy.' He pointed to the right. 'That green promontory beyond the warehouses is called Lochias. It forms the eastern extremity of the Great Harbour. You can see roofs of the Ptolemaic palaces among the palms and cypress trees. Cleopatra's tomb is there, too.'

'Cleopatra!' breathed Flavia.

'Over there to the west, do you see that causeway that looks like an aqueduct? That is the Heptastadium. It leads from the city to Pharos, the island straight ahead of us. It carries water as well as people, and as you can see, ships are able to sail through its arches.'

'And it's over half a mile long?' asked Flavia.

'Of course,' murmured Jonathan. 'Hepta means seven, and a stade is a unit of distance. Eight stades to a mile . . .'

Lupus grunted and pointed towards a temple overlooking the Small Harbour. It had massive columns of red granite.

Thonis nodded at Lupus. 'That's the Poseidium, where we're going now,' he said. 'The Temple of Neptune. Or Poseidon as we call him in Greek.' He flicked the team into motion and the chariot moved smoothly forward.

Jonathan inhaled the fresh sea air and looked up at the gulls wheeling above him in the bright bowl of the sky. On his right were bustling warehouses and to his left the dark blue harbour with its myriad white sails and towering lighthouse.

From somewhere deep within him rose a strange,

sweet sensation. It took him a moment to identify it and when he did, the revelation came as a shock.

It was joy.

Flavia and the boys followed Thonis up the marble steps of the Temple of Poseidon.

'Are you ready to cut off your hair, Lupus?' asked Flavia. 'It is the proper sacrifice for when you survive a shipwreck.'

Lupus shrugged, then nodded.

'And you, Jonathan?' She gave his hair an affectionate tousle. 'Are you going to cut off all those curly locks?'

Jonathan grinned. 'When in Rome . . .'

She gave him a quizzical look. 'Are you all right?' she added. 'You have a strange look on your face.'

'I'm fine,' he said. 'In fact . . .' His voice trailed off as they entered the temple and their footsteps echoed in the vast, cool space.

Before them sat the cult statue of Neptune. It was carved of polished black granite, which made it look as if the god had just emerged dripping from the sea. In one hand he held a bronze trident and the other was open in a gesture of acceptance. His bearded face was noble, his expression kind.

'Master of the Universe!' whispered Jonathan beside Flavia. 'What are all those things on the walls? Are they all votive plaques?'

Flavia turned to look at the walls, which glinted with a thousand copper plaques and other objects. She moved towards the right hand wall.

'Yes!' she exclaimed softly. 'They're thanks offerings. Look! Rings, necklaces, a sandal . . . and each one beneath a plaque. Oh! This one's in Latin. It says: *I,*

27

*Horatius, thank you Neptune – Master of Storms – for saving
me from the foamy brine. To you I dedicate my sodden clothes,
my only remaining possession.'*

'This one's in Aramaic,' said Jonathan. 'The poor man
washed up naked on the beach. All he had to give was
his hair.'

'Maybe that's how the custom began,' mused Flavia.
'A shipwrecked man wanted to thank Neptune but didn't
have anything to give except his hair.'

'Where *is* all the hair?' said Jonathan, scanning the
wall. 'Why haven't they hung it up?'

'We burn it as a thanks offering to the god,' said a
voice behind them in Greek-accented Latin.

They all turned to see the priest standing benignly
before them. He was clean-shaven with short curly hair
and the olive complexion Flavia had come to recognise
as Greek. He wore a floor-length robe of pale blue linen
and around his head was a simple gold band.

The priest smiled. 'Hair begins to smell after a time.
We wouldn't want to offend the god.'

'No,' said Jonathan. 'We wouldn't want that.'

'How may I help you?' said the priest.

'These children were shipwrecked,' said Thonis.
'They want to make the proper sacrifice of thanks.'

'Yes,' said Flavia. 'Neptune saved us and we want to
dedicate our hair to him.'

The priest nodded gravely. 'We've had a few wrecks
recently,' he said. 'That recent storm was most
unseasonable.'

'Oh dear,' murmured Flavia. 'I hope pater is safe.'

Behind them Lupus gave an urgent grunt of
excitement.

'What is it, Lupus?' cried Flavia, turning.

Lupus pointed excitedly at a bright copper plaque. Beneath it hung a cherry-wood flute. It was swollen by the sea, but still recognisable.

'Is it hers?' gasped Flavia, and when Lupus gave a nod, Flavia could not contain a sob of joy. 'Oh thank you, Neptune!' she cried.

Jonathan hurried to stand behind Lupus. He leant forward to read the inscription on the plaque. '*I, Nubia,*' he read, '*daughter of Nastasen of the Leopard Clan, dedicate this my most precious possession to you, Neptune, and also to the dolphin who saved my life.*'

SCROLL VI

'Praise Juno!' whispered Flavia, for the dozenth time. 'Nubia's alive! A dolphin carried her to safety.'

Flavia was sitting in a curtained-off section of the temple, letting the barber priest cut her hair.

Jonathan and Lupus had gone first. The barber had cut their hair, then shaved their heads, but he had promised Flavia he would not be so drastic with her. 'I cut below ears,' he had said, 'with fringe of hair at front. In Egyptian style. As you request.'

The curtain parted and the boys appeared, looking strangely vulnerable with their bald heads. Thonis came in behind them.

'Sorry, Flavia,' said Jonathan. 'We didn't see any other plaques from anybody from the *Tyche*. There was another wreck that same night, but it was a different ship. The priest says apart from Nubia and the three of us, there have been no other survivors from our ship. So far.'

'No Uncle Gaius?' whispered Flavia, feeling tears welling up.

'I'm sorry,' whispered Jonathan.

'Don't despair,' said Thonis with a forced smile. 'Perhaps he made his thanks offering at another temple.'

'But Uncle Gaius couldn't swim,' said Flavia. 'Lupus

taught us last summer. But he never taught Uncle Gaius.'

'Oh,' said Thonis, his smile fading. 'Oh. I see.'

'And Nubia may be alive,' murmured Flavia, 'but we don't even know where she is.'

'I know where Nubia is,' said the barber priest behind her.

Flavia twisted to look at him.

'Careful!' he said with a smile. 'These shears are very sharp.'

'You know where our friend Nubia is?'

'She is dark-skinned? About your age? With gold-brown eyes? From the merchant ship *Tyche*?'

'Yes!' cried Flavia. 'That's her! Where is she?'

'I do not know where, but I know with whom,' he replied.

'Tell us!'

'She went with a eunuch.'

'Eunuch?' gasped Flavia. 'A *eunuch*?'

Thonis turned to Flavia. 'A eunuch is a man who's had his—'

'I know what a eunuch is!' interrupted Flavia, and turned back to the priest.

The priest nodded.

'But who? Why? Where?'

'I do not know,' said the priest. 'All I know is that the Nubian girl who dedicated her flute came to the temple in the company of a eunuch. He was wearing a pale yellow tunic with black edging on the hem and sleeves.'

'A scribe!' exclaimed Thonis.

'Yes,' said the priest.

'What?' said Flavia and Jonathan together.

'A scribe from the Library,' said Thonis. 'The scribes and scholars who work at the Great Library all wear a special livery. Scribes wear yellow trimmed with black and scholars wear black trimmed with yellow. They say the pale yellow represents papyrus and the black stands for ink,' he added.

'What was the scribe's name?' Flavia asked the priest.

'I do not know. All I know is that they came in together and after she made her dedication they departed together. I know her name because of the plaque, but I do not know his name.'

'Did she seem . . . afraid?' asked Flavia. 'I mean, you don't think the scribe kidnapped her, do you?'

'She did not seem afraid,' said the priest carefully. 'But she seemed very sad. Her eyes were red and swollen, as if she had been crying. She asked me if there had been any other survivors from *Tyche*, but at that time there had not. I told her to check back here regularly. Oh! I remember she said to her friend "There's nothing for me here. I will go with you after all."'

'Go?' cried Flavia. 'Go where?'

'I am sorry,' said the priest with an apologetic smile, 'that I do not know.'

An hour later the three friends and Thonis stood in the office of the harbour-master who dealt with non-imperial merchant ships.

'The merchant ship *Delphina* set sail for Ostia ten days ago,' said the man in Greek-accented Latin. 'It was captained by one Marcus Flavius Geminus, and its cargo consisted of linen, papyrus and glassware.'

Flavia felt a strange mixture of happiness and disappointment.

'Rejoice!' said Thonis. 'Your father is alive and well.'

'And probably back in Ostia by now,' said Flavia

glumly. 'He'll find out that I disobeyed his command to not set one foot outside the house.'

Lupus gave Flavia his wry 'you're-in-trouble-now' look.

Jonathan nodded. 'Maybe it's just as well we missed him,' he said.

Flavia took a deep breath and turned to address the harbour-master. 'Jonathan and I have imperial passes from the Emperor Titus.' She took the ivory pass out from beneath the neck of her tunic.

The harbour-master examined it and his eyebrows went up. 'This allows you to withdraw the equivalent of ten thousand sesterces at any town big enough to have a Capitolium,' he said. 'You may also claim food and lodging at Imperial Way Stations. And free passage on any ship. I suggest you go straight to the governor with these.'

Thonis gave a low whistle. 'You could sail to Ostia today,' he said.

Flavia glanced at the boys. They nodded back at her and she turned to Thonis. 'We're not going back to Ostia,' she said. 'Not until we've found our friend Nubia.'

On the way to the governor's villa, Thonis stopped at one of his warehouses and gave Lupus and Jonathan turbans of fine linen, indigo blue for Jonathan and turquoise for Lupus. To Flavia he gave a blue silk palla with a fringe of three colours: orange, dark blue and light blue.

At the governor's villa, the three friends waited while Thonis explained the situation in rapid Greek to a young door-slave not much older than Jonathan. Presently the youth ushered them into a tablinum with frescoed walls and an alabaster floor.

At the far end of the tablinum a middle-aged man sat at a marble desk which was flanked by sphinxes with the heads of Titus and Domitian. The official was writing on a sheet of papyrus and did not look up for some time. As the friends waited, Lupus scanned the room with interest. The walls were decorated with frescoes depicting some of the animal-headed gods of the Egyptians. Lupus wondered if any of their gods were half man and half wolf.

'I am Faustus.' The man looked up at them with heavy-lidded eyes. 'What can I do for you?'

Thonis stepped forward and quickly explained the matter to the official in Greek. Unlike Flavia and Jonathan, Lupus was fluent in Greek and although the two men were speaking with Alexandrian accents, he could understand every word.

'Shipwrecked?' the official was saying.

'Yes, and they appear to be the only survivors. Apparently a girl called Nubia was with them. They believe she also survived but have not been able to locate her.'

'Nubia?' said the official. 'I've read that name recently. Do they understand Greek?'

'Only the basics,' said Thonis in a low voice. 'And only if spoken slowly and clearly. They're Roman.'

The man turned back to Lupus and his friends. 'May I see your imperial passes?' he asked in Latin.

Flavia and Jonathan pulled the ivory tags from around their necks and handed them to the official. Lupus shrugged and opened his hands to the sky, to show he did not have one.

Faustus examined Flavia's pass first. 'Ah!' he said,

turning it over and reading the name on the back. 'You are Flavia Gemina?'

'That's right,' said Flavia. 'Daughter of Marcus Flavius Geminus, sea captain.'

Lupus moved over to the right hand wall to have a closer look. There was an interesting creature painted there: it had the body of a hippo and the head of a crocodile.

'And Jonathan ben Mordecai,' came Faustus's voice behind him. 'A Jew, I take it. And the younger boy?'

'That one is mute. He had an imperial pass, too, but it was lost in the wreck. His name is Lupus.'

'Fine, fine,' said the official in Latin and then, in low rapid Greek: 'I recently had a missive from an official in Sabratha about four children wanted by someone very high up. I'm certain the name Nubia was on the list. The others, too. But I'll need to check. Can you delay them for a day and bring them back tomorrow morning?'

Lupus stiffened and resisted the urge to look around. Because he was mute, people often assumed he was deaf. And neither Thonis nor the official suspected he was a fluent Greek speaker.

'I'll make it worth your while,' said Faustus in a low voice, still in Greek. 'There's a big reward. Very big.'

'Yes,' said Thonis after a short pause. 'Of course.'

Lupus moved on to the next fresco, pretending to be engrossed in the pictures.

'Do you have the documentation to go with these passes?' said Faustus in Latin.

'No,' came Flavia's stammered reply. 'How could we have documentation? We were shipwrecked!'

'The only reason we still have those passes,' added

Jonathan, 'is that we were wearing them around our necks.'

'Well, I'll have to keep these passes overnight so that my scribes can draw up new documentation. In the meantime, I can advance you some spending money – say ten drachmae each – enough for your night's lodging. You can come back tomorrow to collect the rest of your gold along with your passes.'

'But the Emperor told us not to let them out of our sight,' protested Flavia. 'In fact he told us never to take them off.'

'I'll give you a receipt. Come back tomorrow before noon and I'll give you back your passes and the equivalent in gold of twenty thousand sesterces.'

'Don't worry,' said Thonis to Flavia. 'That's how things are done here in Alexandria. You can't blow your nose without filling out a form. You'll get your money.'

'All right,' said Flavia. Lupus could hear the reluctance in her voice. 'If you say so.'

'Now come!' said Thonis, clapping his hands. 'We're here in the greatest city in the world. Let me show you around. Then you must come and stay at my house. Nice quiet street. No noise, good food, soft beds.'

'Tell them I'll try to find out what happened to their friend,' said Faustus in rapid Greek. 'Just make sure you bring them back here tomorrow.'

'Of course,' said Thonis, and turned to Flavia: 'Faustus here says he'll try to find out what happened to your friend Nubia.'

'Oh, thank you!' cried Flavia.

'Now,' said Thonis, 'let's not waste any more of this busy man's valuable time. Let me show you Alexandria.'

Lupus's heart was thumping. They were wanted! And Thonis was prepared to betray them. He needed to warn his friends. But how?

SCROLL VII

As they climbed back up into Thonis's chariot, Lupus gave Flavia and Jonathan his bug-eyed look and mimed writing something.

'Thonis,' said Flavia. 'May Lupus borrow your wax tablet? He lost his in the shipwreck.'

'Of course,' said Thonis. He searched in his belt pouch. 'This is just a little one. Keep it.'

Lupus took it with a smile and a nod of thanks. It fit into his palm and had two boxwood leaves coated on the inside with yellow beeswax. A small bronze stylus had been pushed into the leather thongs which acted as a hinge. He waited until Thonis had taken the reins and was busy driving before he wrote on it and showed it to Flavia and Jonathan.

SOMETHING NOT RIGHT. WE NEED TO TALK. SAY YOU ARE TIRED AND WANT TO REST.

As soon as his friends had seen it, he rubbed out what he had written with his thumb and drew some of the hieroglyphs he had seen, in case Thonis asked to see the tablet. But Thonis was too busy driving.

'Thonis,' said Flavia. 'Could we go to your house now? I'm tired and would like to rest.'

'Me, too,' said Jonathan.

'Yes, of course,' said Thonis over his shoulder. 'In fact I need to do a few errands here in town. Why don't the three of you have a nap? I'll come back around the fourth hour after noon and show you the sights.'

'That sounds perfect,' said Flavia.

'That's very kind of you,' agreed Jonathan, and glanced at Lupus.

Lupus gave them a secret thumbs-up.

'Here we are,' said Thonis, turning into a road with workshops beneath jewel-coloured awnings. 'Gem-cutter's Street in the Gamma District.' He reined in the horses and pointed. 'Mine is the cedar wood door between the red awning and the blue one.'

He followed Flavia and the others down from the chariot and tethered the horses to a marble post with a bronze ring on top. Then he led the three friends across the wide pavement to a cedar-wood door with a lion's-head knocker.

On the left, Flavia saw an old gem-cutter at work in his shop, his face bathed pink in the light filtering through the red awning overhead, his wares laid out on dark blue velvet before him.

The moment Thonis banged the knocker a huge deep barking made them all jump back.

'That's Scylax,' said Thonis. 'My watchdog.'

'Doesn't "skylax" mean puppy in Greek?' asked Flavia.

Thonis chuckled. 'It's one of my little jokes.'

The door swung open to reveal a young door slave holding a massive black mastiff on a thick leather strap.

'Sambas,' said Thonis to the boy. 'Tell Petesouchus to stable the horses. Make sure he gives them a good rubdown. Hello, boy!' This last was addressed to the big dog, whose tail was a blur of excitement.

'Master!' cried a voice and a tall Egyptian emerged from a side room into the bright atrium. 'Back from your party?' He stopped when he saw the three children.

'Helios!' responded Thonis and turned to Flavia and the boys, 'These are some friends of mine. They'd like to spend a few nights here.'

The Egyptian's face betrayed only a moment's surprise. Then he smiled and said, 'Of course. Very good, sir.'

'Children, this is my steward Helios. He'll look after you until I return.'

Helios looked at Thonis. 'No luggage? No bags?'

'No,' said Thonis in Latin, and then added something in Greek so rapid that Flavia did not understand a word.

The steward raised his eyebrows, then said in Latin, 'Of course. I shall take excellent care of them until you return. Come,' he said to Flavia and her friends. 'Follow me.' And he gave them a smile which Flavia did not trust one bit.

'Thonis said *what*?' whispered Jonathan a quarter of an hour later. The three of them had finally been left alone in a bedroom on the first floor. They were having a conference.

HE SAID NOT TO LET US OUT, wrote Lupus.

'And what were they saying back at the governor's mansion?' asked Flavia. 'When they were speaking in Greek?'

WE ARE WANTED BY SOMEONE VERY HIGH UP, wrote Lupus with a trembling hand.

'Faustus said that? The man behind the desk?'

Lupus nodded.

'And Thonis agreed to help him?' whispered Jonathan.

Lupus grunted yes. FAUSTUS SAID THERE WAS A BIG REWARD

'For us?' said Flavia. 'A reward for *us*?'

Lupus nodded again.

'Anything else?' said Jonathan. 'Can you remember anything else?'

HE MENTIONED NUBIA BY NAME, wrote Lupus. He stared up at the ceiling for a moment, then snapped his fingers and added: HAD A LETTER FROM AN OFFICIAL IN SABRATHA.

'Who do we know in Sabratha?' asked Flavia and then answered her own question. 'Taurus! Titus's cousin and friend. The one who sent us on the mission to get the emerald.'

'And then took the gem and the glory for himself,' said Jonathan.

'But Taurus set sail for Italia almost two weeks ago,' said Flavia. 'From North Africa. How can he be back in Sabratha already?'

'It's just about possible,' said Jonathan. 'But I admit, not likely . . .'

WE HAVE TO GET AWAY FROM HERE, wrote Lupus.

'I agree,' said Flavia. 'And we have to find Nubia.'

'But how?' said Jonathan. 'You saw that slobbering hound in the vestibule. And there's no back door. How can we get away? And how will we find Nubia?'

'If we can just get out of here,' said Flavia, 'I know where to start looking.'

Thaemella the gem-cutter was carving a tiny Hermes into a carnelian when a thud on the red canvas awning above him almost made him decapitate the messenger-god with his fine chisel. A moment later a girl in blue dangled from the awning at arms' length, then thumped down onto the pavement. She cursed in Latin as she rolled on the ground, then stood up and brushed herself off.

The girl had short fair hair and grey eyes and she was wearing a long blue tunic with a blue scarf tied around her hips. He was about to ask her what she was doing when she gave him a smile and put her finger to her lips.

Wide-eyed and open-mouthed, Thaemella nodded, then gave a violent start as another body fell onto the awning above, causing it to sag alarmingly. This body belonged to a boy about the same age as the girl. He was wearing a long beige tunic tied in a knot above his knees and a dark blue turban. A moment later a third and smaller body thudded on the awning. Thaemella could see the dents of knees and hands move towards the awning's edge and now a younger boy in a turquoise turban dangled before him. For a moment the boy gazed with green-eyed alarm at Thaemella. The gem-cutter put his own finger to his lips. The boy grinned, and his friends helped him jump down to the pavement. Now the older boy was looking up and tugging something. From somewhere above the awning came a sudden crack and a rope of coloured cloth came tumbling down onto the three children.

'Thank you, sir!' whispered the girl in Latin, a language Thaemella barely understood. She handed him the bundled rope of cloth – bedspreads tied together by the look of it – and she gave him a rapid explanation. But he only caught one word: 'kidnapped.'

The girl put her finger to her lips again and he nodded

his understanding. Then – still open-mouthed and holding the knotted bedspreads – he watched as the three of them ran down the pavement, turned a corner and disappeared from sight.

SCROLL VIII

It was almost noon by the time the three friends found an entrance to the great Museum of Alexandria. After the heat and brilliance of the granite streets, the vestibule was cool and dim. But the entryway was guarded by two soldiers.

'No entry to the public this afternoon,' said one of the guards, without even looking at them. 'There's a lecture this evening at the twelfth hour, but that's in the exedra.'

'We don't want a lecture and we don't need a scroll,' said Flavia in her best Greek. 'We're looking for one of your scribes. A eunuch.'

The guards exchanged a glance and the first one smirked.

'There are some of those working here,' he said. 'But I don't keep track of them.'

'Wait,' said the other guard. He had very hairy legs. 'Weren't they telling us to keep an eye out for a missing eunuch?' He turned to Flavia. 'What's this eunuch's name?'

'I don't know,' said Flavia. 'He was with our friend. We think he kidnapped her.' It was an exaggeration but it had the required effect. Hairy legs turned and disappeared down a hall towards a bright inner garden.

The first guard snorted and stared straight ahead, ignoring Flavia's questions about the Museum: how big was it, how many rooms did it have, where was the Library. Presently she wandered over to Jonathan and Lupus, who were examining the frescoed walls. Lupus was pointing at a composite god with the body of a hippo and head of a crocodile. Near this god were scales with a tiny person on one side and a feather on the other.

'*A man not a man saw and did not see a bird not a bird sitting on a stick not a stick*,' said a quavering voice behind them in Latin.

The three friends turned to see an ancient man bent over a walking stick. He wore a long black tunic trimmed with yellow, marking him out as a scholar of the Museum. Wispy white hair and beard framed a face as brown and wrinkled as a walnut. His bright black eyes were keen and sharp, but his smile was kind. The hairy-legged guard was close behind him.

'Roman are you?' said the old man in Latin, looking from Flavia to Lupus to Jonathan.

'Yes, sir. We are,' said Flavia.

'In search of a eunuch who works here as a scribe?' Flavia nodded.

'I am Philologus, the Head Scholar of this place,' he announced in his tremulous voice. 'At your service.'

'Thank, you, sir,' said Flavia. 'We're actually looking for our friend Nubia. She was shipwrecked a few days ago and doesn't know anybody here in Alexandria. But a priest at the Poseidium saw her yesterday; she was with a eunuch dressed in yellow and black.'

'One of our eunuchs with your shipwrecked friend?' said Philologus, stroking his wispy white beard.

'Fascinating. And you think this eunuch has kidnapped her?'

'We're not sure if he kidnapped her exactly,' stuttered Flavia. 'But they were together.'

'We do have several eunuchs employed here in the chicken coop of the Muses. And one of them is missing.'

'Chicken coop?' said Jonathan with a puzzled frown.

The old man chuckled. 'That is what some call this place,' he said. 'They refer to our scribes as cloistered bookworms scratching endlessly in the chicken coop of the Muses.' He looked up at them with his bright black eyes. 'A bad mixture of metaphors. Bookworms don't scratch; they devour.'

The three friends exchanged puzzled looks. Flavia had no idea what the old man was talking about, but when he beckoned them on, she and the boys followed.

'*A man not a man saw and did not see a bird not a bird sitting on a stick not a stick*,' repeated Philologus. He was slowly leading them back down the corridor towards a bright inner garden with a bubbling fountain at its centre. 'It's a riddle from the fifth scroll of Plato's *Republic*. "A man not a man" means a eunuch, "saw did not see" means caught a glimpse of, "bird not a bird" is a bat, and the "stick not a stick" was a reed. Ergo: a eunuch caught a glimpse of a bat on a reed. Of course, you're not looking for a bat or a reed, just for a eunuch.'

Flavia nodded, then gave her friends a quizzical look.

'My specialty is codes and puzzles,' said the old man, as they passed from the bright garden into a domed room ringed with statues of robed females. 'Also hieroglyphs, the sacred writings of the Egyptians. By the way,' he said, stopping abruptly and using his walking stick to gesture towards the statues of nine women surrounding them, 'this whole place is dedicated to the Muses, hence the name: Museum. It is a shrine to knowledge.'

'Do you know the eunuch who was with our friend?' asked Jonathan.

The old man seemed to nod as he led them out of the cella and along another colonnade – this one with gilded columns. Presently they emerged into a sunny courtyard with a shell of semi-circular benches at its centre, like a small theatre. 'I lecture here at the exedra on the Ides of every month,' he said, leaning on his staff. 'And anyone can attend.' He glanced at Flavia. 'Even women.'

'Can women be scribes here at the Museum?' asked Flavia.

'Sadly, no; we are a community of men. But women can attend lectures.' He gave her a keen look. 'Tell me, young lady, can you answer this riddle? *I thrive on letters, yet no letters know. I love a book, be it codex or a scroll. And though I devour the Muses, no wiser do I grow.*'

'*I thrive on letters,*' repeated Flavia. '*And though I devour the Muses* – I know the answer!' she cried. '*Tinea sum*: I am a bookworm! A bookworm loves to eat through papyrus and parchment but it can't read, of course!'

'Excellent!' said the old man, pounding his walking stick on the marble pavement. 'Excellent.' He happily led them out of the exedra to a lush inner courtyard with bars between the columns.

'This,' said Philologus, stopping to catch his breath, 'this is one of our animal gardens. Creatures from all over the world live here so that our biologists can study them. Stop. Look. Listen. And here,' he looked at Jonathan, 'is a riddle for you: *Although my step is slow, my attire is ravishing. Because I live so long, I should know everything. Alive I nothing say, but when I'm dead I sing.*'

Jonathan repeated the riddle in his mind and gazed thoughtfully into the animal garden. Suddenly he caught sight of a slow-moving creature in the sand beneath a shrub and he grinned. 'I am a tortoise?' he said. '*Testudo sum?*'

'Yes!' Philologus pounded his walking stick. 'Tell me why?'

'Because a tortoise is slow and old and silent, but after he's dead you can make a lyre from his shell. So in a way he sings.'

'Well done, Jonathan!' cried Flavia and Lupus nodded happily.

They moved on to the next animal courtyard. This one had a pool.

'Aaaah!' cried Lupus, suddenly. He pointed at a large crocodile basking in the sun. The crocodile opened one evil yellow eye, then closed it again.

'Ugh!' agreed Flavia. 'I hate crocodiles.'

'And finally, my young lad,' said Philologus to Lupus, 'a riddle for you. *There is a little beast, whom you and I both know. Now if you catch this beast, you'll want to let him go. But if you do not spy him, with you he'll surely go.*'

Lupus thought for a moment. Then his face broke into a smile. He took out the wax tablet Thonis had given him and wrote: I AM A LOUSE? PEDIS SUM?

'Euge! Euge!' Philologus thudded his staff gleefully. 'They say that the great poet Homer died of frustration because he couldn't solve that riddle. And you did it in a moment.'

'That's because Lupus knows all about lice,' said Jonathan with a grin.

Lupus nodded proudly and pretended to scratch himself. They all laughed.

'Come,' said Philologus, 'You have all passed the test. You are worthy indeed.'

He led them down another long double-colonnaded walkway, this one with a medicinal garden at its centre. On both right and left were scroll-filled niches in the wall, with tables and chairs set before each one. Sitting at these tables were dozens of men in pale yellow tunics bordered with black. Most of the men were writing on papyrus with quill pen and ink, but some were making notes on wax tablets and others rolling or unrolling scrolls.

'Do you see?' cackled Philologus. 'Do they not look like chickens in their coop, peck-peck-pecking away with pen on papyrus?' He tapped his staff on the floor. A few of the scribes looked up at this and smiled at him.

Philologus moved forward to peer over the shoulder of a young man with the looks of a Phoenician. 'Good, good,' he murmured, 'but don't ignore that rubric.' He turned back to Flavia and her friends. 'Come,' he beckoned. 'Not much further.'

'Excuse me, sir,' asked Flavia. 'But where is the Great Library? Someone told us it was here in the Museum.'

'Why, it's all around you, my dear girl. A million scrolls and books are spread throughout this place. Volumes and codices on exotic animals are found back there, near the animal garden.' He waved his staff vaguely behind him. 'The apothecaries study here in the medicine garden. The physicians congregate nearby – to perform autopsies and mix their potions – and of course the medical treatises are kept there. The astronomers and astrologers gather near the observatory and the physicists and engineers near Hero's steam engine;

literature and poetry is in another wing of the Museum, and as for religious texts and funerary rituals,' he gestured straight ahead, 'I am taking you there now, to a scribe called Seth.'

'Is he the eunuch-scribe who knows our friend Nubia?'

'He is not himself a eunuch,' said Philologus, 'but he might know where your friend's eunuch has gone.'

SCROLL IX

It seemed to Jonathan that they had been following the old scribe for miles along the colonnades and corridors of the Museum.

'My father studied here,' said Jonathan to Philologus. 'When he was younger. Have you heard of him: Mordecai ben Ezra?'

'I knew him!' said Philologus and stopped to regard Jonathan with his keen dark eyes. 'He was a fine young physician. And a wise man. You are Jewish,' he added. 'Good, good. We have many Jews working here. Jews and eunuchs, Greeks and Egyptians. We exclude no one.'

'Except women,' said Flavia.

'Ah! You have me!' the old man laughed and shot Flavia a keen glance. 'But if it was up to me you would be welcome! Come!'

He led them down another long colonnade to a bright courtyard with grey speckled columns. Instead of a fountain or garden, this one had an elaborate model of a monumental building at its centre.

Philologus leant on his staff and glanced at Jonathan. 'Do you recognise it?' he said. 'Or perhaps you were too young . . .'

'The Temple,' said Jonathan. 'It's a model of the Temple of God at Jerusalem.'

'Indeed,' said Philologus, and his smile faded. 'Sadly now destroyed.' He gestured towards the men working against the walls. 'These scribes work on religious texts,' he said. 'Scriptures, commentaries, spells, curses and invocations. In fact, I believe it was here that the Septuagint came into being.'

'What's the Septuagint?' asked Flavia.

'It's the translation of our holy writings from Hebrew into Greek,' said Jonathan. 'It's called the Septuagint because seventy rabbis translated it.'

Some of the scribes had turned round to see who was disturbing the peace of their sanctuary. But one of them – a plump young man with curly red hair and a black skullcap – remained facing the wall.

It was this youth that Philologus approached.

'Seth,' he said. 'I would like to introduce you to three friends of mine.'

Seth turned and looked up at them with something like alarm.

'The only problem,' said Philologus with a giggle. 'Is that I don't know the names of my friends.'

Jonathan opened his mouth to speak, but as usual, Flavia stepped forward first. 'My name is Flavia Gemina, daughter of Marcus Flavius Geminus, sea captain,' she said. 'This is Jonathan and that's Lupus. Lupus can't speak,' she added.

The youth stared at them.

'This is Seth ben Aaron,' said Philologus, 'one of our most promising junior scribes.'

Jonathan smiled at Seth. The youth had a chubby face and long-lashed hazel eyes. His beard was almost non-existent and Jonathan guessed he was about seventeen or eighteen.

'Shalom,' said Jonathan.

'Who are you?' said Seth to Jonathan in Aramaic. His voice was surprisingly deep. 'Why are you here?'

'We were shipwrecked on our way from Mauretania to Italia,' said Jonathan in Latin, so that the others could understand him.

'We washed up at a place called Canopus,' added Flavia.

'Canopus!' Philologus cackled and rubbed his hands together. 'Canopus: famed for its decadence and debauchery!'

Lupus nodded and staggered in a circle, as if tipsy.

Seth stared at Lupus in astonishment.

'Some of the people there *were* slightly drunk,' admitted Flavia. 'But they were kind. One of them drove us into Alexandria and took us to the Temple of Poseidon so we could make our thanks offering. Then we discovered that our friend Nubia had been there the day before: yesterday. So that means she also survived the shipwreck! The priest said she was with a eunuch wearing pale yellow and black. That led us here.'

Seth looked at Jonathan. 'You were making an offering at a temple of idols?' he said in his husky Aramaic. 'And now you're wearing a turban?'

Jonathan flushed and self-consciously patted his indigo turban. 'It seemed the right thing to do,' he said. 'When in Rome . . .'

'Oh, leave the boy alone, Seth,' quavered Philologus in Latin. 'And help us find the eunuch. I think you know who they're looking for, don't you?'

Seth's face clouded over. 'Chryses?' he said in accented Latin.

'Exactly.' Philologus turned to the three friends.

'There are only three eunuchs employed here in the chicken coop of the Muses. Two of them are at their posts this morning, but one of them, Chryses, did not come down.'

'And you know this Chryses?' said Jonathan to Seth.

Seth glanced at Philologus and nodded. 'He works here in this section. That's his station there. He wasn't here yesterday, either.'

'But he's not the only thing that's missing,' said Philologus. 'Tell them, Seth. Tell them what you told me.'

Seth's chair scraped as he pushed it back and stood up. 'Come,' he said, and led them to an empty table at the end of the colonnade. 'This is Chryses's station. As you can see, there's nothing on his desk and no scrolls in the niche. But two days ago I noticed him examining an unusual-looking sheet of papyrus. It was written in a combination of hieroglyphs, Greek and Hebrew, and with five different coloured inks. When I leaned over to see it more clearly, he quickly put a new sheet of papyrus on top of it, to hide it. But I had seen enough to know it was some sort of map. We have to log all the documents we receive,' he added, 'and keep them at our posts until we've finished copying them.' He lowered his voice. 'When Chryses didn't come in yesterday, I went to have a look at that curious papyrus.'

'And?' asked Jonathan and Flavia together.

'There is no record of a document written in three languages. And as you can see, there is nothing here. Both Chryses and the map are gone.'

A deep booming clang made Lupus nearly jump out of his skin.

54

As the sound of the gong died away he heard his own stomach growl loudly.

'Midday,' quavered Philologus. 'And as the gongs and this lad's stomach attest, it's time for lunch. Seth, why don't you take our three young friends to the refectory and hear their story? I give you full authority to pursue this matter. If you find our missing document and the eunuch, I will be very inclined to promote you to a higher level.'

'To Scholar?' said Seth, his hazel eyes wide.

'Yes, to Scholar. No longer will you be a mere bookworm in the chicken coop of the Muses.' He cackled at his own joke. 'Take a few days. A week. A month if necessary.'

'But sir,' stammered Seth. 'I wouldn't know how to begin to find Chryses.'

'We do,' said Flavia brightly. 'We're detectives.'

It was Philologus' turn to stare open-mouthed. 'Detectives?' His voice cracked with disbelief. '*Detectives?* I'm Head Scholar in the greatest library in the world, and I've never heard that word.'

'It's from *detego*,' said Flavia firmly. 'It means people who uncover the truth. I read it in a scroll of the late Admiral Pliny. I don't think he made it up,' she added.

Philologus stared at her for a moment. Then he slapped his thigh, gave a wheezing cackle and turned to Seth. 'There are no rules to this game, my lad! You can either remain a bookworm in the chicken coop of the Muses or become a "detective" and a scholar. Seth ben Aaron, the decision is yours.'

The three friends and Seth had a lunch of wheat porridge and posca in a vaulted refectory with two

hundred other scribes and scholars. Long tables stretched out beneath frescoed walls showing a vast map
of Alexandria on one side, and a horizontal plan of the
River Nile on the other. The cacophony around them
was immense, but it didn't matter because Seth ate in
sullen silence. Finally he stood, picked up his empty
bowl and beaker, and gestured for them to do the
same. Flavia and the boys followed him out, and when
he left his eating implements on a counter at the end,
they did too.

'We're not slaves, you know,' he said, as they left the
din of the refectory for a relatively quiet corridor. 'We're
paid. Not much, but it's enough. Especially considering
the Library provides food and shelter.' He led them past
a line of red porphyry columns, then turned and started
up a flight of marble stairs. 'Three meals a day in the
refectory, free access to the Museum Baths, and a small
private sleeping cubicle here on the upper level. And we
are well-respected. When you are promoted to Scholar
you get two proper rooms and a bigger salary. This is
Chryses's cubicle,' he said, stopping before a doorway
leading off the balcony walkway of the inner garden. He
hesitated outside.

'This is where the eunuch sleeps?' asked Flavia,
pushing past him and entering the small, cube-shaped
room.

Seth nodded. 'Mine is just a few doors down. It's
virtually identical.'

Flavia studied the eunuch's cubicle with interest. It
had white plaster walls and a small high window. In one
corner stood a narrow bed with a pale yellow coverlet,
a cedarwood chest at its foot, a low wooden table and
stool at its head. On the table were various writing

implements, as well as a life-sized ornamental cat made of polished bronze.

'Oh!' cried Flavia. 'Look at this beautiful statue.' She picked it up and weighed it in her hands. It was smooth, cold and heavy.

'Chryses is a cat-lover,' muttered Seth. 'Wretched idol!'

Even as he spoke, a sleek grey cat entered the room and rubbed up against Seth's legs, purring loudly. 'Get away, you flea-bitten creature!' muttered Seth, and pushed the cat away with his foot.

'Don't be cruel,' chided Flavia. She bent down to stroke the cat, but it eluded her and disappeared back out through the doorway.

'I thought you weren't allowed to hurt cats in Egypt,' observed Jonathan.

'You're not,' grumbled Seth.

'Is it Chryses's cat?' asked Flavia. 'Who will feed it?'

'It won't starve,' said Seth. 'Everybody pampers it. Everybody but me. Yet whom does it want to sleep with every night? Me!' He sighed deeply.

'Do you bring work to your rooms?' asked Jonathan, nodding at the desk.

Seth shrugged. 'Sometimes,' he said. 'But the table is mainly for our private writings. Letters home, practice, that sort of thing. Maybe we should look through those sheets of papyrus. Anything there?'

Jonathan bent and shuffled through the textured sheets of papyrus. 'No,' he said. 'They're all blank. What is your work?' he added, 'I mean, what do scribes do all day?'

'Our work is copying,' said Seth. 'Copying, copying, and more copying. Every ship that comes into

Alexandria is searched for scrolls. If there are any on board which are unknown to us, we confiscate them, copy them, and then give the copies back to the owners.'

'You give back the copies?' said Flavia. 'Not the originals?'

'That's right. The original manuscripts are kept here in the Library. My department deals with religious rites and rituals. I am usually given Hebrew, Aramaic or Latin manuscripts, Chryses gets Demotic and Hieroglyphic texts and my friend Onesimus used to get the Persian and Indian scrolls. Of course if it's a book of the Torah or the Megillot we don't bother. We have enough copies of those already.'

'Lupus,' said Flavia, pulling back the yellow bedcover, 'have a look under the bed, would you? I'll search on top.'

Lupus dutifully squirmed underneath the bed while Flavia examined the mattress. After a few moments she looked over at Seth. He was still lingering in the doorway. 'Do you have a knife?' she said. 'If we want to be thorough we should look inside the mattress.'

Seth sighed and searched in his belt pouch. A moment later he brought out a small folding knife. 'I use it for sharpening quill pens,' he said, opening it.

As Flavia stabbed the mattress, Lupus scrambled out from under the bed with a yelp.

'Oh, sorry! I forgot you were under there.' Flavia gave Lupus a sheepish grin. He scowled at Flavia as he brushed the lint from his long tunic.

'How can Lupus hear what you're saying?' said Seth. 'I thought he was a deaf-mute?'

'He's not deaf, just mute,' said Jonathan.

And Flavia added, 'His tongue was cut out when he

was six years old. But he doesn't like us talking about it. Here, Lupus!' She held the knife out. 'You look in the mattress.'

Lupus's scowl immediately turned to a grin. He took the knife and began to slash the mattress enthusiastically. After a few moments he reached inside and pulled out a handful of camels' hair stuffing. He handed this to Jonathan.

'Thanks,' said Jonathan drily.

'I'll help you look,' said Seth. He moved forward and helped Jonathan pick through the stuffing.

'I thought Julius Caesar burned the Library down,' said Flavia, examining the hieroglyphs carved into the polished surface of the bronze cat.

'Common misconception,' said Seth gruffly. He bent forward to help Lupus pull out more handfuls of mattress stuffing. 'When Caesar first arrived here in Alexandria he was trapped by the Egyptian fleet in the Great Harbour. So he ordered some of his men to sneak out and set fire to the enemy's ships. The fleet was destroyed, but the fire spread to some of the warehouses on the docks, where duplicate scrolls are kept. Luckily, the fire never reached the Library or the Serapeum and only forty thousand scrolls were burned.'

'Only forty thousand!' muttered Jonathan, who was pulling apart clumps of camel hair and looking for clues.

'Nothing here,' said Seth, at last. 'Any other ideas?'

Flavia nodded. 'We'll have to search the chest.'

'But it's locked.'

'I know,' said Flavia, weighing the bronze cat in her hands. 'But we can use this to break it open.'

Seth stretched out his hand. 'Let me have it,' he said. 'I don't mind destroying a pagan idol.' He took the heavy cat from Flavia and brought it down hard on the small bronze lock of the chest. The lock shattered and they all crowded forward as he opened the cedarwood lid. 'Eureka!' muttered Seth. 'Half his clothes are gone and his travelling bag, too. But he's left his scribe's tunic behind. Now I'm sure of it: Chryses has run away.'

'And for some strange reason,' said Flavia. 'He's taken Nubia with him.'

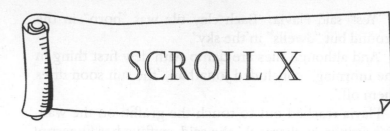

SCROLL X

From behind them, Lupus gave a puzzled grunt. Flavia and the others turned to see him pointing at some graffiti on the wall beside the doorpost.

'What's that?' said Seth. 'Something written on the wall?'

'It's in Latin!' said Flavia, peering over Lupus's shoulder.

Jonathan read it out loud: '*My body is earth, but my strength comes through fire. I was born in the ground but I dwell in the sky. Morning dew soaks me, but soon I am dry.*'

'That's his handwriting,' said Seth, coming up behind them. 'It must be one of his cursed riddles. He loves riddle and codes. Just like old Philologus.'

'A riddle?' said Flavia. 'How exciting! I wonder what it means.'

Seth shrugged. 'That one's easy. Schoolboy stuff.'

'What's the answer, then?' said Jonathan.

'I am a roof-tile, of course. *Tegula sum.* Roof-tiles are made of clay, hence "my body is earth".'

'And "my strength comes through fire",' cried Flavia, 'means fired in a kiln, which is where a tile gets its strength!'

Lupus grunted and pointed out through the doorway to the clay tiles on the sunlit roof of the inner garden.

'Yes!' said Flavia. 'Each clay tile was "born" in the ground but "dwells" in the sky.'

'And although tiles are damp with dew first thing in the morning,' concluded Jonathan, 'the sun soon dries them off.'

Flavia reached out to touch the graffiti on the wall. 'It's written in charcoal,' she said, sniffing her fingertip. 'But why did Chryses write a riddle about a roof tile on the wall of his cubicle?'

Lupus grunted again and pointed to the desk. On it a curved, broken roof-tile was being employed as a pen-rest for three ink-stained reeds.

Lupus picked it up and turned it over, and his green eyes gleamed with excitement. He held up the tile so the others could see letters neatly inked on its curved hidden side.

'Is it another riddle?' cried Flavia, snatching the tile. She didn't wait for his reply but read it out loud: 'A turning post am I, where there is no race-course. A lofty park in the midst of the City. I am not Alpha, nor Omega. Neither Beta nor Delta. But something in between. And on my slopes the goat-god frolics ...'

'Another easy one,' scowled Seth. 'You've only just arrived in Alexandria but even you should guess that one.'

'I know!' cried Jonathan suddenly. 'We saw it from the chariot this morning. Remember?'

'No,' said Flavia. 'Give me a clue.'

'It's a park,' said Jonathan, 'shaped like a pinecone, like the meta of a racecourse. It's in the Gamma District – the letter gamma comes between beta and delta – and it's linked to the goat-god Pan.'

'Eureka!' cried Flavia. But before she could say the

answer Lupus held up his wax tablet. On it he had written PANEUM.

'Too easy,' muttered Seth.

'There's something else written on the tile,' said Flavia suddenly. 'A hieroglyph. What is it?'

Jonathan took the tile. 'It looks like a little dog with an arrow for his tail. But his ears are rectangular and his nose is curved like a crescent moon ...'

'Let me see!' cried Seth. He took the roof tile, examined its underside, then threw it to the ground with an oath. The tile shattered.

'Why did you do that?' cried Flavia.

'It slipped,' said Seth with a scowl.

'Never mind,' said Flavia. 'The clue must mean that he's gone to go to the Paneum, and maybe Nubia's still with him. Come on! We don't have a moment to lose!'

As Jonathan followed the others up the steep path spiralling around the cone-shaped hill, he marvelled at its construction. The Paneum was a man-made mountain, an almost perfect cone, and far bigger up close than it had looked from a distance. Here were trees he had never seen before, their branches full of exotic birds. Every so often there was a marble bench where suppliants could stop and rest and enjoy the view over the city. Halfway up he froze at the sight of a satyr crouched in the shrubbery, but when he came closer, he saw it was a bronze statue.

'Master of the Universe!' gasped Seth, sitting on one of the marble benches about halfway up the hill. 'I'd forgotten what a stiff climb it is.'

Flavia nodded, too breathless to speak, and sat on Seth's left while Lupus scampered off to investigate a life-sized bronze statue of a centaur nearby. Jonathan sat on Seth's right. 'I'm asthmatic,' he said to Seth. 'But I'm hardly wheezing at all after that climb.'

'That is because the air here is so dry,' said Seth, mopping his red face with the long sleeve of his tunic, 'and the climate so favourable. Feel that breeze? Even in mid-summer it prevents the city from becoming too hot.'

'The Etesian Winds,' said Jonathan. 'We heard how Alexander's architect planned the streets to catch that breeze.'

'Look!' said Flavia, standing up and leaning over a bronze and marble rail. 'You can see inside the houses. Look at that one: with the fountains, and flowers and palm trees. Where's Thonis's house, I wonder?' mused Flavia. 'Do you think they realise we've gone?'

'It's in the Gamma District, I think,' said Jonathan. 'But I'm not sure where that is.'

'The Gamma Disctrict is all around us,' said Seth. 'The Alpha is over there, to our far left. Beyond the Museum and the Soma is the Beta District. And over there to the right, towards the Canopic Gate, is the Delta District. That's where my family lives. It has the greatest number of Jews of any other city in the world, now that Jerusalem is no more. Our synagogue is so big that a man has to stand halfway between the front and back and wave a flag to signal the response "Amen".'

'And the Jews who live here aren't persecuted?' asked Jonathan in surprise.

Seth shrugged. 'There have been some bad riots in the past,' he said. 'The Greeks resent our success and the Egyptians don't understand our beliefs. But we hold our own. My rabbi reckons there are a million of us Jews here,' he added.

From their left came a whoop. Lupus had clamboured up onto the back of the bronze centaur and was pretending to whip it into motion.

They all laughed and Flavia turned her back on the view. 'Come on! Maybe Chryses and Nubia are still here. If we hurry we might find them.'

'All the way to the top?' asked Jonathan.

'If that's what it takes,' said Flavia, and added. 'If your asthma is bad then you can wait here.'

'No,' said Jonathan. 'I'm not wheezing at all. Let's go.'

It was the hottest part of the day, and there was no one at the summit of the cone-shaped hill except a statue of goat-legged Pan dancing on a white marble plinth. One of his bronze hoofs was polished gold where a thousand visitors had rubbed it.

Lupus rubbed Pan's hoof, too, then turned to look in the same direction as the statue. He closed his eyes and spread his arms and let the cool Etesian breeze ruffle his damp tunic and hair. It felt wonderful.

'Nubia!' came Flavia's voice from behind him. 'Nubia! Are you here?' Flavia had lingered on the path to look for Nubia.

There was no reply, just the sound of the wind, and a crow cawing in a cypress tree somewhere below them.

Lupus opened his eyes and gazed out over the two vast harbours. Here on top of the Paneum he was almost as high as the flames on the lighthouse. Although it was more than a mile away, his eyes were sharp as a rabbit's and he thought he could see tiny dark figures silhouetted against the deep blue sky. They must be the official fire-feeders.

'Nubia!' Flavia's voice was coming closer.

Lupus was suddenly aware of Jonathan standing beside him.

'I could live here.'

Lupus stared in surprise at Jonathan.

Jonathan gave Lupus a shrug. 'It's beautiful and clean, and I don't suffer from asthma here.'

'I couldn't live anywhere else,' said Seth, who had come to stand behind them. 'I love this city.' After a moment he said, 'Come over here. Look towards the south.'

They dutifully followed Seth around the base of Pan's statue to see a huge expanse of mirror smooth water, dazzling in the afternoon sunshine. Beyond it were vineyards, then wheat fields, then low tawny mountains.

'I don't think Nubia's here.' Flavia arrived breathlessly beside them. 'Is that the sea, too?'

'No, that's Lake Mareotis,' said Seth. 'It's a freshwater lake that leads to the Nile. It is so deep that Homer called its waters "black". See those vineyards? They produce some of the finest wine in the Empire.'

Flavia nodded. 'We've tried it,' she said. 'It's as sweet as mulsum.'

'Is that another harbour down there at the lakeside?' asked Jonathan.

Seth nodded. 'Yes. The Lake Harbour receives goods brought up from the interior and from the trade routes to India. And all the grain grown here in the Delta passes through that harbour. See the canal?' Seth pointed to a bright ribbon within the western walls of the city. 'It leads from Lake Mareotis to Cibotus, that man-made

66

harbour there in the western harbour: Eunostus, as it's called. Cibotus is where all the massive grain ships come to be loaded.' Seth turned back to the inland lake. 'My cousin works down there at the Lake Harbour. He smuggles goods in and out of Alexandria.' Seth shook his head. 'He's the black sheep of the family.'

'So Alexandria has six harbours in all,' said Jonathan.

'Yes, I suppose it does,' said Seth. 'That part of the city down towards the canal is called Rhakotis. That's where most of the Egyptians live. Rhakotis means "building site" in Egyptian. The locals still refuse to call this city by the name Alexander gave it.'

'I heard,' said Flavia, 'that the poet Homer came to Alexander in a dream and told him to build a city here.'

Seth nodded. 'Rumour has it that Alexander stood upon this very hill – it wasn't quite as lofty then – to watch his architect Dinocrates lay out the city grid in the shape of a Macedonian chlamys.'

'A Macedonian what?' said Jonathan.

'A chlamys,' said Seth. 'A cloak shaped like a rectangle.' But the plan of the city was so big that they ran out of chalk. So they cut the corners from bags of flour and drew the lines of the streets by drizzling white flour onto the earth.' Seth threw his arms wide in a dramatic gesture. 'Suddenly ten thousand birds arose from the lake. Imagine! Ten thousand! They flew up in a great cloud, then settled on the site of Alexander's future capital and ate the street plans marked out in flour.'

'Alexander must have been upset,' said Jonathan.

'He was,' said Seth. 'He thought it was a terrible omen. But his soothsayers assured him it was quite the opposite. They told him it meant that many people, from many different countries would flock to his city to feed on its riches. They convinced Alexander and he gave the sign for them to begin building. And they were right.'

'Oh!' cried Flavia suddenly, and pointed to a gold-roofed temple in the area Seth had called Rhakotis. 'What's that building? The one higher than the others. It looks as if the roof is made of pure gold.'

'That's the Serapeum,' said Seth. 'Its roof is made of gilded tiles. Some have called it the most magnificent building in the world, surpassed only by the Capitolium in Rome.'

'Which I burned down last year,' muttered Jonathan.

'What?' said Seth.

Lupus uttered a yelp of excitement. He had just seen some graffiti at the foot of Pan's plinth:

HERBA ANTE NOS, APER MEUS.

'It's another riddle!' gasped Flavia. 'And look! There's that hieroglyph of the dog creature again.' She glanced round suspiciously. 'Has that riddle been there this whole time?'

Lupus shrugged, then nodded.

'*The grass is before us, my boar,*' read Jonathan, and looked at them in puzzlement. 'What in Hades does that mean?'

'It's not a riddle,' said Seth, his cheerful face darkened by a scowl. 'Riddles have a certain form. Two or three lines in dactylic hexameter. That's something else . . .'

He gazed at the letters for a moment, then he went so pale that Lupus could see a light sprinkling of freckles on his nose. 'Master of the—' he said huskily. 'That arrogant idol-worshipper. He's taunting me!'

'Who?' cried Flavia.

And Jonathan said, 'What?'

'It's an anagram,' said Seth. 'A phrase or word whose letters can be scrambled to make a new phrase or word.'

Lupus stared at Seth, then took out his wax tablet and copied down the phrase. He knew how anagrams worked. Their tutor Aristo occasionally gave them such puzzles.

Lupus's heart was beating fast: he had already deciphered the last two words; that only left the first part of the phrase.

'Then you know what the anagram means?' asked Jonathan. 'The grass is before us, my boar?'

'Oh, yes,' said Seth, but before he could explain, Lupus held up his wax tablet with a grunt of triumph. On it he had written:

HERBA ANTE NOS, APER MEUS

Underneath he had shuffled the letters to make the name of a person and the name of a place.

Seth nodded. 'Yes,' he said bitterly, 'You're right.'

SCROLL XI

'Oh, Lupus!' cried Flavia. 'You solved the anagram.' She felt a strange mixture of jealousy and pleasure.

On his wax tablet, Lupus had written:

SETH BEN AARON, SERAPEUM

'Seth ben Aaron is your full name, isn't it?' said Flavia. 'And the Serapeum must be where Chryses wants you to go. Maybe he's in danger and needs your help.'

'He's not in danger.' Seth glared at the letters written on the plinth. 'Do you see that hieroglyph? The dog with the curved nose?'

'Yes,' said Flavia. 'It was on the roof tile, too.'

'It's the sign for confusion,' said Seth. 'Or for something strange. It's called a Seth animal. That was what Chryses used to call me: a Seth animal. If he was in danger he wouldn't use a nickname he knows I hate.'

'Even if Chryses isn't in danger,' said Flavia, 'he might still be with Nubia. If we hurry to the Serapeum, maybe we'll find them both there.'

Seth sighed, then shrugged. 'All right,' he said. 'But I don't like it. For some reason he's taunting me.'

It took them nearly a quarter of an hour to descend the spiral path of the Paneum. Finally they turned onto a side street wider than the Via Sacra in Rome.

'What is the Serapeum, anyway?' asked Flavia.

'It's a huge temple devoted to an imaginary god.'

They all looked at Seth in surprise.

'Serapis is an invention,' said Seth. 'A made-up god to please both Greeks and Egyptians. There's a shrine to him at the Serapeum, but – more importantly – there are also colonnades and courtyards which contain the overflow of scrolls from the Library in the Museum.'

'So there's another library there?' said Flavia.

'Yes. A large annex to the Great Library.'

'So why are we going there?' asked Jonathan. 'Why is Chryses leaving all these anagrams and riddles scrawled about?'

'It is all the fault of Philologus,' said Seth.

'Philologus?' said Flavia. 'That sweet old man at the Library?'

Seth snorted. 'Sweet old man indeed! He's as crafty as a serpent.' He sighed. 'Five years ago, Chryses and I were both taken on as novice scribes, together with a Persian boy called Onesimus. We were all about your age at the time. Novices spend their first year at the Library of the Serapeum. Our teacher at that time was Philologus. He used to send the three of us on Word Quests around Alexandria.'

'Word Quests?' repeated Flavia.

'Yes. A riddle would lead to an anagram, and that to a pictogram and that to a hieroglyph or a famous quote, and so on. Each solution would lead us to a new place, where we would find the next clue. In this way he taught us to recognise and break codes and to identify and translate different languages. Also, we got to know our way around the city.' As if to demonstrate, Seth waved a greeting to a honey-merchant in the colonnade to their right. 'We got to know the markets, temples, harbours. I remember one time a clue sent us to the top of the Pharos. The heat from the fire was intense, even on the second tier. But the view!' Seth guided them around a pile of steaming donkey droppings not yet tidied away by the Alexandrian street cleaners.

'It sounds exciting,' said Flavia wistfully. 'Following clues all over the city. A bit like being a detective.'

Seth smiled at her use of the word. 'Yes, it was exciting,' he said. 'The first one to finish each Word Quest would find a prize: a handful of dates, or a new quill pen and inkpot. Chryses usually won, but occasionally Onesimus or I got there first. The three of us had an agreement: if the prize could be divided, the winner would share.'

'What happened to Onesimus?' asked Jonathan. 'He was Persian, wasn't he?'

Seth's smile faded. 'He died. He died about this time last month.'

Flavia was about to ask how Onesimus had died when they came to a crossroads and her jaw dropped at the sight of the Serapeum, even more impressive from below. It was elevated on a marble platform with at least one hundred steps leading up to it. This platform occupied an entire city block. The highly polished pink granite columns surrounding the lofty temple were massive.

'There it is,' said Seth. 'The great Serapeum of Alexandria.'

Jonathan gave a low whistle of appreciation. 'Those columns must be ninety, even a hundred feet tall,' he said.

'It's so big!' breathed Flavia. 'How will we ever find them in there?'

'I'm not sure,' said Seth, 'but I think I know where to look first.'

'Chryselephantine!' breathed Flavia, as they passed through the massive columns and entered the sanctuary of the god Serapis.

Lupus gave her his bug-eyed look.

'Chryselephantine.' Flavia pointed at the massive sculpture. 'It's made of gold and ivory.'

The cult statue was of a seated man draped in voluminous robes. He was at least eighty feet tall, as tall as the statue of Jupiter on the Capitoline Hill. The god Serapis was shown with long wavy hair and a luxuriant curling beard. On his head he wore a gilded modius, a cylindrical-shaped basket used to measure grain. His robes were gilded, too. The sunshine filtering in from small high windows reflected off the gold and bathed the whole space with a soft yellow light.

There were a few other suppliants in the sanctuary, and also a priest who stood at a table near the wall grinding incense. Flavia could smell its pungent and exotic scent. The priest glanced over his shoulder at them, then turned back to the table.

Flavia gave Lupus a quick nod and the boy hurried up a dozen steps and disappeared behind the statue.

The priest must have heard the slap of Lupus's sandal for he lifted his head again and this time he turned his whole body to look at them.

'Um ... Tell us about Serapis,' said Flavia to Seth, ignoring the priest and gazing with feigned interest at the statue.

Seth shrugged. 'When the Greeks established this city three and a half centuries ago, they tried to find a god that both Greeks and Egyptians would happily worship. Alexander favoured Ammon, but Greeks don't like animal-headed gods, and Ammon has the head of a ram. After Alexander's death, Ptolemy Soter invented this god. He looks human but he's actually a blend of Osiris and Apis, two of the most popular Egyptian gods. The name "Serapis" is a combination of SER – which stands for Osiris – and APIS, the bull god. But they've made him look like Hades, whom you Romans call Pluto. You should know,' he added, 'that Egyptians are obsessed with the afterlife.'

Flavia frowned up at the statue's lofty head. 'Why is he wearing a modius on his head? In Ostia we use the modius to measure grain.'

'The modius of Serapis is filled with grain,' said Seth, 'and sometimes fruit, to show that he brings wealth and prosperity.'

'Like a cornucopia,' said Flavia.

'Exactly.'

For a few moments they gazed at the massive cult statue in silence, then Flavia saw Lupus peep out from behind the statue's throne. He grinned and gave them a thumbs-up.

'He's found something!' whispered Flavia. A quick glance showed her the priest still bent over his table, so she beckoned Lupus to come.

He arrived panting just as the priest turned back towards them with a suspicious glare.

'Was there another clue?' whispered Jonathan.

Lupus nodded and tapped his wax tablet.

'Come on,' said Flavia. 'The priest's coming this way. Let's get out of here.'

A few moments later, standing in bright sunshine at the top of the hundred steps, Lupus pulled out his wax tablet. On it he had written:

I DO NOT FEAR AN ARMY OF LIONS, IF THEY ARE LED BY A LAMB. I DO FEAR AN ARMY OF SHEEP, IF THEY ARE LED BY A LION. AND BEST ARE ARMIES LED BY A RAM.

'Is it a riddle?' said Flavia. 'Or an anagram?'

'Neither,' said Seth. 'It's a quote. At least the first part. But who said it? I can't recall . . .'

'I know!' cried Jonathan. 'I just can't remember . . .'

'Julius Caesar?' suggested Flavia. 'It sounds like something he would say.'

Lupus gave a sudden grunt of excitement and scribbled on his wax tablet. He held it up.

'He's right!' exclaimed Jonathan.

And Seth nodded. 'How foolish of me not to remember.'

'How did you know that, Lupus?' asked Flavia.

Lupus shrugged and grinned. I WAS PAYING ATTENTION IN LESSONS THAT DAY he wrote, then added: HE'S MY HERO

'Well,' said Flavia. 'He's not far away. Let's go and see him!'

SCROLL XII

Lupus gazed in awe at the mummified body of Alexander the Great.

They had hurried down the steps of the Serapeum and run all the way to the Soma, at the great crossroads. It was mid-afternoon and the queue of tourists was not too long. Inside the cool marble building, they were able to catch their breath as they followed a slow-moving line of people past statues, paintings, tapestries and mosaics: all of Alexander and his exploits.

Finally they found themselves approaching Alexander's sarcophagus. The lid was of some kind of thick glass that slightly distorted the figure inside.

'Ugh!' shuddered Flavia as they drew close enough to look in. 'He doesn't look very handsome. His hair is all wispy and his face is shrunken.'

'That's what too much unwatered wine will do to you,' joked Jonathan.

'He is over four hundred years old,' said Seth defensively.

But Lupus felt a surge of pride. To him, the body looked wonderful: both young and old, innocent and wise. The spirit was gone, but it was the earthly body of the man who had conquered the known world and founded dozens of cities. Alexander the Great, his fellow Greek.

'You can see where his nose is glued back on,' said Jonathan.

'Anything written on the sarcophagus?' murmured Flavia. 'Our next clue should be here.'

Lupus shook his head. They were rounding the head end of the sarcophagus and he could see the exit up ahead.

Beside him, Flavia reached out her hand and brushed the stone with her fingertips.

They all jumped as a guard blew a shrill warning blast on a bone whistle. He scowled at them and shook his head sternly.

'Seth,' whispered Flavia. 'What kind of rock is that? Is it marble?'

'No. It's granite. Granite from the quarries of Syene. It's very common here in Alexandria. The granite columns of the Serapeum are from Syene, too.'

'Syene?' said Jonathan. 'I remember that name from the map in the refectory, where we had lunch today. It's not near here, is it?'

'No,' said Seth. 'It's over seven hundred miles away. On the first cataract of the Nile.'

'They can bring a massive block of granite seven hundred miles?' asked Jonathan.

'Maybe Chryses has gone all the way to Syene,' said Flavia. 'Maybe the sarcophagus itself is a clue.' She looked at them, then shook her head. 'No, that can't be right. There must be some graffiti here. There must.'

But now the shuffling queue of people was pushing them out of the inner tomb towards steps that led up to a bright colonnade. There was an inner garden here, with latrines and refreshments for sale.

They found a table under a fig tree and snacked on

salted almonds washed down with a strange soupy drink that prickled the back of Lupus's throat and made him feel light-headed. He almost choked on it. Flavia and Jonathan had to pat his back.

'What is this?' asked Jonathan, peering into his own beaker. 'It's got bits floating in it.'

'It's called beer,' said Seth. 'It's made of fermented grain. It's very good for you.'

Lupus coughed and glared at Seth with watering eyes.

'Well, maybe not for everyone,' said Seth, with a sheepish grin.

'Let's think about this,' said Flavia and looked at Seth. 'Chryses is making a Word Quest, like the ones you used to do with Philologus. We know the clues are intended for you,' she added, 'because the anagram named you: Seth ben Aaron.'

Lupus dipped his finger in his beer and wrote on the table: SETH ANIMAL

'That's right,' said Flavia. 'He sometimes adds a Seth animal, which is his nickname for you. So far, each clue has led us to a place where we found a new clue. But there was no clue here. Where did we go wrong?'

'Maybe the clue was there but we missed it ...' suggested Jonathan.

Lupus grunted no. He had scanned the whole room, top to bottom and the sarcophagus as well.

'We've been going round and round,' said Jonathan, 'like a dog with a flea in its tail. And we haven't got any further. Maybe we're wasting our time.'

'Yes,' sighed Flavia. 'We don't even know if Nubia is still with him.'

'Well,' said Jonathan, draining his beaker of beer and

plunking it down on the wooden table. 'It doesn't matter anymore. The trail's gone cold.'

'No!' cried Flavia. 'I refuse to accept that. We know the last clue pointed to Alexander the Great. If the next step of the trail isn't here, where else could it be?'

Seth frowned into his beaker. 'There is one other place we could try . . .'

'Yes?' cried Flavia eagerly.

'When Alexander first came to Egypt, four centuries ago, he visited the oracle of Ammon at the great oasis at Siwa.'

'Ammon the ram-headed god?' asked Jonathan.

'Yes. Ammon is also associated with Zeus, your Jupiter,' said Seth. 'At Siwa he allegedly claimed that Alexander was his son.'

'Alexander was the son of Zeus?' breathed Flavia.

'Or Jupiter. Or Ammon. Whatever you want to call him.'

Lupus used both hands to make twirling motions beside his ears.

'That's right,' said Seth. 'From that moment on, Alexander had himself depicted with the rams' horns of Ammon, to show the god's favour.'

Jonathan nodded. 'Our tutor Aristo told us that. I remember now.'

'So we have to go to Siwa?' asked Flavia. 'Is it far?'

'Yes,' said Seth. 'At least three days from here by camel. But there is also a Temple of Ammon here in Alexandria. We should check there first.' He was looking over Lupus's shoulder. 'Someone's in trouble,' he said. 'The governor's private guard are here. They wear red trimmed with gold,' he added.

'Governor?' said Jonathan. He and Flavia ducked their

heads, but Lupus slowly turned to look. A pair of burly soldiers had entered the courtyard. One had taken a stand by the exit to the street and the other was scowling round at the crowd.

'Don't tell me they're looking for you?' said Seth in a hoarse whisper.

Lupus nodded.

'Why?'

'We don't know why!' whispered Flavia. 'Seth, you've got to get us out of here. And quickly!'

'How?' said Jonathan. 'We're trapped.'

Lupus took a deep breath and tried to calm his thudding heart. His instinct told him to run. But that would only draw their attention.

'What shall we do?' cried Flavia, looking at the governor's guards out of the corner of her eye. 'There's no way out!'

'How about back the way we came?' whispered Jonathan.

'No,' said Seth. 'The guards by the sarcophagus only let the people move one way. If we tried to go that way, they'd arrest us at once. There's only one exit. And the governor's guard is standing right beside it.'

With a horrible sinking feeling, Flavia saw that the beer seller was pointing their way. But the scowling guard hadn't seen them yet; he was still scanning the crowds.

Suddenly, Lupus dipped a trembling finger in Flavia's glass and wrote on the table: SEE YOU AMMON!

'What?' said Flavia and Jonathan together.

Lupus rubbed out the liquid words and with a whoop he ran towards the guards.

'There's one!' shouted the scowling guard. 'Get him!'

The guard by the door moved forward to intercept Lupus, but with a howl the boy dodged round him and ran under a table.

'Look!' said Jonathan. 'The door's unguarded. Let's go!'

'We can't leave the boy!' said Seth.

Flavia's heart was pounding. 'Lupus is doing that so we can escape. He knows they're looking for three children, not a scribe and two children. Walk, don't run.'

She glanced over her shoulder at Lupus. He was at the far end of the garden. He had scrambled up a fig tree and was jumping up and down on one of the branches. All eyes were on him.

Slowly Flavia, Jonathan and Seth walked towards the exit. Behind them they heard leaves rustling and Lupus whooping like a monkey. They had almost reached the open door and freedom, when another guard put his head round to see what was happening.

'There are three children over there,' said Seth calmly. 'They seem to be giving your friends a merry chase.'

The guard cursed and clanked past them towards the crowd surrounding the fig tree.

Now Flavia, Jonathan and Seth were outside on the pavement.

'Pollux!' cursed Flavia. There was another guard waiting outside. He was talking to a member of the gathering crowd but when he saw them he shouted: 'Stop! Wait!'

'Run!' cried Seth. 'RUN!'

Jonathan lifted the hem of his long beige tunic and ran. The sandals Thonis had given him were cushioned with palm fibre, like the wheels of Alexandrian chariots, and they were perfectly silent. Jonathan could hear the guard clanking and cursing as he pounded after them.

'Stop!' cried the guard in Greek. 'Stop in the name of the governor!'

Jonathan could tell the guard was falling behind. But for how long? Soon the asthma would tighten his chest and make it impossible for him to run. He could see Flavia, her short fair hair bobbing up and down, and in front of her Seth, puffing along in his papyrus-coloured scribe's tunic. Abruptly Seth turned down a broad street with stalls along the pavements. Jonathan's nose told him this was a street of perfume makers and spice-sellers. They hadn't been this way before.

'Hey! Seth!' cried one of the shopkeepers. 'What have you done to upset the governor?'

'Nothing!' Seth stopped and reached for a glass bottle full of yellow liquid. 'I'll pay you back!' he cried, and threw the bottle down onto the pavement. It shattered just behind Jonathan, and the air was suddenly filled with the scent of rose blossoms. 'Perfumed olive oil!' puffed Seth, coming up beside Jonathan. 'Let's hope it slows him up a little.'

'Ohe!' came the soldier's gruff cry behind them, and Jonathan heard the crash of metal armour as the man hit the pavement. The soldier had slipped on the spreading pool of scented oil.

'Clever!' muttered Jonathan, amazed that he was not wheezing. 'Very clever.'

'Flavia!' cried Seth, 'this way!'

On the broad pavement ahead Flavia skidded to a halt, turned and doubled back, following Seth and Jonathan as they wove through the spice stalls in the multicoloured shade of overhead awnings.

'Aeiiii!' came the soldier's cry and Jonathan glanced over his shoulder. The guard had slipped again and crashed into one of the spice-sellers' stalls. Cones of coloured powder had toppled onto him and the stallholders were showering him with curses.

'In here!' gasped Seth from the doorway of an opulent perfume shop. Jonathan and Flavia followed him through the arched doorway and a moment later the guard charged past them, only a few feet away. He was coated in powdered spices of orange and yellow, and he was sneezing. 'That way!' some of the stallholders were shouting, and pointing further into the depths of the spice market. 'They went that way!'

'Herodion!' panted Seth, mopping his brow. 'Are you here?'

A bead curtain tinkled as the perfume-seller emerged from a back room. 'At your service,' he said with a little bow.

'Do you have access to the cisterns? My friends and I are . . . on a quest.'

'Of course, Master Seth. This way.'

The perfume seller held back the curtain and the three friends filed through into the back of his shop.

'Thank you, Herodion,' said Seth, as the perfume-seller opened a low wooden door in a back wall. 'I'll repay you for your kindness soon.'

'I know you will, sir.'

Seth led the way down the stone steps into darkness. Flavia followed him and Jonathan took up the rear, keeping close to the rough limestone wall on his right. He could smell damp and hear the plop of water. When they reached the foot of the stairs he gazed around in amazement. It was dim down here, but as his eyes adjusted he could see that he was not in a tomb-like room but in a vast space of columns and arches with water where the floor should be. Here and there beams of light slanted down from the world above, illuminating the jade green water and throwing back strange wobbling patterns on the vaults and arches above them.

'Great Juno's peacock!' exclaimed Flavia, and her voice echoed strangely in the vast space. 'It's like a massive underground temple.'

'Where are we?' breathed Jonathan.

'The cisterns of Alexandria,' said Seth. 'Underground aqueducts bring water from the Canopic branch of the Nile. Almost every homeowner has access to fresh water and some, like these, are for public use.'

'But they seem to go on for ever,' said Jonathan, peering into the dim vaulted distance.

'Yes,' said Seth. 'The entire city of Alexandria is suspended over air and water.'

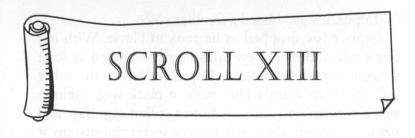

SCROLL XIII

By the time Lupus found the Temple of Zeus-Ammon
it was late afternoon. He had shown his wax tablet to
several stall-keepers before one of them had finally told
him it was in the Brucheion by the Great Harbour, not
far from the Poseidium.

When he finally entered the temple, the thin beams
of sunlight filtering through latticework windows were
almost horizontal. He glanced quickly around, taking
in the cult statue and hieroglyph-decorated walls, while
at the same time alert for either his friends or guards in
pursuit. But there was only a young priest, an old man,
and a veiled Egyptian mother with her two daughters.

Lupus went forward and knelt before the porphyry
statue of Zeus-Ammon and pretended to worship. He
was hungry and tired and he needed to think. Had
Jonathan and Flavia been caught after all? Even after all
his efforts to provide a diversion? Had Seth betrayed
them to the guards?

A hand on his shoulder made him jump and he looked
up into the face of the Egyptian woman. A brown palla
almost obscured her curly red hair. Her long-lashed
hazel eyes were heavily made up with kohl and she had
a few wispy hairs on her chin. It wasn't an Egyptian
mother. It was Seth in disguise.

'Lupus, it's us!' hissed a familiar voice.

Lupus's jaw dropped as he took in Flavia. With her black wig and heavy eye make-up she looked at least sixteen years old. Amazed, Lupus turned to the other girl. Jonathan wore a blue palla, a black wig, eyeliner and a sheepish expression. Lupus stifled a guffaw and made it a cough, then gave them a secret thumbs-up. It was a brilliant disguise.

'Come on,' hissed Flavia. 'We've been waiting for nearly an hour. But we have the next clues and we need to go right away. Seth thinks his black-sheep cousin Nathan might be able to smuggle us out of Alexandria.'

'And Lupus,' added Jonathan, his kohl-rimmed eyes shining, 'wait till you see what's underneath this city.'

An hour later the three friends and Seth were sailing across the surface of Lake Mareotis, watching a huge red sun sink behind the reed beds to the west. They had made their way through the cisterns of Alexandria to the canal and from there to Lake Mareotis, where they found Seth's smuggler cousin Nathan and his flat-bottomed sailing boat, the *Scarab*.

Nathan stood at the stern, at the tiller behind the sail, and the three friends and Seth were having a whispered conference at the front.

'Tell us, Lupus!' hissed Flavia. 'How did you get away from the guards?'

'Yes, tell us,' said Jonathan. He had taken off his palla and black wig. With his bald head and heavily made up eyes, Lupus thought he looked like a young Egyptian pharaoh.

Lupus grinned and took out his wax tablet. EASY, he wrote. THE PEOPLE WERE ALL ON MY SIDE. I JUMPED OUT

OF THE TREE AND THEY USED HANDS TO PASS ME ALONG
OVER THEIR HEADS. THEY SLOWED DOWN THE GUARDS
FOLLOWING ME, he added, LONG ENOUGH FOR ME TO
GET AWAY

Seth nodded grimly. 'Most Alexandrians endure
Roman rule, but they hate Roman soldiers and will
obstruct them at every chance. That's because the
soldiers always accompany tax collectors and they're the
ones who stop you and search you for contraband every
ten feet.'

Jonathan patted Lupus's back. 'It was very brave of
you.'

'Yes,' said Flavia. 'Thank you, Lupus.'

Lupus shrugged and bent his head to retie the strap
of his sandal. He could feel his cheeks flushing with
pleasure and he didn't want them to see.

'Speaking of soldiers,' said Jonathan to Seth. 'How
did you manage to get us past those ones on the dock?'

'They're friends of Nathan's,' said Seth. 'He gives
them a few drachmae every week and they leave him
alone.'

'I'm sure our disguise helped, too,' said Flavia, and
added. 'It's lucky your cousin has a boat.'

Lupus nodded and leaned back to look past the sail
towards the young man at the tiller. Like the other
boatmen they had seen on the docks, he wore a short
one-sleeved tunic and a white cone-shaped cap. He had
curly hair, but unlike Seth's it was dark brown. And
while Seth was pudgy and pale, Nathan was tanned and
lean from long days on the lake.

Flavia leaned over, too, so that she could see Nathan.
She whispered in Lupus's ear. 'Seth was telling us about
Nathan. Instead of becoming a scribe or a rabbi he chose

to be a smuggler, because he loves mammon. Whatever mammon is.'

'It means "wealth",' said Jonathan.

Nathan saw the two of them watching him and winked back.

Lupus leant forward again, so that the sail blocked Nathan from view. WHERE ARE WE GOING? he wrote on his tablet.

'We're going to a place near Memphis,' said Seth glumly.

'We found two clues at the Temple of Zeus-Ammon,' explained Flavia.

'The first clue,' said Jonathan, 'was written in charcoal on the back of the cult statue. It was a riddle:

First I was buried in earth's deep depths: a dark and hidden band.

But flames have changed my looks and name, and now I purchase land.'

Flavia looked at Lupus, her grey eyes shining. 'Can you guess the answer?' she said. 'I got it and so did Jonathan.'

Lupus thought for a moment, then nodded and wrote on his wax tablet: I AM GOLD

'Correct,' said Jonathan.

Suddenly Lupus hit his forehead with his hand.

'What?' they all cried.

His hand shaking with excitement, Lupus rubbed out what he had written on his wax tablet and wrote: NOT WORD QUEST. TREASURE QUEST!

SCROLL XIV

'Treasure quest?' said Flavia to Lupus. 'What do you mean?'

The three friends and Seth were sailing across Lake Mareotis on a flat bottomed boat.

Lupus looked at Seth and wrote: MISSING PAPYRUS LOOKED LIKE MAP. TREASURE MAP?

Seth nodded. 'I suppose it could have been. Egypt's packed with fabulous treasures. If you know where to look . . .'

'Of course!' cried Flavia. 'Chryses isn't looking for a handful of nuts or a new quill pen. He's looking for fabulous treasure.'

Lupus nodded enthusiastically.

Flavia stared thoughtfully over the water. 'But why has he taken Nubia with him?' she asked.

'And why,' added Jonathan, 'is he leaving Seth clues? If there is treasure, you'd think he would want it all to himself. He doesn't want his rival in hot pursuit.'

'I know why!' cried Flavia, and looked at Seth. 'You said some of the words on the treasure map were Hebrew. You are fluent in Hebrew, but is Chryses?'

'He can read the alphabet,' said Seth. 'But he isn't as fluent as I am.'

'Maybe,' continued Flavia, 'he wants you to tag along

a few steps behind so that when he needs help with the Hebrew, you can decipher them.'

Jonathan shook his head. 'Couldn't any Jewish person help him with that?'

'Not really,' said Seth. 'Most Jews who live here in Egypt speak Greek, not Hebrew. They use the Septuagint. So Flavia could be right.'

Flavia clapped her hands. 'Maybe he's taken Nubia with him for the same reason. To translate Nubian clues!'

YOU SAID TWO CLUES AT AMMON TEMPLE wrote Lupus.

'That's right,' said Flavia. 'Remember all those hieroglyphs carved into the wall?'

Lupus grunted yes.

'Well,' continued Jonathan. 'I noticed that a circled group was underlined in charcoal.'

'Luckily,' said Flavia, 'Seth understands hieroglyphs. Once Jonathan pointed out the circled sequence of hieroglyphs, he wrote them down. Seth, show us your wax tablet.'

Seth reached into his belt pouch and handed Flavia his wax tablet.

'See that circle around the hieroglyphs?' said Flavia. 'You only get that around the name of a king or a god. These little symbols – the ball of string, the quail chick, the horned viper and another quail chick – spell out the name Khufu, which is Cheops in Greek. He was a pharaoh of ancient times. Is that right, Seth?'

'Yes,' said Seth. He had turned to watch a heron flying low over the lake, so his voice was barely audible.

Lupus grunted and pointed at the other symbols in front of the king's name – a wasp above a bowl and something like a bending tree above a bowl.

'That bendy thing represents a plant called sedge,' said Flavia.

'It's a kind of rush or reed that grows in rivers,' said Jonathan. 'It represents Upper Egypt.'

Lupus pointed to the wasp. He made a buzzing sound.

'That's right,' said Flavia. 'It's a bee, the symbol for the Delta, where we are now. The semicircle below it is the sign for 'Lord'. Taken all together it says: *Cheops, Lord of the Lands of Sedge and Bee.*'

Lupus frowned at her.

'Lands of Sedge and Bee is just another way of saying Egypt,' said Jonathan. 'Upper Egypt plus Lower Egypt equals Egypt!'

'And Cheops,' said Flavia. 'Is the famous pharaoh whose tomb is considered one of the Seven Sights of the World!'

Lupus shaped a pyramid with his hands.

'That's right!' said Flavia. 'The treasure must be in or near the great pyramid!'

'It's that way,' added Jonathan, pointing south across the water. 'About a day's journey, according to Seth.'

'Master of the Universe,' said Seth suddenly. 'What am I doing? This is madness.'

Lupus and the others looked at Seth, who was resting his head in his hands.

'How did this happen?' moaned Seth. 'This morning I was happily copying scrolls. Then you three arrive and six hours later I find myself dressed like a woman, sailing in a boat owned by my reprobate cousin, in flight from Roman guards and on the way to the great pyramids a hundred miles from here.'

Lupus reached out and gave Seth a tentative pat on the back.

'Don't be sad, Seth,' said Flavia. 'Think of it as an adventure.'

'Adventure?' said Seth. He raised his face and stared at the friends in disbelief. 'Until today I've never set foot outside Alexandria. This is no adventure. This is a disaster!'

SCROLL XV

'You've never been outside Alexandria?' said Flavia to Seth. 'Not in your whole life?'

Seth shook his head. 'I'm a cosmopolitan. A city-dweller. I don't do countryside. The only time I venture outside the city walls is when I visit our family tomb in the necropolis.'

'Great Juno's beard!' muttered Jonathan.

'And why should I leave?' exclaimed Seth. 'The city offers me everything I desire. Books, music, lectures and my synagogue. I can use a marble latrine instead of squatting behind a shrub. There's fresh water beneath every house, enough for a bath every day. I don't have to worry about scorpions, snakes and hippos. Why should I leave?'

'He's got a point,' said Jonathan.

'What about the treasure?' asked Flavia.

'For me the only treasure is books, and I have all I want in the chicken coop of the Muses.'

'Then what about adventures?' said Flavia. 'And quests and mysteries?'

'Plenty of those in the city.'

'So you've never seen the pyramids?'

'We have pyramids in Alexandria.'

'But the great pyramid!' spluttered Flavia. 'It's one of the Seven Sights.'

'We have one of the Seven Sights in Alexandria. The lighthouse.'

'But ... but ...' Flavia was speechless.

'My little cousin is afraid of the big bad countryside!' said Nathan, appearing on silent bare feet from behind the sail. 'All those nasty things that creep on sand and riverbank.' He roughly tickled the back of Seth's neck.

'Get off!' snarled Seth.

'And that fiercely burning sun,' continued Nathan, and added, 'I suggest you either wear a turban or put your veil back on tomorrow. You'll burn to a crisp out here in the real world.'

'Be quiet, Nathan,' growled Seth.

'Better be nice to me. You're sailing on my boat.'

Seth glanced back at the limp sail. 'We don't seem to be sailing at the moment.'

'That's because the wind has died. Also, it will be dark in half an hour and the moon won't rise for another half hour after that. In the meantime I thought I'd make us some dinner. You are hungry, aren't you?'

Lupus nodded and Jonathan's stomach growled enthusiastically.

'Well, I wasn't expecting company, so you'll have to settle for what I've got.'

Nathan moved to the bows of the boat, opened a wooden door beneath the storage area there and removed a small brazier. Using a flint and a handful of palm fibres he expertly lit a fire and stirred the coals. When the tinder had caught, he filled a copper beaker and a copper pan with water from the lake. Into the beaker went a handful of sage leaves. Into the pan went lentils and some salt from a papyrus twist. While the soup cooked and the tea brewed, Nathan laid out a striped rug on the flat bottom of the boat and set a bowl-shaped basket of dates at its centre. He added three discs of hard brown bread.

'Half a loaf for each of you,' he said, breaking one with effort. 'And one for me because I'm doing all the work. Come. Sit on the rug,' he said.

Jonathan and his friends moved to sit in a circle around the dates and bread.

Nathan reached out a hand to take a date but Seth stopped him with a gesture. He covered his head with his brown woman's palla and uttered the prayer of thanksgiving in Hebrew.

'Amen,' said Jonathan and Nathan together at the end.

'You're Jewish!' said Nathan in Aramaic, and looked at Flavia and Lupus. 'All of you?'

'Just me,' said Jonathan, and then added in Latin. 'My name is Jonathan ben Mordecai. These are my friends Flavia and Lupus. Flavia is Roman and Lupus is Greek,' he added.

'You're a girl?' Nathan stared at Flavia in astonishment.

'Of course!' she cried. 'Don't I look like a girl?'

Nathan showed white teeth in a grin. 'Yes, but wearing all that eye makeup, so do these two.' He gestured at Seth and Jonathan.

Flavia lifted her chin a fraction: 'My name is Flavia Gemina, daughter of Marcus Flavius Geminus, sea captain.'

'Pleased to meet you,' said Nathan.

'Ahhh!' cried Jonathan. 'I almost broke a tooth on this bread. It's hard as rock!'

'It's sun-bread,' said Nathan. 'You have to soak it in the soup.' He reached over and took the soup pan by its wooden handle and placed it in the middle of their little circle. 'Like this.' He dipped his bread in the lentil soup, swished it around, then brought it dripping to his mouth.

They all followed suit. Soaked in hot soup, the bread was edible, even tasty.

The heat of the day had died and it was the perfect temperature. As the sky darkened the egrets, herons and geese were flying off to roost, until only the ducks were still with them.

When they had finished and the soup pan was wiped clean, Nathan burped.

'So,' he said to them. 'What are you three doing with my little cousin Seth? Did I hear you mention the word "treasure"?'

Seth groaned and dropped his head. A moment later he raised it again and sighed. 'We may as well tell him everything,' he said. 'He'll find out anyway. Besides, if you can't trust family, who can you trust?'

I will be a rich man!' sang Seth's cousin Nathan in a pleasant tenor voice. *'Countless gold of Ophir and of Cush!'*

It was morning of the next day. A strong breeze had risen with the sun. They had left Lake Mareotis shortly after dawn and were now sailing on a tributary of the Nile.

'Countless gold of Ophir!' sang Nathan from the tiller. *'Yadda, yadda, yadda dee dee dum.'* He had been singing since sunrise.

'We don't *know* there's any treasure,' observed Jonathan. 'It's only Lupus's theory.'

'No treasure!' Nathan stopped singing and gazed at Jonathan in mock horror. 'No countless gold of Ophir and of Cush? Only a theory?'

'Well, *I* think there is gold,' said Flavia. 'I agree with Lupus: this is a Treasure Quest. Imagine Chryses, pecking away in the chicken coop of the Muses, a "man not a man", scorned by many. Then someone brings in a tub of scrolls taken from a ship. Routine copying. One scroll has little pictures on it, so it is given to the scribe who specialises in hieroglyphs: Chryses. As soon as he sees it, he realises it's a map showing the location of a fabulous treasure! Heart pounding, he takes it to his cubicle, gets his travelling bag and extra clothes and sets out immediately on the quest.'

Nathan's eyes lit up. 'So you think the treasure is hidden inside the great pyramid? Many have searched it before, you know.'

'Maybe the map tells of a secret chamber in the pyramid. One nobody has found.'

'Assuming you're right,' said Jonathan, ' do you think we'll get there in time to find them? They have at least a day's start.'

'If we don't find them there,' said Flavia, 'then maybe we'll meet them coming back as we sail down the Nile. We'll have to keep a sharp lookout.'

'This river isn't actually the Nile,' said Nathan. 'It's one of the seven main tributaries that forms the Delta. We'll join the proper Nile at a place called Heliopolis. Also, we're not sailing down it. We're sailing up.'

Jonathan frowned. 'But we're going south. Away from Rome. Isn't that down?'

'No,' said Nathan. 'It's up. When you sail away from the mouth of the river, towards the source, it's called going up river. At the moment we're travelling against the current and that's why we can only sail when the wind is blowing.'

'Luckily,' said Seth, 'the Lord decreed that the wind would always blow south and the current always flow north.'

'Really?' said Jonathan. 'The wind always blows from the north?'

'Not always,' grinned Nathan. 'But most of the time.'

'Excuse me,' said Flavia suddenly. 'Where's the latrine on this boat?'

Nathan laughed. 'For us boys, it's easy. And if we want to do the other, we just do it over the side of the boat. I suggest you do the same.'

Flavia looked at him aghast. 'What? Pull up my tunic and hang my bottom over the side? With all of you watching? Can't we just go to the bank of the river?'

Nathan gestured around. 'As you can see, there are reed beds on either side of the river. We'll have to wait until we find a place where you can disembark. You should have gone earlier.'

'But I have to go now,' said Flavia.

Nathan shrugged. 'I do have a chamber pot around here somewhere,' he said. 'But you won't get any more privacy.'

'I told you the city was better than the country,' muttered Seth.

Jonathan felt a wave of sympathy for Flavia. Her face was bright pink.

'All right, then,' she said at last. 'Keep your backs to me and don't turn around.'

Jonathan grinned at Lupus and they obediently turned their backs to the port side.

Jonathan felt the boat rock as Flavia walked to the side. Then he heard her breathing heavily. Presumably she was negotiating herself into position. Then silence.

'I can't do it while you're all quiet,' came her voice. 'Sing. Or whistle. Do something!'

Without hesitation, Seth began to sing one of the psalms in Hebrew: *'I lift my eyes to the mountains,'* he sang. *'Where does my help come from?'* He had a wonderful deep voice and after a moment Nathan and Jonathan joined in. *'My help comes from the Lord, the Maker of Heaven and Earth,'* they sang. Lupus patted the beat on his knees.

When they finished the song, Jonathan said. 'Can we turn around yet?'

'Just a moment,' came Flavia's voice.

'I wouldn't hang your rear end over the boat for too long,' remarked Nathan. 'Those reed-beds are a favourite haunt of crocodiles.'

Behind them came a squeal and a splash.

Flavia had fallen into the river.

SCROLL XVI

Jonathan and the others ran to the side and pulled a spluttering Flavia out of the water.

'Flavia!' cried Jonathan. 'Are you all right?'

'Oh, Pollux! My sandal fell in the river.' Flavia pulled a slimy strand of duckweed from her hair.

Lupus grunted and pointed to something floating downstream. Nathan hurried to the stern, grasped his punt pole and fished out the dripping sandal. Meanwhile, Lupus had found a rough brown blanket in one of the little cupboards beneath the bench which ran around the inside of the boat's hull.

'Thanks, Lupus,' said Jonathan, and to Flavia: 'Here. Wrap yourself in this.'

Flavia pulled the blanket round her and scowled up at their concerned faces. Then she burst out laughing. 'At least I finished doing what I had to do,' she said, when their laughter subsided.

Nathan bowed and extended a dripping object. 'Your sandal, Princess Rhodopis, has captured my heart.'

'Rhodopis?'

'She was a rich and beautiful girl from Naucratis, a town not far from here. An eagle snatched her gilded sandal from one of her slave-girls and dropped it hundreds of miles away, right into the lap of pharaoh. After one glance at the enchanting object, he vowed to find its owner and make her his queen.' Nathan looked at Flavia with his dark eyes. 'And so he did.'

'Stop flirting with the child, Nathan,' growled Seth. 'It's not seemly.'

Flavia felt her face growing hot so she turned and pretended to look out over the smooth surface of the river, opalescent under the pink and blue sky of dusk. 'Are there really crocodiles in there?' she murmured.

'Not so many this far north,' admitted Nathan. 'I was just teasing you.'

'Aaaah!' she squealed, as a quacking duck came flapping out of the reeds and across the water.

'Look out, Flavia!' said Jonathan with a grin. 'It's a duck!'

Lupus guffawed.

'Actually,' said Nathan, 'some Egyptians are very afraid of ducks. They believe they have demons which will possess you if they follow you into a tomb.'

'Superstitious pagans,' muttered Seth.

Jonathan grinned at Flavia. 'Better watch out for those evil ducks!'

Flavia sat on the bench and dried her legs with the blanket. 'I'm not afraid of ducks,' she said. 'But I have good reason to be frightened of crocodiles.'

'What is this reason?' said Nathan, and winked at Jonathan.

'I had to face one last year in the big new amphitheatre at Rome. The arena was flooded and I was in a boat with some other girls. We were supposed to be nymphs,' she added. 'But then they released some hungry crocs and hippos, and sank the boat we were in.' She shuddered.

'Master of the Universe!' exclaimed Seth and Nathan together.

'I was nearly eaten by a lion,' said Jonathan. 'And Lupus exposed a plot against the Emperor.'

Nathan looked from one to the other. 'Who are you children?'

'We're detectives,' said Flavia firmly. 'We solve mysteries. And the mystery we're trying to solve now is what treasure Chryses is after and whether Nubia is still with him.'

'Wake up, Nubia. We've arrived.'

Nubia opened her eyes to see a good-looking youth in a cream tunic smiling down at her. He had slanting grey-green eyes, honey-coloured skin and straight dark eyebrows beneath a small white turban. Behind him the sky was vivid orange. There was a strong smell of sweet green fodder.

Nubia had been dreaming of Ostia. It took her a moment to remember where she was and what had happened. Her heart sank as it all came flooding back.

She had been shipwrecked in Egypt.

Now she was travelling with a young man called Chryses, riding in a donkey cart full of sweet-smelling clover. He had found her wandering the beach the morning after the shipwreck and he had taken her to the Temple of Neptune to fulfil her vow. When Nubia told him she wanted to go home, he had offered to travel with her. He said he had been planning a trip to the Land of Nubia for some time, in order to collect an inheritance. He suggested that the gods had brought them together for this purpose. Nubia agreed. As

Neptune had provided the dolphin, so he must have provided this travelling companion.

Also, something about the youth's laughing eyes and soft voice made her trust him. Nubia's eyes welled with tears at his kindness and at the overwhelming ache for her lost friends.

'We're here,' said Chryses gently: 'And it's later than I hoped. The sun has set.'

Nubia sat up on the soft bed of clover and blinked back tears. Beyond Chryses, she saw an undulating plain of stony ground with jagged mountains silhouetted against a copper sky. Her head felt oddly cool and light and as she reached up to touch it, she remembered that the priest had cut off her hair and that she was pretending to be a boy.

'Look behind you,' said Chryses.

Nubia turned and gasped. Rearing up above her, and blocking out half the sky, was a massive pyramid, black against the fiery sunset.

'Great Neptune's beard!' she exclaimed.

Chryses laughed. 'You say the funniest things.'

The cart driver turned his head and said something to Chryses in rapid Egyptian. Chryses replied in the same language and the cart driver whipped his tired donkey into a trot.

'He told me there's a camel market here every fourth and seventh day,' explained Chryses in Latin, 'but they usually pack up at dusk. If we miss them we'll have to wait another three days. I told him I'd pay him double if he got us here before they left.'

The cart driver began to babble excitedly and whooped and waved his arm.

'There!' said Chryses. 'There they are!'

Nubia saw a line of camels moving out from behind the pyramid.

The cart driver reined his donkeys to a halt and said something to Chryses. They had a short, heated exchange. Finally Chryses shook his head in exasperation, reached into his shoulder bag and took out a coin. He flipped it to the driver and jumped down from the cart.

'Come on,' he said to Nubia. 'He claims he's done his part. He promised to take us to the pyramid and no further. We've got to catch up to those camels.'

Nubia gripped Chryses's outstretched hands and jumped down onto the stony ground, then almost tripped as she hurried after him. She was wearing one of his cream linen tunics and she was not used to a garment that touched the ground. Also, his spare pair of sandals were slightly too big for her.

'Walk quickly,' said Chryses, 'but don't look like you're hurrying. And for Serapis's sake, walk like a boy! Stomp, don't glide.'

Nubia nodded and followed him over the stony undulating ground. As they approached the rear of the camel train, the last driver in the line glanced over his shoulder at them.

'Pretend we're deep in conversation,' said Chryses. 'Discussing some philosophical point or other. We don't want to seem too eager. On the one hand,' he gestured with his right arm, 'and on the other ...' here he flung out his left. 'You know: that kind of thing – Look! It's worked!' he hissed. 'He's stopped.'

'Camel?' called the trader in Greek as they passed by. He was an elderly Egyptian in knee-length tunic and tattered leggings. 'Hey! Pretty boys! Want to buy a camel? This camel here is gentle as a dove but fast as a hawk. I'll give you a good price.' He recited the words without much enthusiasm, but when Chryses stopped and casually asked 'How much?' the trader ran towards them.

'Not much,' replied the old Egyptian eagerly. 'I give you very good price. She is very good camel but I sell her very cheap to such pretty boys.'

'What do you think, Nubia ... er, Nubian boy?' said Chryses. 'Is she a good camel?'

Nubia reached into the leather belt pouch Chryses had given her and took out a date. The camel accepted it eagerly, spat out the stone and opened her mouth for another. Nubia leaned forward and studied the animal's teeth. 'How old is she,' Nubia said to the trader in Greek. 'About five years old?'

'Oh,' said the trader, throwing up his hands in admiration. 'I can tell you are very wise Nubian boy. Very wise. Very handsome. You know all about camels. Yes, she is five years old. But only just. Very young. Very strong. Very wise. You are also very handsome,' said the trader to Chryses.

Chryses rolled his eyes, and winked at Nubia.

Nubia fed the camel another date, then knelt to examine the creature's feet.

By now all the other camel traders were hurrying back with their beasts and clamouring for attention.

Nubia glanced up at the ring of men and animals around her. Although most of the camels were thin, they were in good condition, and she saw two or three that would easily be able to make the journey back to her native land.

She stood up and turned to Chryses, the kind youth

who had befriended her, and who had promised to accompany her to her desert home. And for the first time since the shipwreck, Nubia smiled.

SCROLL XVII

As the moon rose over the east bank of the Nile, Chryses and Nubia finished their dinner of sun-bread washed down with water, and mounted their new camels.

'Hold on with your hands and toes,' instructed Nubia, as Chryses's camel pitched him forward and then back. 'The way we practised. Once you are up it is easier.'

'Ugh!' Chryses wrinkled his nose. 'This camel smells.'

'Yes,' said Nubia. 'I like this smell,' she added. 'It makes me think of home. Yours is called Castor,' she added. 'And mine is called Pollux.'

'How do you know that?'

'I just named them.' Nubia smiled and patted Pollux on the neck. She had grown up with camels and their presence consoled her. 'I cannot believe you are Egyptian but have never been on camel,' said Nubia, clicking the camels into motion.

'I'm not Egyptian,' said Chryses. 'I'm Greek. I'm Alexandrian born and bred. No need to ride a camel in the city. Are you sure this is safe?' he added. 'Travelling by moonlight?'

'Yes,' said Nubia. 'Behold the moon is almost full. And see how the road here is level and smooth.'

'You're not afraid of bandits?'

'I pray to Mercury, god of travellers, that he will protect us. But we have camels. They are lofty and swift.'

Somewhere nearby a dog began to bark, setting off other dogs further away.

'And you're not too tired?' asked Chryses.

'Little bit; not so much. I slept in clover. Are you tired?'

'Yes, but I want to put as much distance between us and Alexandria as possible.'

'We will travel while it is still bright.' Nubia slowed her camel so that Chryses could come up beside her. In the brilliant light of the rising moon, she studied the youth who had helped her. Although he had a male name, and although he acted like a young man, Chryses looked like a girl. He had told her he was eighteen years old, yet he did not have the slightest trace of a beard.

Nubia reached up and touched the white turban on her head. A gift from the camel seller. 'If people come,' she said. 'We must be covering faces with turbans, with only eyes showing. That way they think we are men.'

Chryses must have felt Nubia's gaze on him because he turned his head to look at her. With his slanting eyes, small mouth and fringe of straight hair emerging from the front of his turban, Chryses did not look the least bit like a man.

'Excuse me being rude,' said Nubia suddenly. 'But are you being a girl in disguise? Like me?'

Chryses stared at her in astonishment, then threw back his head and laughed. 'Silly girl. I'm a eunuch. Don't you know what a eunuch is?'

'I have heard of a eunuch but I am not knowing what it is,' said Nubia.

Shaking his head, Chryses reached into the canvas

bag slung over his shoulder and pulled out a gourd. 'Before I tell you I need a strong drink. This is the palm wine that old camel trader gave us. I think he was pleased with the sale.' Chryses uncorked the gourd and brought it carefully to his mouth, trying to accommodate the camel's rocking stride. 'O Lord Serapis Helios!' he gasped, as he finally succeeded in taking a mouthful. 'That's strong!' He held out the gourd. 'Want some?'

'No, thank you,' Nubia shook her head politely. She could smell the pungent drink even over the camel's odour.

'Please yourself,' said Chryses, and took another swig. 'Aeiii!' he said. 'It burns. But it's good.'

He replaced the cork in the gourd and said: 'A eunuch is a man who is not a man. Neither male nor female.' He looked over at her, his slanting eyes almost black in the silver moonlight. 'Do you know what they do to make a boy a eunuch?'

Nubia shook her head.

'They geld him.'

'Oh!' cried Nubia. 'Like male camels and horses? They are chopping off testicles?'

Chryses nodded grimly. 'I was lucky,' he said. 'They didn't chop anything off. They only made a little cut at the top. It does the same job. Prevents a boy from ever becoming a man. But it hurt like Hades and they swelled to the size of— No. You don't want to hear all the details . . .'

'But why?' asked Nubia. 'Why were they doing this to you? Was it punishment?'

Chryses laughed. 'No. It wasn't punishment. I was only eight years old when they did it,' he said. 'My parents were slaves. Greeks from Tralles, a town near

Ephesus. The master's wife liked the idea of a little Greek eunuch to serve her. And so they cut me. It turned out I wasn't very good at serving, but I did have a gift for languages. The master was Roman and the mistress Egyptian, so I learned Latin and Demotic. My parents spoke Greek to me so I'm fluent in that, too.'

'You can speak three languages?'

Chryses shrugged. 'It's not difficult if you learn them as a child. I can write four: Greek, Latin, Hieroglyphic and Demotic.' He took another swig of palm wine. 'My mistress was kind to me. When she realised my gift, she had her husband's scribe teach me to read and write. After that, she used to take me to the baths with her and I would read from a scroll. Then one day, she asked one of her husband's Egyptian secretaries to teach me hieroglyphs. Do you know what they are?'

'Yes,' said Nubia. 'Little picture writing of Egyptians.'

'That's right. I loved learning what the little pictures meant. I mastered the basics in only a month. From then on my mistress used to take me out in her litter. We would visit the tombs and monuments of the ancient Egyptians and I would decipher the hieroglyphs for her. Then she decided to go all the way up the Nile, and visit the shrines of her forefathers. I was about your age at the time.'

Chryses took another drink and wiped his mouth with the back of his hand. 'We sailed on a beautiful cedarwood barge, with lotus blossoms painted on its side and a shady cabin for the heat of day. We visited marvellous places: deserted cities and painted tombs. But then one day, my mistress died suddenly.'

From a dark sycamore grove an owl hooted.

'When we returned to Alexandria,' continued

Chryses, 'I discovered that my mistress had set me free in her will. I went to work in the Great Library. I had no savings, you see, and my parents were slaves with no possessions. But because I can read and write four languages – including hieroglyphs – the Museum employed me. It is one of the few places in Alexandria where a eunuch freedman can get a job.'

'Were you liking it there?'

'I did at first, I was only thirteen and it was my first taste of freedom and the world outside. I was studying with two other novices and we had a wonderful teacher. I loved it. But then,' he said, 'I made an enemy.'

'Who?'

'One of the other novices. A Jew named Seth.'

'Why is he your enemy?'

'He calls me a pagan, and he hates me because I'm a eunuch.'

'But you cannot help being eunuch,' murmured Nubia.

'He made my life miserable. That's why I left.' Chryses took a swig of palm wine, and Nubia heard him add under his breath: 'But I'll show him!'

The smell of sage tea and the cheerful squeak of a moorhen woke Flavia early the next morning. She was wrapped in a coarse brown blanket and lying on one of the thin mattresses that Nathan had unrolled the night before. For a moment she lay looking up at the pale yellow sky of dawn, feeling the gentle rocking of the boat and wondering what was different. Then she realised. They were not moving. The sail was furled and the *Scarab* was moored to the bank. She could hear the soft smack of ripples on the boat's hull.

She sat up, looked around, and gasped. Two great pyramids stood on the horizon, flattened by the morning mist and framed by shaggy palm trees.

'Great Juno's beard!' she exclaimed.

A pile of blankets on the mattress beside her stirred, and Lupus's bald head emerged. He blinked sleepily and looked around. Then his eyes opened wide as he saw the pyramids.

'Aren't they amazing?' she breathed.

Lupus nodded.

'Jonathan!' Flavia turned to her other side and saw Jonathan, Seth and Nathan sitting on the bench at the boat's stern. Jonathan and Seth had covered their heads with shawls and Nathan wore his white conical cap. All three of them were rocking gently and murmuring in Hebrew.

'Amen!' they said together, and pulled the shawls back from their heads.

'Good morning!' said Nathan, jumping up. He walked over and grinned down at them and held out his calloused hand to help Flavia to her feet. 'As you can see, we had a favourable breeze as well as the full moon. We passed Heliopolis in the night and now we are only a few hours from Memphis. I can't offer you breakfast; you've devoured my store of bread. But I've brewed some sage tea. *Countless gold of Ophir!*' he sang cheerfully. '*Treasure, treasure, treasure in my boat!*'

'Is this the proper Nile?' asked Flavia.

'Yes,' laughed Nathan. 'This is finally the proper Nile. We have left the Delta behind. Everything to the right, on the west bank, we call Libya. And on the left is Arabia.'

'But we're still in the province of Egypt?'

'Yes, of course. Though some call this Middle or even Upper Egypt. Upper Egypt really begins at Hermopolis. And it ends at Syene, where the first cataract marks the border of Nubia.'

'According to Strabo,' said Seth, 'This river is more than a thousand miles long, yet nowhere is it more than five hundred feet wide.'

'Have you seen the pyramids?' Jonathan sat beside Flavia and began to put on his turban. 'They're impressive, aren't they?'

'They're wonderful!' sighed Flavia and added under her breath. 'I wish Flaccus was here. He wanted to see all Seven Sights.'

Jonathan looked at Seth and Nathan. 'May we go and investigate them?'

'Of course you must go,' said Nathan, squatting down beside the brazier. He began to pour out the tea into five small, thick glasses. 'That's where the treasure is hidden, isn't it?' He stood and extended a glass of sage tea to Seth. 'That reminds me: we need to talk about how we divide it up.'

Seth paused for a moment, took the glass and said. 'What do you mean?'

Nathan opened his arms, palms up. 'Well, you couldn't have got here without me,' he said, 'but I can't come to the pyramids with you. Someone has to stay here to guard the *Scarab*. And someone has to buy bread and supplies for the journey back to Alexandria. I don't want to miss out. I should have a share of the treasure.'

'And providing we find this hypothetical treasure,' said Seth acidly, 'what do you suggest?'

'I suggest we divide it four ways,' said Nathan. 'One part for you, one part for me, one part for the children and one part for *Scarab*, who's been doing all the work.'

Lupus made a grunt of protest and Jonathan frowned. 'Lupus is right. That's not fair. That means you get half and each of us only gets um . . . a twelfth. Shouldn't we divide it into fifths?'

'It doesn't matter,' said Flavia. 'All we care about is finding Nubia.'

'That's all right for you to say,' muttered Jonathan. 'Your family is rich. Mine could use the money.'

'My family is not that rich,' said Flavia. 'It's just that I care more about Nubia than I do about treasure.'

'I care about Nubia, too,' said Jonathan. 'But we'll need to pay for our passage home now that we don't have our imperial passes any more.'

'Good point,' said Flavia, and turned to Nathan. 'We want a bigger share of the treasure.'

'All right! All right!' said Nathan, showing his white teeth in a smile. 'We'll split the treasure five ways. But you must pay me back for food and services. After all, I'm funding this expedition.'

'That sounds fair,' said Jonathan.

'So what do we do now?' said Seth, draining his tea and putting the glass down on the bench beside him. Behind him the lemon yellow sky was turning pink.

'We need to find Chryses and Nubia,' said Flavia. 'We didn't meet them coming back, so they've probably gone into the pyramid to get the treasure. Using the map,' she added.

'Speaking of maps . . .' Nathan, reached into one of the storage areas under the bench. 'This is my most valuable possession.' He unrolled a map of soft leather. 'It shows the Nile from the Delta to Nubia.'

'That's interesting,' said Jonathan, taking the map.

'The Delta really does look like a capital Greek delta. Look! Here we are. By these little pyramids.'

'And there is your transportation,' said Nathan, pointing behind them.

Flavia turned to see the shapes of a dozen boys and their donkeys emerging from the mist on the riverbank above them. As soon as the boys saw them, they started calling out, pointing at themselves and at their donkeys.

'Where did they come from?' asked Jonathan.

'There's a village over there,' said Nathan, nodding to the south. 'They probably saw our mast. I imagine the bread- and fruit-sellers will be along shortly.'

'Do we need donkeys?' said Seth with a frown. 'Couldn't we just walk?'

Flavia nodded. 'It can't be more than half a mile from here.'

'You could walk,' said Nathan, 'but it might upset them. Ride their donkeys. Give them a few small coins. These people aren't rich.'

Seth scowled. 'I'm not rich either. And I don't have much money left; I only thought we were going out for the afternoon. And I refuse to pay for a journey which I can easily make on foot.'

But the boys with their donkeys were not easily discouraged. Begging and pleading, they followed Seth and the three friends all the way from the riverbank to the great pyramids.

SCROLL XVIII

The sun was rising behind them as they reached a collection of reed shacks and stalls pitched before the great pyramid. Half a dozen men rushed up to them with goods for sale, but the only one they took notice of was the bread-seller. He lowered the circular tray from his head and let them each choose a flat round loaf, still warm from the oven. Seth said something in Egyptian, gave the man a copper coin and pointed back towards the place where the *Scarab* was moored.

'Juno, it's big!' said Flavia, gazing up at the dazzling pyramid, now gleaming gold in the light of the rising sun.

'And there are two more of them,' observed Jonathan. 'Plus those three little ones.'

Flavia nodded. 'I wonder how tall this big one is?' She took a bite from her piece of bread.

'Three hundred feet?' suggested Jonathan.

Lupus shook his head and pointed up, as if to say: higher.

An Egyptian youth about their age skidded up to them in a cloud of dust. 'Five hundred of feets!' he said in Greek. 'This pyramid five hundred of feets tall. And yes, many others here. More than nine. You want guide?' He wore a long striped tunic and a little black turban.

At this two of the boys from the village began to yell at him and make rude gestures. The boy in the black turban shouted back at them and imitated a braying donkey. Then he winked at Flavia. 'I tell them they are only donkey boys. I am proper guide, speaking good Greek.' He gave a little bow. 'My name is Abu. You want guide to the pyramids and Sphinx?'

Flavia was about to rebuff him, then thought better of it.

'My name is Flavia Gemina,' she said in her halting Greek. 'Daughter of Marcus Flavius Geminus, sea captain. These are my friends Seth, Jonathan and Lupus. We are looking for some friends. They might be inside the pyramid of Cheops. Can you ask if anyone has seen them?'

'Of course! You very pretty girl with camel-coloured hair. You married?'

'Yes,' said Jonathan, slipping an arm around Flavia's shoulder, 'She's married to me. Our friends are a Nubian girl of about thirteen and a young eunuch.'

'Eunuch? You are meaning man-girl?'

'That's right,' said Seth. 'Have you seen them?'

'I have not seen them, but I will ask my friends.' The boy ran off towards the reed huts.

'That was very bold of you, Jonathan,' said Flavia, when Abu was out of earshot. 'Saying I was your wife.'

'Don't get any ideas,' said Jonathan, removing his arm from her shoulder and winking at Lupus.

'Flavia,' said Seth. 'Seeing as you're wanted in Alexandria, do you think it's wise to tell people your name?'

'Oh!' Flavia brought her hand to her mouth. 'You don't think they're still after us?'

'He's got a point,' said Jonathan. 'Until we know

who's after us and what we're supposed to have done, we'd better adopt disguises.'

'Eureka!' cried Flavia, after a moment's thought. 'I've got it!'

'What?' said Jonathan drily. 'Shall we pretend to be a troupe of pantomime actors? Or maybe acrobats?'

Lupus nodded enthusiastically, performed a neat back flip and took a bow.

Flavia laughed. 'Actually, that's not a bad idea, but I have a better one. Seth can pretend to be our father and we are his three sons.'

'I'm only eighteen!' grumbled Seth. 'How can I possibly be your father?'

'Then you can be our mother! It worked last time we tried it.'

'I will not dress in woman's clothing again. It is an abomination to the Lord.'

'Well, luckily *our* gods don't forbid dressing up,' said Flavia. 'Jonathan, give me your turban. I'm going to pretend to be a boy!'

Jonathan sighed, unwound his indigo blue turban and handed it to Flavia.

As Flavia began to wrap the turban around her head, Lupus chuckled and wrote on his wax tablet: I AM USUALLY THE ONE IN DISGUISE.

Seth narrowed his eyes at Flavia. 'How does a highborn Roman girl know how to bind a turban so expertly?' he asked.

'Simple,' said Flavia. 'Last month we travelled on a caravan from Sabratha to Volubilis, on a mission for the Emperor. I had to put my turban on every day. You should wear one, too. Otherwise you'll be burnt by the sun.'

Seth shook his head. 'I refuse to look like one of these heathen peasants. My skullcap is fine. I will not wear a turban.'

'Well, I will!' said Flavia, tucking in one end of the turban and adjusting the tail over her shoulder. 'From now on I am an Egyptian boy.'

Jonathan pointed with his chin. 'Here comes our guide,' he said. 'Doesn't look as if he's had any luck.'

Abu came running up to them and shook his head. 'Sorry,' he panted. 'Nobody has seen Nubian girl . . . or Alexandrian eunuch . . . But I can take you inside pyramid to look. There is a secret door high up. Not ground level. But door is hard to find. I show you for small fee.' He looked at Flavia. 'Ah! Wearing turban you look like boy. Very good, very good.'

Suddenly Lupus grunted and wrote on his tablet:
WHAT IF NUBIA IS IN DISGUISE?

'Great Juno's peacock!' cried Flavia. 'You could be right. She cut her hair at the Temple of Neptune. She might be pretending to be a boy, too!'

Flavia turned to Abu: 'Our friends could have been travelling as a eunuch and a Nubian boy! Or even as two boys, one dark-skinned and one fair.'

'Or as two girls?' said Jonathan.

'Two girls travelling alone would draw too much attention,' said Seth.

Their young guide shook his head and led them towards the north face of the pyramid. 'My friends do not see any Nubian here yesterday. Young or old, male or female. But that does not mean they were not here. There was camel market. Many people. Very crowding. Look.' Abu bent down and picked up a handful of stone chips lying at the foot of the pyramid. 'Do you see the lentils and half-peeled grains here, all made of stones? These were foods of a million workers who are building pyramids three thousands of years ago. These foods are now petrified over time. I know many other interesting facts.'

'Oh!' cried Flavia. 'Some of them do look like lentils!'

Lupus put one in his mouth and tentatively bit down. Then he made a face and spat it out.

Flavia gazed up at the north face of the pyramid. 'You say there's a secret entrance?'

'Yes, indeed.'

'I don't see anything,' said Jonathan.

Abu smiled. 'That,' he said, 'is because entrance is secret.'

'Wait!' said Seth. 'Is this the pyramid with a moveable stone which leads down a sloping passage to a vault?'

Abu stared at the scribe. 'How do you know this? You have been here before?'

Seth shook his head. 'A Greek traveller called Strabo visited this place a hundred years ago. He wrote about it.'

Abu scowled. 'He is correct.' Then his face brightened. 'Look! Here is my friend Psammiticus with oil lamps. I call him Psammi. He will accompany. If your friends are in pyramid, I promise we will find them.'

Abu led them up a slope of sand and now they could see shallow handholds cut into the white limestone slabs which formed the facing of the pyramid. Abu went up like a monkey. After a few pushes one of the great slabs gave a groan and tipped inward. It was not a wide entrance but Abu slithered through first, after taking the two oil-lamps from Psammi, a thin youth in a yellow tunic and turban. Psammi followed, then Lupus swarmed up and in. A moment later his grinning face appeared and he beckoned them on. Seth should have been next, but he stopped halfway into the entrance and wiggled back out, forcing Flavia and Jonathan to retreat.

'Too narrow and too dark,' he panted, moving over to the side. Although the morning was still cool, his plump face was red and sweating. 'I'll wait down there in the shade,' he added, mopping his brow with his sleeve.

'You are coming?' Abu's face appeared above them.

'We're coming,' called Flavia. 'All except for Seth.'

She found the footholds going up and eased herself into the entrance, trying not to think what would happen if the stone slipped and fell back into place. Abu and Psammi helped her jump down to a narrow corridor sloping steeply up. It was dark and surprisingly warm after the cool morning air, and there was barely enough room to stand upright. She looked around the dim, cramped tunnel. Already she was envying Seth's decision to stay outside.

Jonathan thumped down onto the floor behind her and Psammi held up the lamp so he could dust himself off.

'Ready?' Abu's voice echoed in the narrow space. 'Let us find your friends.'

It was not the dust or the darkness or the oppressive stuffy heat of the pyramid that convinced Flavia to turn back. It was not the sense of foreboding or the knowledge that a million tons of rock hung over her head.

What sent Flavia whimpering back down the corridor to freedom and light were the giant bats in the Great Gallery.

When the explorers emerged from the pyramid two hours later, Flavia saw that Jonathan's face was pale. When he reached ground level she could hear him wheezing.

'Was it very terrible?' she asked.

He nodded. 'Awful. We went down one musty corridor after another and found nothing but cobwebs and dust and more bats.' He wrinkled his nose. 'And someone had used one of the corridors as a latrine.'

'Ugh!' said Flavia, with a shudder. She turned to the others. Abu and Psammi looked tired, but Lupus was beaming.

'You liked going inside the pyramid?' she asked, in disbelief.

Lupus nodded vigorously.

'Nubia wasn't in there, was she?'

Lupus shook his head, and his smile faded.

'Sorry, Flavia,' sighed Jonathan. 'It was all for nothing.'

'Don't be disappointed!' said Flavia. 'Seth and I found another clue! And something else. Something wonderful!'

'Oh!' groaned Jonathan. 'Don't tell me we went in there for nothing!'

'Afraid so. Come look.' She led them back to the east face of the great pyramid and pointed. Here at ground level, the slabs of white limestone covering the pyramid were crowded with graffiti, but Chryses's fresh charcoal letters stood out clearly:

I navigate the waterless waves more easily than you'd think.
I take my cisterns with me, and rarely need a drink.
And though some call me ship, never will I sink.

SCROLL XIX

'I navigate the waterless waves ...' Jonathan read the riddle a second time, then frowned at Flavia.

'Do you want me to tell you the answer?' she said.

'You know the answer?'

'Of course!' she said. 'And Seth didn't have to help me at all.' She glanced over to a reed stall, where Seth sat nursing a beaker of mint tea.

She turned back to the boys. 'Come on. It's easy!'

Lupus held up his wax tablet. On it he had drawn a camel.

'Well done!' cried Flavia.

'Of course!' said Jonathan. 'The camel navigates the sand sea and has its own water supply. And some people call it the ship of the desert.'

'Now look at this,' said Flavia. She pointed to another small graffito among all the others. It was also written in charcoal: NUBIA WAS HERE

'It's her handwriting, isn't it?' said Flavia, her eyes shining.

Lupus nodded, and gave Flavia a thumbs-up.

'That means she's still with Chryses,' said Jonathan.

'Exactly!' Flavia looked at them eagerly. 'We've got to solve that next riddle and find her. You didn't see a camel inside the pyramid, did you? Not a real one, of course, but a drawing or hieroglyph. Anything. We need to find a camel.'

'There was no camel inside the pyramid,' said Jonathan.

Flavia thought for a moment and then turned to Abu. 'Are there any big statues of camels around here, like that one?' She pointed at the massive head of a sphinx emerging from the sand nearby.

The boy laughed. 'No, he said. 'We do not have big statues of camels here in Egypt. Camels are not known to pharaohs. You Romans are bringing them time of my father's father's father's father.'

'Oh,' said Flavia.

Suddenly Lupus grunted. He was pointing at two hieroglyphs, a hand's-breadth from the riddle.

Jonathan nodded. 'What about those? They're drawn with the same piece of charcoal.'

'Great Juno's peacock!' exclaimed Flavia. 'I was so excited about seeing Nubia's message I didn't even notice them . . .'

'It's the Seth animal again,' said Jonathan. 'The dog with the arrow tail. And the other is a drawing of a man with a crocodile head.'

'Alas!' cried Abu, 'those signs are most ill-omened! Pay me so that I might flee!'

'What?' They all turned to look at him.

'Pay me! Pay me!'

Flavia gave him a copper coin. Abu snatched it and ran off towards the village without saying thank you or goodbye.

The three friends stared after him, astonished. The donkey boys had been resting in the shadow of a stall and Flavia noticed them getting to their feet and looking after Abu's retreating form with alarm.

She shrugged and turned back to the hieroglyphs.

'Which god do you think that one is?' She said examining the crocodile-headed god. She turned to look for Seth and saw him draining his beaker of tea in the shade of a stall near the donkey boys. 'Seth!' she cried, 'Come here for a moment!'

At this, the donkey boys turned to stare at Seth. As the scribe trudged past them they shrank back in horror. Seth ignored them. 'That was the worst mint tea I've ever had. It was full of sand.' He shook his head with disgust and drops of sweat fell from his curly red hair.

'Seth, we missed some more clues! Those hieroglyphs!' Flavia pointed. 'I know the Seth animal is you, but what does that one mean?'

'That's Sobek, the crocodile god.'

'They have a god of crocodiles?' Jonathan's eyebrows went up.

'Yes,' said Seth. 'Sobek is worshipped in— Ow!' He put his hand to his forehead and brought it away covered with blood.

'What was it?' cried Flavia.

'A rock!' cried Seth in disbelief. 'Someone threw a rock at me.'

Even as he spoke two more rocks flew past and one hit Seth on the shoulder.

They all turned to see the donkey boys watching Seth with narrowed eyes. One was poised to throw a stone. For a moment the two groups stared at each other, then the donkey boy threw his stone at Seth, striking him on his upraised arm. And now all the donkey boys were tossing small stones or handfuls of gravel, and calling out something in Egyptian. Flavia heard them chant the name: 'Seth! Seth!'

Flavia screamed as a stone struck her arm.

'Let's get out of here!' cried Jonathan. 'Quickly!'

The four of them ran back towards the boat.

'Crouch down!' cried Jonathan. 'Keep low. Lupus! No!'

Lupus had stopped to throw stones back at the boys. One of his stones struck down a donkey boy and the others gathered around him. For a moment the hail of stones ceased.

'Come on, Lupus!' cried Flavia and Jonathan together.

At last they saw the *Scarab's* mast rising above the riverbank.

'Nathan!' screamed Flavia. 'Help!'

As the boat came into sight below them they saw Nathan look up, his eyes wide.

'Help!' cried Flavia and Seth together.

'Donkey boys!' wheezed Jonathan. 'After us!'

'Get in!' cried Nathan, hurriedly untying the rope which moored them to an acacia tree. 'Hurry!'

Flavia and Seth thudded across the small gangplank but Jonathan and Lupus both jumped from the shore. While Nathan started to loose the sail, Jonathan grasped the gangplank and used it to push the boat away from the riverbank. A moment later he held the plank like a shield in front of him, just in time to ward off a shower of gravel. A fist-sized stone bounced off the *Scarab's* mast and clattered into the boat. Lupus grabbed it and hurled it back with a guttural cry. The boys on the shore cringed, then looked around for more stones.

But now the wind was filling the sail and they were

moving past reeds and papyrus, out into the centre of the river. Stones splashed into the water nearby, and a pair of geese rose honking from the reeds. The donkey boys ran along the bank, trying to keep up, but by now the *Scarab* was out of range and their stones splashed harmlessly into the Nile.

'Did you find the treasure?' called Nathan from the tiller. 'Is that why they're after you?'

'No,' said Flavia. 'No treasure.'

Blood was dripping from Seth's forehead and Jonathan was trying to staunch the flow with his sleeve.

'Then why were they stoning you?'

'I don't know,' said Flavia, tearing a strip of cloth from the hem of her long tunic. 'But they were angry at Seth.' She handed the strip to Jonathan, who grunted his thanks.

'Seth, what on earth did you do to make them so angry?'

Seth gave his cousin a wounded look. 'I didn't do anything. They were throwing rocks at me for no reason at all.'

Nathan frowned back at the donkey boys, now small figures on the retreating riverbank. Suddenly he looked at the three friends. 'Did one of you address him by name? Did you call him "Seth" in front of them?'

Lupus nodded yes and pointed at Flavia, who was rubbing the place on her arm where the stone had hit her.

She looked up to see them all looking at her. 'What? What did I do wrong?'

'You frightened them,' said Nathan, and shook his head ruefully. 'Why Aunt Rachel chose to give you that name, I will never understand.'

'Why?' asked Flavia 'What's wrong with the name Seth?'

'It's a good Jewish name,' said Jonathan.

'But here in Egypt,' said Nathan, 'Seth is the red-haired god of death and destruction.'

'The Egyptian god Seth,' said Nathan, 'was the brother of Osiris. Their sisters were Isis and Nephthys . . . They were the four children of the sky goddess Nut and Geb, god of the earth. Osiris married Isis and Seth married Nephthys, but Seth preferred Isis and grew jealous of his brother. He tried to kill Osiris several times. Finally he succeeded. Seth chopped up his brother and tossed the pieces in the Nile.'

'Oh!' cried Flavia. 'That must be why the Seth animal stands for destruction and confusion.'

They were safely out on the river now, and although two of the bigger pyramids still loomed on the horizon, they could no longer see the angry boys on the river-bank. Jonathan had cleaned Seth's head wound and was bandaging it with a strip of linen torn from the hem of Flavia's tunic.

'Osiris's faithful wife Isis found most of the pieces,' continued Nathan, 'and she put him back together. And even though his most vital bit had been eaten by a sharp-nosed fish, they managed to have a son called Horus. When this son grew up, Seth persecuted him, too, and in one terrible battle young Horus lost an eye. So you see, the Egyptians regard Seth as a powerful and evil persecutor.'

'But the name "Seth" means something completely different in Hebrew,' said Jonathan, tying off Seth's bandage.

'Most Egyptians don't know that,' said Nathan. 'Especially here in the countryside.'

'That's another reason not to leave the city,' grumbled Seth. 'This never happened to me in Alexandria.'

Nathan ignored him. 'Also, red is an unlucky colour. It reminds Egyptians of the desert, and that represents death. To have red hair and be called Seth is doubly ill-omened. And if they guessed you were a Jew, you'd really be in trouble.'

'These Egyptians are crazy,' muttered Jonathan.

'You should wear a turban like us, Seth!' said Flavia.

Lupus pointed at his own turban and gave Seth a thumbs-up.

'And change your name,' added Jonathan.

Nathan nodded. 'Good advice. The further upriver we travel, the worse it will get.'

'We're not going up river.' Seth touched his bandaged forehead and winced. 'We're going back. This quest is over.'

'No!' cried Flavia. 'We can't go back to Alexandria! We have to find Nubia!' She looked at Nathan. 'There wasn't any treasure, but we did find another clue. A riddle whose answer was "camel" and a hieroglyph of Sobchak, the crocodile god.'

'Sobek,' corrected Jonathan. 'I think his name is Sobek.'

Lupus grunted and pointed at his wax tablet.

'And also,' said Flavia, glancing at what Lupus had drawn there, 'the hieroglyph of the Seth animal.'

'So where do we go?' asked Nathan, frowning. 'Seth?'

'Nowhere,' growled Seth. 'I'm finished with this quest.'

'Don't you care about the treasure?' asked Nathan.

'It's probably a trap!' said Seth.

'A trap?' Nathan stared at him.

Seth nodded. 'I've told you a dozen times, Chryses isn't my friend. He's my enemy. I'm sure he was trying to cast spells on me in Alexandria.'

'What kind of spells?' asked Flavia.

Seth ignored her. 'Now he probably wants to kill me. And I wouldn't be the first one.'

'What kind of spells?' repeated Flavia.

'You're not the first what?' said Jonathan at the same time.

'Remember I mentioned Onesimus?'

'The scribe who died last month?' said Jonathan.

Seth nodded. 'They found his body at the foot of the stairway leading up to our cubicles. His neck was broken.'

'Maybe he slipped and fell,' said Flavia.

'Maybe,' said Seth. 'But one of the other scribes said he heard Chryses and Onesimus arguing. A few moments later he heard a cry and found Onesimus lying dead at the foot of the stairs.'

'Great Juno's peacock!' breathed Flavia. 'Do you really think Chryses could be a murderer?'

Seth shrugged.

Flavia gripped his arm. 'That gives us even more reason to find Nubia. If Chryses is with her then she might be in danger!'

Seth sighed deeply, then nodded. 'I think I know where they're going,' he said, and looked at Flavia. 'But when you find out you may not want to go on.'

'Where?' asked Flavia. 'Where are they going?'

'To Crocodilopolis, the city of crocodiles.'

SCROLL XX

'Crocodilopolis?' gasped Flavia. 'There's a place called Crocodilopolis?'

Jonathan and Lupus exchanged looks of amazement.

'Several,' sighed Seth. 'Entire towns devoted to worshipping crocodiles. The nearest Crocodilopolis has a tame jewel-encrusted crocodile who takes food from your hand.'

'A tame crocodile? Is that true?' Jonathan asked Nathan.

'Yes,' said Nathan. 'And it's only a day or two from here, near Lake Moeris in the region called Fayum, in the nome of Arsinoe.' He frowned at Seth. 'But how did you know that?'

'Strabo,' said Seth. 'He also mentions a labyrinth at Crocodilopolis, and calls it the Eighth Sight of the World.'

'And you think that's where they're going?' asked Flavia in a small voice. 'To the city of crocodiles?'

Seth shrugged. 'It's the nearest place where the god Sobek is worshipped . . .'

'But I thought the main clue was the camel riddle!' protested Flavia, and added hopefully: 'Is there maybe a place called Camelopolis?'

Nathan laughed. 'As far as I know, there is no place or sanctuary associated with camels.'

Jonathan added: 'You heard what Abu told us at the pyramids, Flavia. Camels are new to Egypt. Aren't they Seth?'

'Yes.'

'Then what did the camel part of the riddle mean?' asked Flavia.

Seth shrugged. 'Perhaps it means they are going by camel. Although I doubt Chryses has ever ridden a camel in his life.'

'But Nubia has!' cried Flavia. 'Nubia loves camels. She's very good with them.'

'Of course!' said Seth. 'I completely forgot: Chryses hates water! He'd never sail in a boat if he had a choice. The only other way upriver is by donkey or camel. That must be why he took Nubia with him; camels are much faster.'

'And Abu told us there was a camel-market at the pyramids, the day before we arrived,' said Jonathan.

Seth nodded and glanced at Flavia. 'Now that you know they're probably on their way to the City of Crocodiles, are you still determined to follow them?'

Flavia looked at her friends. Jonathan and Lupus nodded their encouragement and she swallowed hard. 'We must find Nubia,' she said, and turned to Nathan. 'Take us to Crocodilopolis.'

'I'd be happy to take you there,' said Nathan, 'but there's a slight problem. The wind has just died.'

By noon they had all taken a turn at punting, except for Seth.

'Come on, Seth!' cried Nathan impatiently. 'The punt pole and I are waiting.'

'I'm busy teaching Flavia the hieroglyphic alphabet,'

replied Seth, without looking up from his wax tablet.

'I don't mind if you punt for a while,' said Flavia.

'I'm wounded,' whined Seth. 'My head is throbbing.'

'It wasn't bothering you a moment ago,' said Nathan.

'Well, it is now.'

'Oh, don't be an infant!' snapped Nathan. 'Even the girl here has tried her hand at it.'

'I don't even want to be on this boat.'

'Listen, Seth!' growled Nathan. 'Either you punt or I'll make you a eunuch and feed your bits to the sharp-nosed fish.'

Jonathan and Lupus both laughed. Seth glared at them, then sighed and rose and went to the back to the stern.

Flavia bent her head over her wax tablet. With Seth's help, she had written out the hieroglyphic alphabet and now she was trying to memorize the characters. Lupus and Jonathan were fishing with a plank of wood and a net. Standing in the bows of the boat Jonathan would strike the water hard with Nathan's small gangplank, while at the stern Lupus used a net to scoop up the stunned fish as they floated to the surface. They had already caught several good-sized pike. Soon they would be grilling them for dinner.

'Lupus!' called out Flavia. 'Here's a riddle for you. What do a lion and a quail chick have in common?'

Lupus looked at her and shook his head.

'They're both hieroglyphic letters in your name.'

Lupus gave her a thumbs-up and a grin.

'And Jonathan,' continued Flavia, 'you have a cobra and two vultures. I also have two vultures, and two horned vipers.' She looked up at Nathan. 'What is a horned viper, anyway? Do they really exist?'

134

'Oh, yes,' said Nathan. He was showing his cousin how to punt. 'You don't want to meet one of those.'

Flavia stared hard at the riverbank, but she couldn't see any horned vipers, just lush green fields and shaggy palms, and beyond them the barren desert, hot and shimmering in the midday heat. A white egret rose out of the reeds and flapped away to the east.

'Hallelujah!' said Seth, as a breeze ruffled the sail and then caused it to balloon. 'I think the wind is rising.'

'Master of the Universe, you're lucky!' Nathan shook his head in wonder. 'You were only at it for a few moments and this breeze gets up.'

'That's because the Lord in his wisdom wants to spare my hands, these skilled hands of a scribe and scholar.'

Flavia put down her tablet and went to Jonathan in the bows of the boat. She lifted the tail of her turban and let the breeze cool the damp back of her neck.

'Look,' said Jonathan, shading his eyes. 'I think I see some pyramids.' He was wearing a nut-brown turban which Nathan had found in one of his storage spaces.

'Yes,' came Nathan's voice from behind them. 'There are more than one hundred of them here in Lower Egypt. And all of them pillaged.'

'Which pyramids are those?' asked Flavia.

'The pyramids of Acanthus,' said Nathan. 'They say the oldest of all the pyramids is there.'

Seth came up behind them, mopping his cheeks. Flavia noticed that his face and the back of his neck were very pink.

'When do we stop?' he asked.

'Stop?' Nathan frowned at his cousin. 'Tonight the moon is full. If we carry on through the night and if this good wind holds, we might reach Crocodilopolis before they do.'

Seth shook his head. 'The Sabbath begins this evening,' he said. 'And I do not travel on the Sabbath.'

Before the first stars pricked the evening sky, Nathan guided his boat to the west bank and moored it to a pink-blossomed mimosa at the water's edge.

Lupus shared Nathan's frustration as they furled the sail. Flavia's eyes were red from crying and even Jonathan was annoyed. He had pointed out that it was permitted to travel on the Sabbath if it was an emergency.

'This is not an emergency,' Seth had grumbled. 'It's a wild-ibis chase.'

Suddenly Lupus's head went up.

'What's the matter, Lupus?' asked Flavia.

Lupus grunted for them to be quiet and put his finger to his lips. He had seen someone in the sycamore grove on the bank above them.

SCROLL XXI

'Just as I suspected,' said Chryses, coming into the sandy clearing. 'Seth won't travel on the Sabbath.'

'Seth?' said Nubia, looking up from her work. She was lying on her stomach near the fire and making a reed flute. 'The scribe who hates you? He is here?'

Chryses seemed flustered. He eased the bulging basket from his shoulder onto the ground and went over to the camels.

'Er . . . yes. About a stade upriver from here, not far from the village. He . . . um . . . he thinks I took something of his and he's pursuing me. I should have told you before. But don't worry. They won't be travelling tomorrow.' Chryses opened his canvas pack and took out a rolled up reed mat.

'They?' Nubia put the glowing end of an acacia twig to the reed. 'Is Seth travelling with others?'

'With his cousin and some boys,' said Chryses, unrolling his mat beside the fire. 'Seth's cousin owns a boat. The boys are probably his nephews. I didn't get a very good look,' he added, 'because I didn't want to get too close to the riverbank.'

'You do not like the river?' asked Nubia. The twig had burned a hole in one side of the reed.

'I hate the river.'

137

'Why?'

'I'll tell you sometime. At least it means we don't have to travel tonight. My bottom couldn't endure one more hour on that creature.' He glared at Castor. The two camels were sitting at the foot of an acacia tree, smugly chewing their cuds.

'What is he thinking that you took?' Nubia held the acacia twig in the fire and waited for the end to glow again. The sun had set an hour before and now the twilight was turning to dusk. The sky above was a deep vibrant blue, and the stars growing brighter by the moment.

'Nothing of importance,' said Chryses. 'He just likes to persecute me. Anyway, I had luck in the village. Some stalls in the market were still open. Food is so much cheaper here than in Alexandria.' Chryses reached into the bulging basket and began to bring out food: two flat loaves of brown bread, four onions the size of apples, several papyrus twists and a fat disc of white cheese wrapped in a woven palm leaf basket. There was a gourd, too.

'Palm wine,' said Chryses, taking out the cork with his teeth. 'But this is weaker and sweeter than the last lot. Want some?'

Nubia shook her head.

'Go on. Try some. Look, they make these cups from some kind of plant that grows around here. The stall-holder gave me some gratis. Here.' Chryses poured some brown liquid from the gourd into the leaf and extended it to Nubia.

She put down her reed and sniffed the liquid in the leaf cup. It smelled slightly sweet and yeasty. And there was another vegetable smell, too. She wasn't sure if it was the wine or the cup. She took a tentative sip.

'Oh,' she said. 'It is good. It is tasting like dates.' She took another sip, swallowed and coughed. 'But it is burning the back of my throat.'

'That's the fun part,' said Chryses, tearing one of the loaves in half and putting it back on the mat. He unrolled one of the papyrus twists and tipped out a handful of raisins. Then he began to peel a large white onion.

The palm wine made Nubia dizzy, so she put it down and picked up her reed again.

'Here's a riddle for you, Nubia,' said Chryses. 'See if you can tell me the answer. *I bite the biters, no one else in sight. To bite me, biting, most are ready, quite. Because I have no teeth, they do not fear my bite.*'

Nubia stared at him, wide-eyed. He was always posing riddles and writing them on monuments. She could never understand them.

'I do not know.'

'Simple,' he said, taking a bite of his onion. 'The answer is an onion!' His green eyes watered and he grinned at her. 'It has quite a bite! But it's delicious.'

'Oh,' said Nubia.

'What are you making?' asked Chryses presently, nodding at the reed. 'A flute?'

'Yes. Music comforts me.'

'Aren't you hungry, Nubia? Don't you want some bread and cheese? It's camel's-milk cheese.'

'No. Grief makes my stomach unhappy.'

Chryses put down his onion. 'Tell me about your friends,' he said gently. 'What were their names?'

Nubia felt her throat tighten and the familiar tears fill her eyes. 'Flavia Gemina was my mistress. She bought me two years ago in Ostia. I was to be her slave but I do not think she knew how to have slave. She set me free a few months later. She was very kind and good at solving mysteries.' The tears spilled over and Nubia let them fall. 'Flavia was like sister to me and I miss her so much.'

'Go on,' said Chryses. 'Tell me about the others.'

'Jonathan was living next door to us. He was Jewish and good hunter and he liked making things. He was pessimist but funny.' Nubia smiled through her tears. 'I remember first meal I have with him. He sticks snails up his nose. It was funny.'

Chryses nodded. 'He sounds very amusing. You said there were three of them?'

'Lupus is youngest. His name means wolf. He has no tongue and cannot speak. The first time I see him he is swinging through branches of graveyard like monkey.' Nubia wiped her cheeks. 'Later Flavia writes an ode to him for his birthday: *Then, like Icarus he fell from the sky, not onto billowing waves, his native element, but onto hard earth, which jars the bones and bruises the flesh. For wolves may swim and wolves may run, but never do wolves fly in the air.*'

Nubia was laughing and crying at the same time.

'Poor Nubia,' said Chryses. 'Don't despair. Maybe you'll see your friends again one day.'

'No,' said Nubia, and now there was no laughter mixed with her tears. 'They drowned in the storm. I will never ever see them again.'

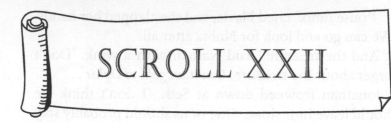

SCROLL XXII

The next morning Seth woke them at dawn by vomiting over the side of the boat. He returned to his mat, shivering and sweating, his face and arms burned red.

'He's suffering from sunstroke,' said Jonathan, covering Seth with the lightest blanket they had. 'It's probably just as well we're not sailing today.'

'The fool,' muttered Nathan, looking down at his cousin. 'I told him to wear a turban instead of that little skullcap. We all did. But would he listen? Just because he can read and write four languages, he thinks he knows everything . . . What else can you do for him?'

'We must keep him out of the sun,' said Jonathan, looking towards the brightening eastern horizon.

'Very well,' said Nathan, rising to his feet. 'Help me put up the awning.'

'That should do,' said Jonathan, when they had fixed the reed awning in place.

'You know,' said Nathan as they sipped their mint tea after breakfast. 'Crocodilopolis is not far from here. Further up the Nile is a canal that leads to Lake Moeris, but we could cover the same distance by donkey, perhaps even faster now that the river is low. I'm sure we can hire donkeys from the village near here.'

'Praise Juno!' cried Flavia, and she clapped her hands. 'We can go and look for Nubia after all.'

'And the treasure,' said Nathan with a wink. 'Don't forget about the treasure. *Countless gold of Ophir . . .*'

Jonathan frowned down at Seth. 'I don't think we should leave him alone. One of us should probably stay here and bathe his forehead with a sea-sponge or damp cloth.'

Nathan nodded. 'Which one of you wants to stay with him?'

Jonathan looked at Lupus, who was whistling and pretending to gaze off into the distance. Jonathan turned to Flavia.

'Don't look at me!' she hissed. 'I'd rather face a thousand crocodiles than stay with him.'

'Well I don't want to stay either,' whispered Jonathan. 'I want to see the labyrinth and the tame crocodile.'

'Me, too!'

'Lupus? Do you want to stay here with Seth?'

Lupus stopped whistling and shook his head vigorously.

Nathan laughed. 'Why don't you choose lots?' He reached out and plucked a reed from the water, then broke it into three bits and showed them that one was shorter than the rest. 'The one who draws the short piece stays with Seth.'

Lupus drew first, and whooped when he saw his reed was one of the long ones.

Flavia went next, and groaned when she saw the short piece.

'Don't worry, Flavia,' said Jonathan. 'We'll tell you all about the jewel-encrusted crocodile and the labyrinth.

Just make sure Seth drinks plenty of water and keep him cool in the shade.'

'My grandmother recommended black Nile mud for sunburn,' remarked Nathan. 'If he becomes too hot, plaster him with mud. Just the sunburned areas,' he added quickly. 'His face, neck and arms.'

'Mud?' groaned Flavia. 'Instead of looking for Nubia, I have to put mud on him?'

Nathan nodded. 'Nice cool river mud. Cures anything. Ready boys?'

Jonathan and Lupus nodded. They were both dressed in loose beige tunics and sandals, with their coin purses round their necks. Lupus wore his turquoise turban and Jonathan the nut-brown one.

Nathan turned back to Flavia. 'We should be back by sundown tonight,' he said. 'But don't worry if we don't get back until tomorrow.'

'Tomorrow?' she yelped. 'You might not get back until tomorrow?'

'That's right. But we'll try to be back tonight.' He gestured around. 'These trees should camouflage you, but if anyone bothers you, tell them Seth is a leper. He certainly looks the part.'

Flavia tried to concentrate on learning the hieroglyphic alphabet but presently she put down her wax tablet and began pacing back and forth in the small boat. 'What if they miss a clue?' she muttered under her breath. 'What if Nubia's in disguise and they don't recognise her? Oh, why did I have to draw the short reed?'

'Stop pacing,' came Seth's feeble voice. 'You're making the whole boat rock. I feel nauseous.'

Flavia glared down at him. It was mid-morning and

the heat was like a furnace. She had to get away from him, if only for a few moments. She kicked off her sandals, stomped to the side of the boat and slipped over the side, tunic and all. The black Nile mud squelched between her toes and the flowing water came up to her neck, cooling her temper as well as her body. It was delicious and when she pulled herself on board again her wet tunic continued to make the heat bearable. This gave her an idea. She dipped Seth's blanket in the river, then wrung it out and draped it over him.

'Oh, that's good,' he murmured and soon his breathing told her he was asleep.

Flavia sighed and picked up her wax tablet again. She wrote down questions about the case. Why had Nubia gone with Chryses? Was the mysterious eunuch really evil? Had he killed Onesimus? And if Chryses was Seth's enemy, why was he leaving him clues to the treasure?

She lay back on the thin mattress and tried to think. But even in the shade of the awning the ferocious heat acted like a drug, and soon she was skimming below the surface of sleep.

She had restless dreams of Ostia. Of her father – grieving for her – and of Alma and Caudex and her beloved dog Scuto. She also saw Flaccus, the young lawyer who had asked for her hand in marriage a few months before. In her dream she saw him: tall dark and patrician, with his straight glossy hair falling over his eyes, wearing the garments of a groom and going to fetch his bride, a girl whose name was not Flavia.

Finally she dreamt of her Uncle Gaius. And with the certainty only a dream can bring, she knew he was dead and that she would never see him again.

Flavia woke to find her cheeks wet with tears.

Miserably she stood and went to the side of the boat. Without even checking for crocodiles she jumped in and struck out upstream. Soon the cool water cleared her mind and washed away her tears. For a moment she stopped and floated on her back. She let the current carry her back downstream and she thought of home. High above her a vulture wheeled slowly in the pure blue expanse of sky.

The vulture made her think of death and dead things. That reminded her of crocodiles. Fear replaced her sadness and set her heart pounding. *Silly girl!* she chided herself. She swam back to the boat as quickly as she could, praying with each stroke to every god she could think of. At last she pulled herself into the boat with a gasp of relief.

As she unwrapped her damp turban she looked down at Seth, who seemed to be sleeping peacefully. Maybe he was right to honour his god. Without the protection of the gods, you were lost.

At that moment a rustle among the shrubs on the riverbank set her heart pounding again. Someone – or something – was in the sycamore grove.

SCROLL XXIII

Flavia crouched down inside the boat, then pulled herself slowly up and peeped over the side. Her eyes widened as she caught sight of the culprit. It was not a bandit, but rather a kind of weasel with brown fur and a long, pointed nose. It was rolling in the mud at the water's edge. Abruptly it sat up and regarded her with bright black eyes.

'Hello, little creature!' she said softly.

'Hello, yourself,' came Seth's feeble voice from behind her.

'Oh! You're awake!' Flavia turned to look at Seth. 'How are you feeling?'

'A little better.'

Seth pushed himself up on one elbow. His face was blistered and peeling and horrible to behold. Flavia averted her eyes and continued as cheerfully as she could. 'Jonathan says you're suffering from sunstroke. He says you'll have to wear a turban from now on, whether you like it or not.'

'Ichneumon,' said Seth. 'Herpestes ichneumon.'

'What?'

'That creature on the river bank. It's an ichneumon. Also called mongoose. There are some in the animal enclosure in the Museum. According to Strabo there is an entire city near here which is devoted to its worship.'

'Some people worship the mongoose? Like the people of Crocodilopolis worship the crocodile?'

'Yes.' He lay back onto his pillow and closed his eyes. 'The inhabitants of Cynopolis worship the dog but eat the sharp-nosed fish, whereas the inhabitants of Oxyrhynchus worship the sharp-nosed fish but eat dog meat. Those two towns are bitter enemies. So it is with the inhabitants of Heracleopolis. They worship the mongoose and are rivals with the inhabitants of Crocodilopolis because the mongoose and the crocodile are enemies. That little creature is one of the few animals that can kill a crocodile.'

'That sweet little thing can kill a crocodile? How?'

'When the crocodiles are basking in the sun with their mouths open – as they often do – the mongoose leaps into the crocodile's open jaws and eats through its entrails and belly to emerge unharmed from the dead crocodile.'

'Great Juno's peacock!'

'It doesn't seem so sweet now, does it?' he added drily. 'May I have something to drink? And something to lift my head.'

'Oh, yes! Sorry. I was supposed to be giving you lots of water.' She rolled up a blanket and put it under his head, then handed him one of the water gourds. Seth drank long and deeply.

'I'm also supposed to be putting Nile river mud on your burns,' said Flavia. 'Would you like that?'

'I'd prefer a damp cloth,' he said. 'It was nice when you did that.'

Flavia duly soaked a cloth in the river and draped it

gently over his face. 'Do you want me to soak your blanket, too?'

'Yes, please,' came Seth's deep voice from beneath the cloth. 'It's unbearably hot. What time is it?'

'I think it's about four hours past noon,' said Flavia, as she dipped his blanket over the side of the boat. 'Maybe five. Nathan and the boys have gone to Crocodilopolis to look for Chryses and Nubia.'

'You really care for her, don't you?' said Seth.

'Nubia? Yes. She's like a sister to me. Or a best friend. I miss her so much.' Flavia gently draped the damp blanket over his body.

'Ah, that's good,' said Seth with a sigh, and added: 'I wish I had a friend like you. I mean, someone who missed me when I went away ... Did you really mean what you said?'

'What?'

'That you'd rather face a thousand crocodiles than look after me?'

'Oh!' said Flavia. 'You heard me say that? I didn't ... It was a figure of speech.'

'No, it wasn't.' His voice was muffled beneath the cloth. 'You don't like me. Nobody likes me.'

'I *do* like you,' protested Flavia. 'But ...'

'I'm not very good with people,' said Seth. 'That's why I became a scribe.'

'So you could read books all day, and not have to get on with people?'

He gave a low, throaty chuckle. 'Exactly.'

'Sometimes I prefer books to people, too,' said Flavia. 'But people are good for you. Take Nubia for example. She's the opposite of me. I'm impetuous and impulsive, and sometimes a little bossy. She's kind and gentle and says "behold!" and loves all animals. Before I met her I never would have said hello to a mongoose. She makes me think about things in a new way. So do Jonathan and Lupus,' she added.

Seth lifted the cloth from his face. 'How old are you again?' he asked.

'I'll be twelve next month,' said Flavia.

'Well, Flavia Gemina,' said Seth, replacing the cloth. 'You are the most amazing girl I have ever met.'

Jonathan, Lupus and Nathan arrived back from Fayum shortly after sunset, while it was still light. Nathan carried a shoulder basket full of provisions.

'No Nubia?' grunted Flavia, as she put down the gangplank for them.

'Sorry, Flavia,' said Jonathan. 'Not a trace of her. But the labyrinth was superb. It wasn't a real labyrinth, but a kind of massive temple. We only saw part of it but our guide said it had over two thousand rooms with another level underground.'

'It did?' said Flavia wistfully.

A grubby but happy Lupus touched his elbows together and smacked his forearms shut.

'And the crocodile!' added Jonathan. 'A rich lady from Alexandria arrived just before we did and the official let her feed it pieces of meat and wine mixed with honey. The priest's assistants had to force its jaws open and when the crocodile finished eating it ran away to the other side of the pool.'

Lupus puffed out his cheeks and patted an imaginary belly as if to say: it was full to bursting.

'Oh,' cried Flavia wistfully, 'I wish I'd seen it. Was the crocodile jewel-encrusted?'

Lupus shook his head and pointed to his throat.

'But it was wearing a golden necklace,' explained Jonathan. 'With lapis lazuli and carnelian, I think.' He shook his head. 'These Egyptians are crazy.'

Lupus chuckled and kicked off his sandals. Then he pulled off his turquoise turban and his beige tunic and jumped off the side of *Scarab* into the river. His splash rocked the boat and Nathan held on to the mast.

'There may have been a labyrinth and a tame crocodile,' Nathan said bitterly. 'But there was no treasure. And we couldn't find any clues, either.'

'No clues anywhere?' cried Flavia.

'Did you ask people?' said Seth from his mattress.

'Of course we did!' snapped Nathan. 'We asked the priests if they'd seen any graffiti, eunuchs or Nubians. We asked all the officials and would-be guides and beggars. I even asked the shopkeepers.' Nathan threw down the shoulder bag in disgust. A wheel of cheese rolled across the floor of the boat.

'Don't despair, cousin,' said Seth, sitting up. 'I think you went to the wrong sanctuary of Sobek.'

Flavia turned to Seth in amazement. 'There's another place where they worship crocodiles?'

At the word 'crocodiles' Lupus's alarmed face appeared over the side of the boat. Jonathan pulled his dripping friend into the boat and handed him his tunic.

'Yes,' said Seth. 'If Strabo is to be trusted there are at least two more places where the crocodile is worshipped.'

'You can't possibly mean . . .' said Nathan.

'Where else?'

'But what if you're wrong? What if you misunderstood the clue?'

'Remember I told you I caught a brief glimpse of the treasure map before Chryses hid it?'

'No.' Nathan scowled at his cousin. 'You never told me any such thing.'

'Well, I told these three, then.'

Lupus had been struggling to put on his tunic. Now his head popped out and he nodded eagerly.

'That's right,' said Flavia to Seth. 'You said it was written with five different coloured inks in Greek, Hebrew and hieroglyphs.'

Seth nodded. 'And now I remember: One of the hieroglyphs was of Sobek, the crocodile god. And there were two names in Greek near the top of the sheet. They didn't make sense then, but they do now.'

'What two names?'

'Ombos and Syene.'

'Well, that's just wonderful!' cried Nathan bitterly, 'I'm sure you'd love to search for the treasure now.'

'I'm willing if you are,' said Seth quietly.

'You what? Are you mad?'

'I said I'm willing. I'll even help punt if necessary.' Seth pushed himself up on his elbows.

'You moan and whimper about a day-trip to the pyramids, force us to stop for the Sabbath, and now you say you're willing to go five hundred miles?'

'I am.'

'I don't believe it. What prophet appeared to you in a vision and told you to go?'

'She did,' said Seth, and pointed to Flavia. 'She didn't exactly tell me, but she inspired me.'

As usual, Chryses was taking a long time in the bushes.

Nubia sighed and stroked Pollux's nose. 'He always

takes so long when he does latrine,' she said to the camel. 'I suppose he's ashamed of being a eunuch. I wonder what it looks like.' Nubia sighed again and gave a date each to Pollux and Castor. The sun had set but it was still light enough to ride. They had rested during the hottest time of the day and were ready to set out again.

At last Chryses appeared from behind the bushes, dressed in his usual white turban and cream tunic. As he pushed some rags into the camel's hempen saddlebag, Nubia could see he was flustered.

'Are you unwell?' asked Nubia.

'Cramps,' said Chryses.

'Your stomach is unhappy?'

Chryses gave her a weak grin. 'You could say that.'

Nubia clicked at the camels and they dutifully knelt to be mounted.

'Lord Serapis Helios!' cried Chryses. His camel had risen to its feet before he was settled and he was dangling from the creature's neck.

Nubia ran to Chryses and put a hand on either side of his waist, in order to help him down. Beneath his tunic she felt something like bandages binding his ribs.

'What is that?' she said with a frown.

'What?' Chryses had turned pale.

'What are you wearing underneath?'

Chryses took a step back. 'It's not what you think!'

'I do not know what to think.'

Chryses turned away from her and hid his face in his hands. After a moment he turned back. 'All right. I'll tell you.' He reached into the neck of his tunic and after a moment of fumbling he pulled out a folded piece of

152

papyrus. 'It's the only way to keep it safe from robbers or cutpurses. To bind it to my body. It is the document giving me the right to claim my inheritance.' He held it out to her.

Hesitantly, Nubia reached out and took the piece of papyrus. It was still warm from being pressed against his skin. As she opened it she caught the sweet blue scent of lotus blossom, his perfume.

For a moment she felt dizzy. Then her eyes focussed on the papyrus. It was still light enough for her to see that on one side there was writing in Greek. On the other side was a picture of something like an upside down papyrus plant with a wavy stem. Along the stem on either side were words and symbols. Some of the words were in Latin, some in Greek and some in hieroglyphs. At the top of the sheet were two crocodiles inked in black and green, and shown facing each other. Between them was a strange symbol like a cross, but with a loop for a top. It was filled in with gold ink.

'What is this?' said Nubia.

'It's a map of the Nile. That's the Delta,' said Chryses, pointing at the upside-down flower of the blossom, 'and that's the river. These are some of the towns, and this,' his fingertip moved all the way up to the looped-top cross, 'this is an ankh, the Egyptian symbol for life. That is Syene, where my inheritance awaits.'

'Syene?'

'It's a town on the first cataract.'

'So you are not going all the way to Nubia?'

'It's the border of Nubia. The first cataract marks its border.'

Nubia's throat felt tight. 'But Nubia is very big. How will I find my family, if any are even left?'

'Let's worry about that when we get there. It's still a long way.'

Nubia swallowed and blinked back tears. 'Show me.'

Chryses came up beside her and again she smelled his sweet scent. He was only a little taller than she was and his honey-coloured skin was very smooth. 'Here is Alexandria, here are the pyramids, and this bud is Lake Moeris in the region called Fayum. And here,' he moved his elegant forefinger all the way up the wavy stem to the top of the papyrus, 'are Ombos and Syene.'

Nubia frowned. 'But where is Nubia my homeland?'

Chryses shook his head sadly. 'I'm afraid it's off the map.'

SCROLL XXIV

'Five hundred miles to Ombos and Syene?' gasped Flavia. 'But that will take us weeks!'

'Maybe months,' said Nathan. 'I have never been that far up the river. Syene is at the very border of Egypt and the Land of Nubia.'

'The Land of Nubia,' repeated Flavia and looked at Jonathan and Lupus. 'Are you thinking what I'm thinking?'

The two boys nodded.

'What?' asked Seth and Nathan together.

'Our friend Nubia thinks we're dead,' said Flavia. 'I think she's going home. All the way to Nubia.'

Seth looked at them. 'So are you still willing to go with us? Five hundred miles, if necessary?'

Flavia looked at her friends. Lupus nodded happily but Jonathan frowned. 'If we end up going all the way to the Land of Nubia,' he said, 'then it could be months before we get back to Ostia. Our families will think we're dead.'

'We should have sent them letters when we were in Alexandria!' cried Flavia.

'We were going to,' said Jonathan, 'but then we had to leave in a hurry. Remember?'

'Then let's write some now,' said Flavia. 'We can send

155

them from the next town.' She looked at Nathan. 'We can send letters from the next town, can't we?'

He shrugged. 'Even the smallest village has its scribe. The trick is finding someone who can take your letters to Rome. That will not be easy. Are you still willing to come with us?'

'Of course we'll go with you,' she said. 'But if there is any way we could catch them before they go much further. If we could just let Nubia know we're still alive . . .'

'That's fine with me,' said Nathan with a grin. 'I want to have a look at that treasure map. Come! Let's set sail now! The Sabbath has ended, the moon is rising, and so is the wind. Lupus, cast off. Jonathan, help me unfurl the sail. Flavia, light the brazier for dinner. Lie down, Seth. I don't expect you to do anything tonight. But enjoy your rest,' he added drily. 'From tomorrow, you'll be pulling your weight.'

The rhythmic forward motion of the camel comforted Nubia a little. So did the luminous moon rising over the palms on the east bank and the quacking of ducks on the river.

At least they were travelling towards her homeland. Even if Chryses would not go with her all the way. She had been lucky to find a companion for part of the journey. She had dreamt of this moment so many times. Of returning to Africa and going back to her desert home.

But what was waiting for her there? The slave-traders had killed her father and she had seen her mother and little sister abandoned by the roadside. One of her brothers had died in a burning tent. Was the other alive? And what of her cousin, Kashta, whom she was to marry?

At the thought of her lost family she felt tears filling her eyes again. She had cried so many since the shipwreck, she thought she had no more left. But she was wrong.

For three nights and three days a strong steady wind filled the *Scarab*'s sails. And for three nights and days they sailed without stopping.

Seth wore a black turban to cover his unlucky red curls and he dutifully smeared his sunburnt face and arms with a greasy white balm Nathan had bought in Crocodilopolis.

Each day after morning prayers, they would grill fish or duck over the brazier and eat it with leeks or onions. Jonathan organized a latrine for them in the bows of the *Scarab*, with the chamber pot and a blanket which could be pulled across for privacy. At the hottest time of the day Nathan unrolled the reed awning to make a patch of tiger striped shade.

They all took turns sailing and steering, even Seth. The tiller was a low fat piece of wood, as thick as Jonathan's thigh. You could either sit and hold it, or stand with it between your knees and steer with your legs. Nathan showed them what to look out for: a patch of rough water on a smooth surface meant underlying rocks, water of a paler colour warned of a sandbank, a half-submerged branch could spell danger.

He showed them how to angle the sail to catch the wind or to spill it.

They also took turns scanning the west bank for riders on camels, but only once did they see a rider on his camel, and he was heading north. Most people in this region rode donkeys or travelled on foot.

The cool green scent of the river mingled with the tang of human sweat and the sweet smell of the blue lotus, just beginning to bloom. The sun grew hotter and the river glittered with a myriad of silver spangles. They saw water buffalo up to their necks and donkeys drinking thirstily. Men fished with plank and net or with lines, little boys splashed in the river, girls washed clothes, and at dusk the village women came down to fill their jugs.

As soon as the sun set, the moon rose. It bathed the world in a light unlike any Flavia had ever seen. In Italia, Greece and even the deserts of Libya, the moonlight made the world silver and black, but here in Egypt the moon was like a pale sun. Colours were not deadened, but softened: the tufts of palm trees were emerald green, a sand bar white as snow, the river a luminescent blue. Even the mud villages looked beautiful, their white-washed domes became pearls and their waterwheels dripping sapphire bracelets.

The warm wind hummed in the rigging, but apart from that they ran silent. Silent enough to hear a distant donkey's bray or the desert jackal's haunting cry at night. There were other boats taking advantage of the miraculous wind and they did not want to draw attention to themselves. If a boatman hailed them, Nathan always answered in Egyptian, making the correct remarks and ending with prayers for a good journey.

Five days after they had first set out, shortly after midnight on the Ides of May, they were rounding a bend in the river when Flavia heard the distant sounds of revelry. She stood up to get a better look. A town emerged from the darkness, on the west bank of the river. It was lit by a thousand torches, perhaps for some festival. Above the mud domes and palm-thatched roofs loomed the massive head of the jackal-god, lit eerily from below.

'Anubis,' said Nathan, who always took the tiller at night. 'God of graveyards and deserted places.'

Flavia made the sign against evil, and nudged the others awake with her foot.

'Mnnnph!' said Jonathan. 'Who's kicking me?'

'Look!' whispered Flavia. 'Look at that massive statue of Anubis.'

'That must be Cynopolis,' said Nathan. 'City of Dogs. It looks as if they are having a feast. This might be a good chance for us to stop under cover of night and pick up provisions.'

Flavia nodded eagerly. 'And see if we're any closer to finding Nubia.'

The sounds of revelry grew louder as they approached the town. Flavia could hear women singing, men laughing, children shouting, the shrill piping of flutes and the patter of drums. The moon was lopsided, but bright enough to show the way over sandy ground. Flavia glanced back at Nathan, who had agreed to stay behind to guard the boat. She could see his white conical cap and his white teeth as he waved at her.

A path of yellow torchlight stretched out from the arched door of the town gate and they followed this in.

Flavia had never seen so many dogs in one place. Yellow dogs, brown dogs, white dogs, cream dogs with brown or black spots. There were even dogs who looked part jackal. Most of them were gnawing bones or sleeping. Plump puppies slept beside their well-fed mothers.

'Oh, look at the sweet puppies!' she exclaimed. 'They look much happier than the dogs in Ostia.'

'They may be better-fed,' said Jonathan, 'but they're not very healthy. Look how diseased most of them are. It would be kinder to cull some of them.'

'I wonder what they're celebrating?' said Flavia as a fresh burst of laughter reached her ears.

'Of course!' cried Seth, suddenly. 'Dogs are honoured here. Strabo talks about a sacred feeding for all the dogs of the town. I believe it is a festival for the townspeople, too.'

'That must be what's happening tonight,' said Flavia.

Lupus nodded his agreement and pointed at two yellow dogs happily gnawing marrowbones.

The sound of pipes and flutes guided them to a torch-lit square crowded with couches and tables. Men, women and even children reclined on the couches, eating food and tossing scraps to the packs of dogs which had congregated there. A group of male musicians were playing pipes, flutes and drums, and nearby a man in a loincloth was juggling goose eggs. Lupus's jaw dropped as two girls danced past; they wore only loincloths and they were bending so far back that their hands almost touched the ground.

The great statue of Anubis gazed sternly towards the river, like an angry father stoically ignoring the antics of his children. In the centre of the square, near a small sphinx with the Emperor Titus's face, was a colourful notice board.

As Flavia wove through the tables towards this board, she glanced around nervously; most of the revellers were dressed in white linen and had their heads uncovered. She and her friends wore turbans and dusty tunics.

'Don't worry,' came Seth's voice in her ear. 'I think they're too drunk to notice us.'

Flavia nodded and leaned forward to read the board. There were various pieces of papyrus tacked to it. One announced the lease of a palm grove. Another offered interpretation of dreams. A third asked for information about a runaway slave called 'Limping Heraclous'.

Then Flavia's breath caught with excitement. The flickering torchlight was bright enough to show two lines at the bottom of the board, written in charcoal in the now familiar hand: *Evil on four legs am I. As deadly on the river bank as in the Nile. Which land animal lacks a tongue? It is I!*

Beneath the riddle was a drawing of Sobek and of a Seth animal.

'I am a Crocodile!' she cried. 'The answer must be crocodile.'

'And the Seth animal is for me,' muttered Seth.

'At least that means we're still on the right track,' said Flavia.

Jonathan shook his head. 'But look how smudged the charcoal letters are. I'd guess we're still at least two days behind them.'

'Oh, no!' cried Flavia. 'They're even further ahead than before.'

'Oh dear,' said Seth. 'I think the townspeople have noticed us.'

Flavia followed his gaze and felt her blood chill at the sight of two dozen youths appearing from one of the dark side streets. They were moving menacingly towards her and her friends, and they all carried bows and arrows.

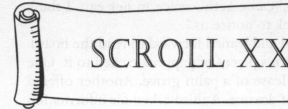

SCROLL XXV

'You!' cried the leader of the archers. 'You dog-eaters! How dare you come here on our holy day?'

Flavia was about to protest that she had never eaten dog in her life – or even considered such a thing – when she heard a voice behind her.

'No! You have eaten our holy fish! Now *you* die!'

Flavia and the others whirled to see a group of men standing near the biggest banqueting couch. They carried spears and swords and wore leather cuirasses with the painted emblem of a sharp-nosed pike. One of them held up someone's plate, and tipped it to show the bones of a fish. Already, people were screaming and running. Plates shattered and wine goblets clanged as they struck the hard-packed dirt. A dog yelped as one of the fish-men bent and cut its throat with his sword.

'You kill our sacred dogs?' bellowed the leader of archers. 'Then you DIE!' He turned to his men. 'Shoot them!'

'Down!' cried Seth, pushing Flavia. 'Get down!'

She heard the whoosh of arrows flying overhead, and now Seth was pulling her towards the nearest street. 'Run!' he cried, his voice hoarse: 'Run!'

Women were screaming and men were crying out. A spear glanced off an empty banqueting couch beside her and thudded to the ground. Flavia stumbled after Seth, Jonathan and Lupus, then tripped over a scavenging dog and fell awkwardly at the feet of the colossal Anubis. For a moment she was staring up at the torchlit underside of his lofty head, then hands were pulling her to her feet.

'Come on, Flavia!' wheezed Jonathan. 'If we don't get out of here, we're dead.'

'Well, we didn't manage to get any provisions at Cynopolis,' said Seth as they sailed up the moonlit river half an hour later. 'But at least we got away with our lives.'

'What on earth is happening back there?' asked Nathan, from the stern. He held a dripping punt pole and was staring towards the town. They could all hear the screams and Flavia knew the growing orange light was from more than torches. The giant head of Anubis seemed to glare reproachfully at them as they moved slowly upriver. Flavia shuddered and made the sign against evil.

'At first we thought it was us they were after,' wheezed Jonathan. 'But it was some men with leather breastplates and spears.'

Lupus grunted and pointed to his chest, then made a face like a fish.

'Yes,' said Flavia. 'They had fish painted on their breastplates.'

'Oxyrhynchites!' exclaimed Nathan. He pushed with his punt pole and sent *Scarab* gliding silently past moonlit reed beds. 'They must have been Oxyrhynchites. The two towns are always at war. It's because the citizens of Oxyrhynchus worship the sharp-nosed pike but eat dog meat.'

'Whereas the people of Cynopolis,' cried Seth excitedly, 'eat fish and worship the dog! I read about this. They had a terrible battle once and as a fish-worshipper was fleeing the dog-worshippers tore him to pieces and ate him raw!'

'Oh!' cried Flavia. And although it was a warm night, she shivered.

Jonathan put a blanket around her shoulders and shook his head. 'These Egyptians are crazy,' he wheezed.

'I don't believe that story about cannibalism,' said Nathan. 'But people *are* killed during their battles. You were lucky to get away.'

'Oh, I hope Nubia is safe,' murmured Flavia. 'Nathan, we found another riddle! But it looked at least two days old. We need to find Nubia before something terrible happens!'

As usual, Nubia went down to the water to fill the goatskins.

'Why do you fear the river?' she asked Chryses, when she returned to the clearing.

The eunuch poked the small fire. 'I will tell you why I fear water,' he said, 'if you tell me about Aristo.'

'Aristo?' Nubia felt her face grow warm.

'You called out his name in your sleep last night.'

'I did?'

'Yes,' said Chryses. 'You did.'

Nubia took a deep breath. 'He is our tutor,' she said. 'He comes from Corinth in Greece. He is almost twenty-three. He plays very wonderful music.'

'What does he look like?'

'He has curly hair the colour of bronze and smooth

tanned skin and brown eyes. He is taller than you or I, but not too tall. He is muscular, but not too muscular, and his legs are very fine.'

'By Serapis!' said Chryses. 'He sounds like a Greek god.'

'Yes,' said Nubia solemnly. 'He reminds me of statue of Mercury or Hermes.'

'I suppose all the girls like him?'

'All the girls like him,' sighed Nubia. 'All except Flavia. She likes Floppy.'

'Floppy?' said Chryses, and laughed. 'She likes floppy men?'

'No,' said Nubia. 'Flavia likes Gaius Valerius Flaccus. And he likes her. He asked her to marry him but she refused him.'

'And who does Aristo like?' asked Chryses.

'Nobody. He used to love Miriam,' said Nubia. 'But she loved another and Aristo's heart was wounded.'

'Poor Aristo,' said Chryses. 'And poor Nubia.'

'Why do you say "poor Nubia" to me?'

'Because you love Aristo and your heart is wounded.'

'Yes,' said Nubia. 'I love him. But it could never be.'

'Why not?' asked Chryses. 'You're one of the most beautiful girls I've ever seen. You are kind and gentle and good. Why shouldn't he love you?'

Nubia had no words.

'Did you ever tell him how you felt?' asked Chryses.

'I tried to, once,' she whispered. 'But then . . .'

'What?'

'I thought if I told him how I feel then we could not be friends.'

'What do you mean?'

'I wanted to stay his friend.'

'And you would have been happy to see him marry another, even though you loved him?'

'No,' whispered Nubia. The ache in her chest was almost too painful to bear.

'Do you still love him?'

'I will always love him,' said Nubia.

'Then you must do anything you can to gain his love,' said Chryses fiercely. 'Anything!'

Nubia stared wide-eyed at the eunuch. For the first time she felt a tremor of apprehension in his presence.

'I have told you of Aristo,' she said. 'Now you must tell me why you fear water.'

Chryses sighed and nodded. 'Do you remember that I was the slave of a rich Greek woman? And how we sailed on her barge from pyramid to temple, from sphinx to tomb, with me interpreting the hieroglyphs? Well, we were nearing a place called Thebes, passing tombs cut into the cliffs beside the river. My mistress ran to the side of the barge to look. Somehow she slipped and fell in the water . . . I called for the other servants. I reached out my hand. I tried to help her but I couldn't save her. They were too quick for me.'

'Who?'

'The crocodiles. They devoured her before my eyes.'

SCROLL XXVI

After Cynopolis, Flavia and her friends began to see dom-fruit palm trees. Unlike date palms, the trunks of this type of palm were thin and forked and the leaves spikier. Each brown dom-fruit was about the size of a man's fist. The pit was hard as rock, and inedible, but the chewy husk had a taste that reminded Flavia of Alma's gingerbread.

One day they spotted a group of antelope that had come down to drink on the east bank. Jonathan was taking aim with a bow he had made but just as he was ready to loose the arrow, a crocodile rose up from beneath the water and took a young one in its fearsome jaws. The antelope thrashed and writhed but soon the water was full of blood and the crocodile swallowed his twitching prey almost whole.

They stopped bathing in the river after that.

Two days after the Ides, they spied a group of excited villagers standing on the riverbank looking at something in the water. When the crowd saw their boat approaching they began to yell and gesticulate.

'Hippo,' said Nathan suddenly, and pointed to wet brown humps rising from the surface of the river. 'He's not with the rest of his herd. Must be a rogue.'

He steered as close as he dared to the opposite bank,

so close to the reeds that they sent a family of ducks flapping across the water.

'Watch out for the evil ducks, Flavia!' called Jonathan.

'Ha ha,' she muttered, not taking her eyes from the hippo, which was now only six boat lengths away.

The hippo blinked at them, but did not attack.

Flavia noticed that most of the children on the riverbank were naked and some of the men wore only tattered loincloths.

'That hippo could feed those poor villagers for a week,' said Nathan. 'But they won't kill him. They consider him to be sacred.' He spat into the river and shook his head.

'*The Nile is the gift of Egypt,*' quoted Seth, and then added. 'Herodotus said that.'

'I'm hoping for a proper gift,' said Nathan, and sang his treasure song.

While they scanned the riverbanks for signs of Chryses and Nubia, Nathan recounted stories of the Egyptian gods and Seth told them facts from Strabo and Herodotus. Seth also insisted that they speak only Greek. 'Otherwise,' he said, 'anyone will know you are Roman the moment you open your mouths.'

'But Nathan told us to keep our mouths shut when other people are around,' protested Jonathan.

'That's right. But if you have to talk, I want your Greek to be faultless.'

The Sabbath came again, bringing the usual strong morning breeze and a silver half moon – like a bowl – sinking over the western horizon. They had made good time, but the charcoal riddles showed that Chryses and Nubia were still at least a day ahead. Seth agreed to let them sail, but he spent the day beneath his prayer shawl, reciting Torah and offering up Sabbath prayers.

The next day they reached Hermopolis, a town where the ibis-headed god Thoth was held sacred. It was also the site of a large Roman garrison and a toll station. As they approached it, Nathan cursed in Greek.

'I was afraid of this.'

'What is it?' asked Flavia, looking up from her hieroglyphs.

'They're searching all the boats, and I only have room to hide two of you.'

Flavia lay with her knees touching her chin in one of Nathan's storage areas under the bench of the *Scarab*. He had removed a false partition to one of his compartments and she had wriggled down inside as far as she could go. When he replaced the false wall she was plunged into darkness. It was dry here, but dusty and her nose suddenly prickled. She mustn't sneeze! That would give away her location.

Presently she heard the resounding thud of the gang-plank coming down and heavy footsteps, as two pairs of hobnail boots came on board.

'From where have you come, and where are you going?' asked an official-sounding voice in Greek.

'From Memphis, sir. On our way to Tentyra,' came Nathan's voice. 'We are three brothers going home for our mother's birthday.'

'Jews, are you?' came another voice.

'Yes, sir.'

'The boy, too?'

'Yes, sir; he's the youngest of us.'

'No Romans aboard?'

'Excuse me?'

'We've been told to look out for three Roman children, two boys and a girl.'

In her dark hiding place, Flavia's stomach writhed. They were still wanted! Even here in Hermopolis, hundreds of miles from Alexandria.

'No,' came Nathan's voice. 'There are no Roman children on board.'

Suddenly Flavia felt her nose tickling again. She took a deep breath and pinched her nostrils.

'Any other goods you want to declare? Gold, linen, wine or honey?'

'No, sir.'

'Then you won't mind if we have a little look, will you?'

'Praise Juno!' breathed Flavia an hour later, as Nathan helped her out of her dark cubbyhole. 'I thought I was going to sneeze when the soldiers were on board.'

'Just as well you didn't,' said Nathan grimly. 'They were looking for you.'

'I know,' said Flavia. 'I could hear.'

Seth and Jonathan were helping Lupus out of the corresponding compartment on the port side of the Scarab. He brushed the dust off his tunic and gave Flavia a thumbs-up.

'There had better be a very big treasure at the end of this quest,' grumbled Nathan. 'I've used up almost all my emergency funds and have put my livelihood at risk for you three.'

'We're very grateful to you, sir,' said Flavia. 'And you can have half of my share of the treasure when we find it.

Jonathan took a deep breath. 'You can have half of my share, too,' he said.

Lupus pointed at himself and gave a thumbs-up.

Nathan gave a curt nod. 'There had better *be* a treasure at the end of this,' he muttered. 'That's all I'm saying.'

They sailed on, and a few days later, they watched the sun rise on the wrong side of the boat. Nathan explained this was because the river curved like a snake, and sometimes doubled back on itself. For three days they had to punt against the double opponent of wind and current.

At Lycopolis, City of Jackals, they found a cryptic phrase on an obelisk: PAVO PARIDIS SOL.

'The peacock of Paris is the sun?' said Flavia, with a frown. 'That's nonsense.'

'It's an anagram for Diospolis Parva!' cried Jonathan. 'A town a few days upriver from here.'

That night was their third Sabbath since they had begun their quest, the end of two weeks sailing. The very next day they saw their first crocodile pit.

They had stopped at Diospolis Parva on the west bank of the Nile, in order to look for clues and buy provisions. On the riverbank near the docking place was an enclosure with a limestone balustrade. Three veiled women stood looking over this low wall.

'Crocodile pit,' said Nathan. 'I've seen that once before. Why don't you children have a look while I go into town? Seth can stay on board.'

Seth nodded. 'Remember,' he said. 'If anyone speaks to you, don't say anything. Act dumb. Oh. Sorry, Lupus.' He grinned and patted Lupus's turquoise turban.

Flavia, Jonathan, Lupus and Nathan went across the

gangplank and along the wooden dock. They pushed through the usual crowd of pleading beggars and as Nathan went towards the town walls, they hurried to the balustrade around the crocodile pit. Flavia shuddered as half a dozen crocodiles came into view below, basking on a kind of limestone stage which slanted so that it went into the water; some of the crocodiles were half in and half out.

'Ugh,' said Flavia. 'They're so horrible. Those cold yellow eyes with the evil black slit.' She made the sign against evil.

'And their bumpy green mud-coloured skin,' added Jonathan. 'Like armour.'

Lupus bared his teeth and snapped his jaws.

'Yes,' agreed Flavia. 'Horrible.' She quoted the riddle left by Chryses. *'Evil on four legs am I. As deadly on the river bank as in the Nile. Which land animal lacks a tongue? It is I!* Is it true the crocodile has no tongue?'

'I don't suppose they need one,' said Jonathan. 'You saw that crocodile eat the antelope. He practically swallowed him whole.'

Flavia shuddered. 'Juno's peacock! That one must be twelve feet long.'

'What about that one?' said Jonathan, pointing.

'Where? Oh!' squealed Flavia, as the glassy surface of the water bulged and then parted to reveal a massive crocodile.

Lupus nodded and flashed the fingers of both hands twice, as if to say: twenty feet long.

'It's bigger than our atrium at home!' gasped Flavia. A pang of homesickness mingled with her horror at the creatures below them.

An excited buzzing made them turn and they saw

172

a crowd following half a dozen men coming towards them.

'Those must be the crocodile fighters Nathan was telling us about,' whispered Jonathan.

The men wore leather loincloths and body oil, and their only weapons were nets and daggers. As they passed by, Flavia caught the sweet scent of jasmine oil, with pungent undertones of sweat and fear. Now other people jostled up beside them at the balustrade. A couple shoved roughly in beside Flavia. She gave them a glare, then turned hastily away: it was a very Roman-looking man and his wife. He wore the tunic of a patrician and she was dressed in a pink stola with a matching parasol.

'Look, Cornelia!' said the man in Latin. 'They're like the ones I saw in Rome last year, at the games. They're called Tentyrites, I believe.'

As the men vaulted the wall and landed lightly on the highest part of the basking-place, most of the crocodiles retreated; all but the twenty-footer.

'All Egyptians fear crocodiles, of course,' said the man in his loud patrician accent, 'but whereas most worship them, the men of this region despise them.'

Down on the limestone basking-place, the crocodile-hunters suddenly moved forward, three on each side, and each tossed his net. As quick as lightning the colossal crocodile writhed towards one of the men, his terrible jaws snapping shut.

The crowd screamed, but the man had moved away just in time. Then the crocodile tried to catch a man on the other side. Again he failed. For a time the men danced round it, taunting it and tiring it. Finally one of them looped a leather strap around the crocodile's jaws.

'That's the way!' said the patrician beside Flavia. 'I

once saw a young girl disable a crocodile with nothing more than a garland of flowers,' he added. 'That was during the opening games of Titus's new amphitheatre.'

Flavia gave Lupus and Jonathan a wide-eyed look: she had been the girl with the garland! They nodded back, and Jonathan put his finger to his lips.

Flavia turned her head away from the couple. Had the man recognised her? But how? She was wearing a turban and long tunic, like all the boys of this region. Only her pale skin and grey eyes might give her away.

'She disabled a crocodile with a garland?' said the woman, also in Latin. 'I don't believe it!'

'It's true,' said the man, 'their jaws are so long that it requires much more strength to open them than it does to close them. Of course it was just a small crocodile, nothing like that brute. My dear Cornelia,' he added. 'If you should ever find yourself gripped in the jaws of a crocodile, simply gouge his eyes and he will let you go at once.'

Flavia shuddered, then gasped along with the rest of the crowd as the crocodile hunters took knives from their belts and began to stab the thrashing, netted creature to death.

SCROLL XXVII

'Excuse me, *kyria*,' said Flavia in Greek. 'Are you Roman?'

The crocodile slaughter was over and the crowd was dispersing.

'Oh!' cried Cornelia, covering her face with her pink linen parasol. 'The impertinence! Marcus, tell these wretched beggar boys to leave me alone.'

The man turned and swore at Flavia in Greek.

'Please, sir!' cried Flavia in Latin. 'We're not beggars. We're Romans! And we need your help.'

'Oh, Marcus!' gasped Cornelia. 'He speaks perfect Latin.' The woman lifted her parasol and looked closer. 'And he looks Roman, with those lovely grey eyes. What do you want, boy? Money?'

'We need to tell our parents that we're alive and well,' said Flavia. 'We've written some letters but we need someone to take them back to Ostia.'

'Oh, poor lads!' She turned to Jonathan. 'Are you Roman, too? Are you lost? Were you kidnapped?'

'We're fine,' said Jonathan. 'But we need to get word to our parents.'

'Oh, Marcus!' cried Cornelia, 'can't we help them?'

'I suppose we could ask Paniscus,' said her husband. 'He's going down to Alexandria next week.'

'Aren't you Roman?' asked Flavia, disappointed.

'Yes, but we're not going back until the inundation. And even if I give it to our friend, I can't afford to send a letter all the way to Rome.'

'Two letters,' said Flavia, and pointed at Lupus, who was running back from the *Scarab* with two papyrus letters in his hand. 'But our houses are on the same street – next door to each other – and here . . .' She pulled the gold and carnelian signet ring from her finger. She had lost weight in the past few weeks and it slipped off easily. 'This is worth something, isn't it?'

'It's lovely.' Cornelia took the ring. 'But it's a girl's ring!' she said, looking up sharply.

'It was my mother's,' lied Flavia. 'It's all I have to remember her by.'

'Oh, you poor thing!' Cornelia slipped the ring on her smallest finger. 'Marcus, can't we help these poor boys?'

'The courier will be well-rewarded at the other end, too,' said Flavia. 'Our families will be very grateful when they find out we're alive and well.'

The man examined the letters.

'My father is Marcus Flavius Geminus, sea captain,' said Flavia. 'He lives in Green Fountain Street in Ostia. See? I've written it on the outside.'

'Very well. I'll try to get these letters to Rome. But tell me, what are you three boys doing here in Upper Egypt?'

'We're searching for our friend.'

'Your friend must be very dear to you,' said Cornelia, looking up from admiring the ring on her finger.

'She is.'

Two days later, on the Kalends of June, Flavia was woken by a strange rhythmic splashing and the sound of a man shouting.

'Hello there!' came the man's voice in authoritative Greek. 'Hello! Who are you?'

Flavia opened her eyes but did not move. She had kept watch during the night and had been fast asleep. Disoriented, she blinked up at Seth, who stood at the tiller with the blue sky behind him.

Nathan was curled up on a mattress, fast asleep and snoring gently; he had been up all night, too. Flavia nudged him with her foot as the man's voice came again: 'Hey there!'

Flavia slowly raised her head and peeped through the reed awning. Lupus's head rose up beside hers. Then they both ducked down again. Less than ten feet away and sailing beside them was a magnificent red and yellow boat with twenty oarsmen and a soldier at the stern.

'I say: who are you?' cried the soldier for a third time. 'Where are you going?'

'My name Pthammeticuth!' Seth yelled back in the lisping accent of middle Egypt. 'Fitherman, come from visiting my thick thithter in Diothpolith Parva.'

Flavia stared at Seth in amazement. In the past three weeks the chubby scribe's sunburn had deepened to a tan. He had lost weight and grown lean. Wearing his turban, he looked just like a native. And he sounded like one, too.

Nathan was awake now, and also looking at his cousin in open-mouthed astonishment.

'Where are you going?' called the soldier.

'Home. Theebth.'

'Thebes?'

'Yeth! Who you?'

'We're officials from the governor's office in Alexandria. We seek three Roman children! Two boys and a girl, aged from nine to fourteen. Have you seen them?'

Flavia's grin faded. She and Lupus looked at each other in alarm.

'No. I have theen no Roman children.'

'What about you, boy?' the soldier called to Jonathan.

Jonathan stared blankly at the man and stayed quiet as Nathan had instructed them.

'You get no thenth out of that one,' said Seth. 'A thcorpion thtung his ear and now he deaf and addled.'

There was a pause. Finally the soldier called out: 'Well, if you do see these children, tell any village magistrate or temple priest and you will be rewarded. They are enemies of Caesar. Farewell.'

'Seth!' cried Flavia. 'You were wonderful! Who taught you to do that accent?'

The scribe smiled shyly. 'I've always been quite good at accents. It just came to me.'

'Are those the people you were fleeing in Alexandria?' asked Nathan. 'They looked like the governor's guard.'

'Yes,' said Flavia. 'I thought we were safe by now.'

'I can't believe they've come all this way to find us,' said Jonathan.

'Me neither,' said Seth. 'They must have searched Alexandria for weeks before they realised we'd gone upriver.'

'Master of the Universe!' said Nathan. 'You didn't tell me it was the governor's guard after you. And what did he mean, saying you were enemies of Caesar? You've been telling us Titus is your friend!'

'He is.'

'Then why did he order your arrest?'

'I don't know!' cried Flavia.

'I can't believe they've followed us all this way,' repeated Jonathan. 'We should try to find out why.'

'I agree,' said Nathan. 'And I have an idea of how to do it. We're coming to Tentyra.' He turned to Lupus. 'Flavia's told us many times how good you are at spying. Do you want to prove it now?'

Lupus's eyes were shining and he nodded eagerly.

'Good,' said Nathan and added: 'The governor's galley is pulling into the port. That means they'll be in town for at least a few hours. Go and see if you can find out why they're after you.'

Lupus ran quickly past the other boats on the wooden jetty and started for the town walls. Although he was wearing neither pack nor bag, a clutch of beggars had surrounded him and were stretching out their hands and calling for alms. Several of them were blind or lame. Lupus kept his head down and moved on quickly. It seemed the further south they went, the poorer the towns and the more numerous the beggars.

Suddenly a boy about his own age darted forward and stood directly in front of Lupus. 'Ungh!' said the boy, blocking Lupus. 'Ungh!'

Lupus felt a flash of anger: the boy was mocking him. Then his anger died. There was no way the boy could know Lupus was tongueless.

'Ungh!' said the boy again, his eyes pleading and Lupus realised that the boy was also mute. Lupus felt a strange pang: the boy reminded him of what he had been two years ago, a beggar at the town gates. Lupus longed to help him. But he had nothing.

Lupus held out his hands – palms up – and shrugged, to show he had no money. The boy nodded his under-standing, then touched Lupus's turquoise turban long-ingly; his own was a greasy grey rag. Lupus saw that the boy's brown tunic was in tatters and that the soles of his bare feet were thick and cracked.

Lupus sighed and gave the boy a rueful smile. He knew what he had to do.

Lupus kept to the shady side of the street and then moved cautiously forward to look at the notice board.

The newest notice still looked wet. Painted in Greek and Egyptian on a whitewashed board, the red letters made his blood run cold.

REWARD OFFERED FOR THREE
ROMAN CHILDREN:
    IOANATAN SON OF
MARDOKHAIOS, AGED ABOUT
FOURTEEN YEARS, OF MEDIUM
HEIGHT, OLIVE SKIN, CURLY-
HAIRED, STRAIGHT-NOSED, NO
VISIBLE BLEMISHES.
    LYKOS SON OF MARDOKHAIOS
AGED ABOUT NINE YEARS, SHORT
HEIGHT, FAIR-SKINNED,
STRAIGHT-NOSED, MUTE.
    FLAVIA DAUGHTER OF GEMINOS,
AGED ABOUT TWELVE YEARS, OF
MEDIUM HEIGHT, FAIR-SKINNED,
ROUND-FACED, STRAIGHT-NOSED,

BLUE-EYED WITH NO VISIBLE
BLEMISHES.
INFORMATION LEADING TO
CAPTURE, 1000 DRACHMAE PER
CHILD. APPLY TO HOR, THE PRIEST
OF HATHOR OR ANY ROMAN
OFFICER.
INFORMATION ALSO REQUIRED
ABOUT A NUBIAN GIRL
TRAVELLING WITH A EUNUCH. 500
DRACHMAE.
(POSTED THE 7TH DAY OF PAUNI,
THE KALENDS OF JUNE, IN THE
SECOND YEAR OF TITUS)

Lupus swallowed hard and glanced around. For people this poor, one thousand drachmae was a fabulous price. He had to warn the others. And quickly.

'Where is Lupus?' muttered Flavia, looking up from mending a tunic. 'It's been nearly an hour.'

'Nathan's gone to look for him,' said Jonathan. 'I'm sure he'll find him.'

'Maybe I should go and look, too,' offered Seth.

'No!' cried Flavia. 'If you go, then Jonathan and I will be all alone. Our Greek may be good enough, but neither of us speaks Egyptian. What if someone questions us?'

'What's happening over there?' said Jonathan suddenly. 'That looks just like the crocodile pit at that last town.'

Flavia put down the needle and thread and stood up.

A crowd had gathered by a painted limestone balustrade at the water's edge. As they watched, the crowd parted and she saw a soldier holding a struggling boy in his arms. The boy wore a turquoise turban.

'Oh no!' whispered Flavia, her stomach plunging. 'It's Lupus!'

Suddenly the soldier dropped the boy into the pit, and she heard the crowd gasp. For a terrible moment there was silence, then women started screaming and boys and men shouting.

Flavia took the gangplank in one jump and ran as fast as she could towards the crocodile pit. She heard Jonathan and Seth close behind her. She pushed her way through the crowd, her heart pounding like a drum. But when she reached the balustrade and looked down into the pit, there was nothing left among the crocodiles but blood and a ribbon of turquoise cloth.

It was Lupus's turban.

SCROLL XXVIII

The bright world around Flavia dimmed and tipped and she heard Jonathan cry 'Catch her!'

She felt strong hands grip her arms and heard Seth's voice in her ear. 'Breathe!' he commanded. 'Breathe!'

And now someone else was there, too. A barefoot beggar boy in a greasy grey turban and tattered tunic. The boy was looking up at her with sea-green eyes.

The world was suddenly bright again, and she could breathe. 'Lupus!' she cried, and threw her arms around him. 'Oh, praise Juno! You're alive!'

Jonathan hugged Lupus, too: 'Praise God!'

'Shhh!' said Seth, his hazel eyes anxious. 'People are looking. Come on.'

Lupus nodded. He took Flavia's hand and pulled her urgently towards the boat. She could see the fear in his eyes and followed.

When they reached the *Scarab* they saw Nathan was already there, pacing back and forth. 'Master of the Universe!' he cried. 'Where were you? The place is crawling with officials. I had to hide in the public latrines for nearly half an hour. Come on! Let's get out of here!'

Lupus untied the mooring rope while Jonathan used the boarding plank to push the *Scarab* away from the pier.

Seth was already at the stern, punt pole in hand, but as they reached the centre of the river a breeze filled the sail.

'Lupus,' cried Flavia. 'What happened? We thought that boy was you.'

Lupus nodded and gestured for his wax tablet.

They all watched as he wrote on it with a shaking hand.

'You traded clothes with him!' said Flavia, reading over his shoulder. 'And then went to the town square.'

Lupus nodded and continued to write.

'Great Juno's peacock,' muttered Seth. 'One thousand drachmae each! And they know about Chryses and Nubia?'

'Then what happened?' asked Jonathan.

Lupus imitated a soldier, with his stiff bearing and chin pressed in.

'You had to hide from the soldiers?'

Lupus grunted yes and Nathan explained: 'They were everywhere.'

THEY WERE ASKING ABOUT US wrote Lupus. BUT THEY WOULDN'T SAY WHY

'And one of them killed that poor boy,' said Flavia, 'because he was wearing your clothes and they thought he was you.'

Lupus nodded and hung his head.

Jonathan patted his back. 'You were just doing a good deed,' he said. 'You weren't to know they would kill him. Master of the Universe,' he whispered. 'They killed him!'

Behind her, Nathan suddenly leaned forward and was sick over the side of the boat.

'I can't believe it,' breathed Flavia. 'The Emperor wants us dead!'

'Do you think it might be something to do with the emerald we stole for Titus in March?' asked Jonathan.

'But we completed the mission.'

'You'd better tell us,' said Seth grimly. 'Tell us about that.'

'Titus sent us on a mission to find an emerald,' said Flavia. 'His cousin Taurus told us where to find it. After we got it, Taurus took it away from us and said that he would take the emerald to Titus.' She looked at Jonathan and Lupus. 'What if he kept it for himself?'

'That's still no reason for Titus to order our execution,' said Jonathan.

'Well, somebody did,' said Nathan.

'Juno!' exclaimed Flavia. 'They probably mean to kill Nubia, too.'

'Dear God!' whispered Seth. 'Poor Chryses.'

'I thought you hated Chryses.'

'I do. But I don't want him to die!'

'And I don't want Nubia to die,' said Flavia grimly. 'We have to catch them and warn them that their lives are in danger.'

'I think we've made a terrible mistake,' said Flavia as Tentyra disappeared in the distance. They were sailing up the Nile with the strong afternoon wind, and she was examining Nathan's parchment map. 'Look at this big curve in the river.'

Jonathan, Nathan and Seth came over to look. Lupus was at the tiller.

'We call it the Caene Bend,' said Nathan. 'What of it?'

'Chryses and Nubia are on camel,' said Flavia. 'What if

they went straight from Diospolis Parva to Hermonthis instead of following the curve of the river? We'd never catch up with them.'

Nathan shook his head. 'I doubt they'd do that. Once you leave the Nile, it's nothing but desert. And not flat desert either. There are mountains here. No, they must follow the river. Even if your Chryses does hate water, he needs it to live.'

'I wish we could be sure,' said Flavia.

'I'm sure,' said Nathan. 'When I was looking for Lupus in Tentyra, I saw another one of their riddles.'

'Why didn't you tell us?' cried Flavia.

'I was a little distracted by the crocodiles,' said Nathan.

'Praise Juno!' breathed Flavia. 'That means they are staying close to the river. What did the riddle say? Do you remember?'

'Of course. *Out of the desert I came, leading my dusky men to Mount Ida. The son of Peleus killed me, but the gods took pity and granted me immortality. Now I sit beside my companion and sing to the dawn.*'

The four of them stared at Nathan for a moment, then looked at each other.

'I know Mount Ida means Troy,' said Jonathan.

'And the son of Peleus is Achilles!' cried Flavia. 'But did an Egyptian fight in the Trojan War?'

'Yes,' said Seth. 'Strabo calls it Aethiopia, which was an ancient name for parts of Egypt and Cush. His name was Memnon.'

'Eureka!' cried Jonathan, looking up from the map. 'There is a place across the river from Thebes called the Memnonium.'

'Exactly,' said Seth.

'The Memnonium,' said Nathan, 'is known by some

as the Valley of the Kings. There are dozens of tombs there, filled with gold and jewels of the pharaohs. That must be where the treasure is!'

Nubia was woken by Chryses's voice in her ear.

'Nubia, wake up. It's almost dawn.'

Nubia nodded and sat up groggily. The previous evening they had reached two massive stone statues and had slept at their feet.

'See these colossi?' said Chryses. He was brewing tea over a flame of palm fronds. 'They are famous. One of them sometimes sings at sunrise. It's a mark of the gods' favour if you hear it.'

Nubia stared up at the colossal seated statues, dark against the deep blue pre-dawn light. It was early June and the temperatures during the day were almost unbearable. But for the moment it was deliciously cool. She could smell the mint tea and dust and the faint scent of Chryses's lotus-blossom body oil.

Chryses sighed. 'We need a blessing. I spent the last of my money yesterday. I didn't think I would run out so soon.'

'No money left at all?' asked Nubia.

'No,' said Chryses. 'None at all.' He handed Nubia a piece of leathery bread and the skin of soured milk. Nubia took her bread and tore at it with her teeth. The food had become worse and worse the further up the Nile they went. For the past few days they had eaten nothing but bread and milk and a little tough goat meat. These days an onion was a rare pleasure. Nubia sighed again. She missed the variety of food she had been accustomed to in Ostia, and especially Alma's cooking. She missed the baths, and the peaceful inner gardens, and her walks in the pine woods with Nipur. She missed making music with Aristo.

Chryses handed Nubia a cup of fragrant mint tea. Nubia sipped it, and smiled. Mint tea always made her think of Jonathan's father, Doctor Mordecai. Mint tea was his cure for almost anything and it always comforted her.

Suddenly she stiffened at the sound of footsteps in the onion field. Looking up, she saw a globule of light approaching through the morning mist: a torch. As it came closer she saw a turbaned Egyptian man and his little boy leading a group of men and women.

Automatically, Nubia and Chryses drew the tails of their turbans across their faces, so that only their eyes were visible. The Egyptian was speaking to his group in a low voice and as they came close to the colossus he greeted them in Greek. Nubia and Chryses nodded back but did not reply; they had discovered the best tactic was usually silence.

The guide turned back to his group – wealthy Greeks and their servants – and said in a dramatic whisper. 'You must now wait in silence, if you want to hear the Memnon to sing.'

The guide nodded at them, then glanced down longingly at Chryses's teapot. Chryses wiped his cup with his sleeve, raised the pot and poured a stream of tea, then offered it to the guide.

The guide mimed his thanks and gratefully sipped the drink. Nubia gave his little boy their last date. He thanked her with a radiant smile.

Everyone was so quiet that Nubia could hear Castor and Pollux chewing their cuds a short distance away. The guide gestured silently towards the eastern mountains on the other side of the river. His group diligently turned to look. So did Nubia and Chryses.

The sky to the east was growing lighter and for a magical moment the sky above the distant mountains glowed pale green.

'Oh!' breathed the tourists softly.

A few moments later the sky flamed orange and the sun's molten edge appeared above the jagged mountains. Within moments its brilliance was dazzling and Nubia had to avert her eyes. Already she could feel its pounding heat.

At that moment came a faint sound, like a low whistle. She could not tell its exact source, but it deepened and swelled to a breathy hum, as if a giant was blowing into a thick glass bottle. Then it faded and died, and all that could be heard was a donkey's distant heehaw.

The tourists clapped and exclaimed and a balding man in a scarlet cloak stepped forward to give the guide a tetradrachm. Nubia saw its silver glint and the guide's deep bow of delight and she had an idea. Pulling the tail of her turban away from her face, she took out her reed flute and softly began to play Slave Song, a song she had composed about her home country of Nubia.

The tourists grew quiet again, and the guide's little boy watched her with huge dark eyes.

When she finally finished they broke into enthusiastic applause. Nubia boldly held out her empty cup. One or two of the men stepped forward and coins clanged in her cup, and the bald man gave her a silver tetradrachm, too.

The tourists departed, chattering happily and when they were out of earshot Chryses pulled the turban's tail away from his mouth and lifted his face to the sky.

'Thank you, O gods! You answered our prayers!' He looked at Nubia. 'How much did they give you?'

'This much,' said Nubia, tipping the coins into Chryses's cupped hands. 'Is it enough?'

Chryses showed his sharp white teeth in a broad smile. 'It's enough.'

The sun was up now, and it was growing hotter.

Nubia unhobbled Castor and Pollux and took them to drink at a nearby canal. When she returned, Chryses stood with his piece of charcoal, searching the graffiti-covered base of the statue for a place to write his latest offering. There was none. Chryses turned and whistled for Castor, who plodded obediently towards him. Chryses clicked for the camel to kneel, mounted it, then whistled it up. Manoeuvring the creature right up to the Colossus of Memnon, he stretched out his hand and began to write his usual riddle, clear and dark, and well above the tangle of graffiti below.

'Come, Nubia,' he said. 'Our journey is almost finished.'

SCROLL XXIX

'Thebes!' said Nathan, as the town came into view on the east bank.

'Or even "Theebth",' said Jonathan with a grin.

Lupus chuckled and gave Seth a thumbs-up.

'Look,' said Seth. 'A whole avenue of ram-headed sphinxes leading to that temple.'

'It must be a temple dedicated to Ammon,' said Jonathan.

'That's strange,' mused Flavia. 'Oedipus came from Thebes and he had to answer the sphinx's riddle. But that Thebes was in Greece, not Egypt.'

'You do realise that yesterday was the Sabbath?' said Nathan to Seth.

Seth nodded. 'This is an emergency,' he replied. 'We need to warn Nubia and Chryses before that galley finds them.'

'Speaking of the governor's galley,' said Jonathan.

They followed his gaze.

The water to the north sparkled with a myriad of spangles in the morning light but they could clearly make out the dark shape of a boat, and the rise and fall of twenty oars.

'Why are they behind us?' said Flavia.

'They must be searching all the towns along the way.'

'It looks as if they're heading for the port of Thebes,' said Nathan. 'On the east bank. But we want the Memnonium. And that's on the other side.'

Flavia and her friends shaded their eyes from the noonday sun and squinted up at the two massive statues.

They stood at the edge of a flat green onion field near the great Theban necropolis on the west bank of the Nile. According to Nathan, dozens of pharaohs were buried in the valley before them.

There were a few Greek-looking tourists here, with an Egyptian guide and his young son. The boy was playing a reed flute.

'Great Juno's beard,' muttered Jonathan, mopping his forehead with his sleeve. 'It's hot.'

'Which of these two statues sings?' murmured Flavia.

'According to Strabo,' said Seth, 'the northern one sings. But only at dawn.'

They moved over to the right-hand colossus.

'It must be sixty feet tall,' said Jonathan. 'Look. It's cracked.'

Suddenly Lupus grunted and pointed to the statue's knees. Written above the mass of graffiti was a riddle in Greek: *My tress is a sign of childhood, my protective eye the moon. I conquered the one from the red land. If you would find my word, go through the pylon.*

'That's Chryses's handwriting!' said Flavia. 'But what does it mean?'

'It must refer to Horus,' said Seth, brushing away a fly. 'Horus is the falcon-headed god who is often shown with a moon for his eye. He conquered the one from the desert, the red land.'

'Who was the one from the red land?' asked Jonathan.

'Seth.' The scribe gave them a wry grin, and added: 'Strabo mentions a Ptolemaic temple at a place called Apollonospolis, which holds the falcon in honour.'

'What does Ptolemaic mean again?' asked Flavia. 'I forget.'

'Anything from the time of the Ptolemies,' said Seth, and added. 'The Ptolemies ruled Egypt from the death of Alexander the Great to the death of Cleopatra.'

Lupus was tapping Flavia's shoulder.

'What?' she asked, turning.

Lupus pointed at the boy playing the flute. Then cupped his ear, as if to say: Listen!

Flavia listened, and her heart skipped a beat. The boy was playing a haunting, familiar tune.

'What is that?' murmured Flavia. Suddenly she gasped. 'It's *Slave Song!*' she cried.

'What?' said Seth.

'That's a tune Nubia made up herself! There's only one way that boy could have heard that song.'

Flavia ran over to the boy. 'Where did you hear that song?' she asked, in Greek.

The little boy stopped playing and frowned at her.

Seth spoke to the boy in Egyptian, and the boy smiled and replied. For a few moments they conversed. Finally the boy pointed towards the east bank.

Seth gave the boy a small coin and turned to them. 'He says two youths were here yesterday, one Nubian, one Egyptian. He says the Nubian one played that song. They left on camels and they went that way.'

Flavia clapped her hands. 'They were here yesterday!' she cried. 'If we hurry, we might catch up with them tomorrow!'

*

The wind sang in the rigging, the sail billowed and *Scarab*'s prow sent up a fine wave, but as the sun sank behind western palms Lupus thought he saw the governor's galley coming up behind them again. Nathan steered the *Scarab* towards the west bank, to a marshy inlet screened by trees, and dropped the sail. They crouched in the boat and waited for the oared ship to approach.

Flavia's heart was pounding and her mouth was dry: it was the governor's red and yellow galley.

The sun had set, and they all held their breath, hoping the silhouette of the *Scarab*'s mast could not be distinguished from the silhouettes of the slender palm trees around them.

The galley's oars fell and rose, dripping golden water, causing a gaggle of geese to rise honking from the reeds.

Finally the galley passed out of sight.

'What shall we do?' whispered Flavia. 'We want to catch up with Nubia and Chryses and warn them. But we don't want to run into those soldiers.'

Two days later, Lupus cautiously approached the great Temple of Horus at Apollonospolis. He was wearing his greasy grey turban and his tattered brown tunic. Luckily he had put on his sandals, for the pavement leading to the temple was as hot as coals. It was midday on the Nones of June and the sun pounded down like Vulcan's hammer.

The gateway – *pylon* in Greek – looked like part of a town wall. But even the walls of Rome were not this high. Lupus's head tipped back as he took in the massive, brightly painted figures of the falcon god and his friends carved into the sandstone. Like all the other Egyptian figures he had seen, they were shown striding forward in profile, but with their shoulders square to the viewer.

On either side of the gateway were two granite falcons, each as tall as two men. At the base of one of them was a charcoal arrow, pointing inside.

Dutifully, Lupus passed through the lofty pylon into a furnace-hot courtyard. It was ringed by massive columns, and here, too, painted figures told their silent stories. A doorway straight ahead lead into another shadowed hall.

There were even bigger columns in here and the shade was like a blessing. Here and there, the sun pierced holes in the roof and sent down dusty shafts of golden light. Lupus crept from shadow to shadow, from column to column.

He moved past stalking pharaohs and animal headed gods, past a silent babble of hieroglyphs etched into the honey-coloured walls. Presently he found his way into the innermost sanctuary. A curtain hung in front of it, but when he peeped inside, he saw no priest, only a black granite shrine with a golden statue of a falcon-headed Roman emperor: a hybrid of Horus and Titus, no doubt. The cult statue was clothed and wearing jewels. Beside it, two oil lamps showed the midday offering of food, plus many votive offerings, in the Greek and Roman manner. Lupus crept in and searched for messages. At last he found the riddle – this time in chalk – in tiny letters at the bottom of the shrine.

Lupus was coming out of the sanctuary of Horus, when his acute senses warned him of danger. He had caught a turpentine-sweet whiff of terebinth.

He knew of only one person who wore that scent. It

was faint, but distinctive, and as he moved into the hypostyle hall, the smell became stronger.

Presently he heard a man speaking in Greek. 'I told you, we need proof. Without proof, no reward.'

Lupus moved forward to peer round a fat column.

Two men stood beneath a vertical beam of sunlight, so that their heads seemed to glow. The big bald one wore a one-sleeved pink tunic. The other man had curly dark hair, greying at the sides. He wore a cream tunic with a blue chlamys.

'We were lucky to rescue the mute boy's turban,' said Thonis, holding the bloody tatters of turquoise linen. 'We mustn't make the same mistake with the three others. Ideally,' he added, 'we need their heads.'

SCROLL XXX

'Thonis!' breathed Flavia, a short time later. 'He's pursued us all this way. The reward for us must be huge. More than a thousand drachmae each . . .'

'And Pullo,' said Jonathan. 'The man with him was Pullo, wasn't it?'

Lupus nodded. He had made his way safely back to the *Scarab*.

'Who's Pullo?' asked Seth.

'Pullo,' said Flavia, 'is the slave of Titus's cousin Taurus, our contact in Sabratha.'

'Ah, yes,' said Nathan. 'You mentioned this Taurus before. You said you stole a gem for Titus and he took it to give to the Emperor.'

'Yes,' said Flavia. 'And now I think I know what happened!'

'What?' they all cried.

'What if Taurus kept the emerald for himself but told Titus that we had kept it for ourselves? That would make Titus angry, wouldn't it?'

'Angry enough to want our heads?' said Jonathan.

'Maybe he wants to frighten us into telling him what we've done with the emerald.'

'Was this gem so very valuable?' asked Nathan.

'Yes, but the real value was the prophecy,' explained

Jonathan. 'That whoever possessed the gem would rule Rome.'

'And you didn't keep it for yourselves?' asked Nathan.

'Of course not!' cried Flavia and Jonathan together. Lupus put his fists on his hips and glared at Nathan.

'All right! All right!' said Nathan. 'I was just asking.'

'And he said he wanted our heads?' said Flavia to Lupus. Her hand went to her throat.

'Was there a riddle?' asked Seth.

Lupus nodded and beckoned for a wax tablet. *Not on Tiber's boat-shaped island, nor at green Epidauros do I heal, nor even near fair Alexander's tomb, but rather at the double shrine of the biter.*

'Aesculapius is the healing god on the Tiber Island,' said Flavia. 'And his Greek counterpart heals at Epidauros, near Corinth . . .'

'And some of the scholars treat people at the Museum near Alexander's tomb,' said Jonathan.

'But what is the double shrine of the biter?' asked Flavia.

Seth pursed his lips. 'At Ombos,' he said, there is a double sanctuary to Horus in his guise as healer. He is known as Haroeris. He shares the shrine with Sobek.'

'Sobek the crocodile god!' cried Flavia. 'The biter.'

'That's easy enough,' said Jonathan, examining Nathan's leather map. 'Ombos is only a day or two from here.'

But now Lupus was holding out a piece of papyrus and Jonathan saw something he rarely saw in his friend's face. Fear.

'What's this?' said Flavia. 'A notice?'

Lupus nodded and mimed ripping it off a wall, rolling it up and slipping it under his tunic.

'Great Juno's peacock!' breathed Flavia, 'it's a revised description of us. It must be recent, because they don't mention you, Lupus; they think you're dead.' She looked at Jonathan. 'But they know about the brand on your arm! Listen: *Reward offered for two children: Jonathan son of Mordecai, aged twelve years, of medium height, olive skin, short curly hair (may be wearing turban), scar on left shoulder. Flavia Gemina, daughter of Marcus Flavius Geminus, sea captain, aged almost twelve years, medium height, fair-skinned, grey-eyed, no visible blemishes. Reward also offered for Nubian girl travelling with a eunuch on camelback. 1000 drachmae for any information leading to their capture. Posted the Nones of June in the second year of Titus.*'

She looked up at them in horror.

'Do you know what this means?' said Flavia.

Seth, Nathan and Jonathan nodded. But Lupus shook his head.

'It means that in the five days since we left Tentyra, someone has betrayed us. But who?'

They reached Ombos the following day at about the fifth hour past noon.

Rounding a bend in the river, they saw the temple on the east bank, its columns golden in the late afternoon sun. On the sandy bank below it, lay half a dozen massive crocodiles, basking in the intense heat.

'Are you sure they'll be here?' asked Nathan, wiping his brow. 'This site is on the east bank.'

'Yes,' said Seth. 'They could easily have crossed on one of the ferries.'

'Look!' cried Flavia, as Nathan steered the boat towards a high part of the riverbank, well past the crocodiles. 'There's the governor's galley!'

'And look there,' added Jonathan. 'Those two camels kneeling in the shade of that tamarisk tree. It looks like that little boy is guarding them.'

'Do you think those camels belong to Nubia and Chryses?' asked Flavia. 'That they've crossed over?'

'If they are, then Nubia's in danger,' said Jonathan. 'She doesn't know there are people after her.'

'Chryses knows that Seth is after him,' said Flavia. 'But he doesn't know Nubia's wanted by the governor.'

Nathan moored the *Scarab* to a landing place below the imposing temple.

'That Temple,' said Seth, 'is a double temple. The left hand side is devoted to Haroeris and the right to Sobek. I spoke to a local guide when I was waiting for you at Thebes,' he explained. 'It must be the double shrine the riddle referred to.'

'Look at those village women!' cried Flavia. 'They're coming to draw water from the river. The crocodiles will eat them!'

'Don't worry,' said Seth. 'The guide also told me that the crocodiles here are tame and used to being fed. It's their way of keeping them under control.'

'They don't kill them, the way they do at Tentyra?' asked Flavia.

'No,' said Nathan, 'Here at Ombos the crocodile is revered. There is even a special pool inside the Temple precinct, and the sacred crocodile lives there. When it dies,' he continued, 'the priests mummify its body and the people give it a great funeral, and put it in a tomb with the previous sacred crocodiles.'

'Great Juno's beard!' exclaimed Jonathan. 'That boy is doing a handstand on the crocodile's back!'

'Where?' cried Flavia, and then gasped as she spotted

a boy on the basking place. He was about their age and wore only a loincloth. There were two other boys with him. They were also somersaulting over the crocodiles and doing handstands.

'They'd better not try that with the crocodiles at Tentyra,' muttered Jonathan. 'They'd be dead in an instant.'

Nathan had finished mooring the *Scarab* to a post. Now he took a deep breath and faced them.

'I have to tell you something,' he said. 'Something bad.'

The three friends and Seth looked at him.

'When we were in Tentyra,' he said. 'I went to the soldier from the boat and told him I had information about you.'

Flavia and the others stared at Nathan, uncomprehending.

'I'm the one who betrayed you.'

'What?' said Flavia.

'I began to doubt there would be any treasure,' he said, turning away from them. 'And the reward . . . it was so great!'

'What did you tell them?' asked Flavia.

'I told them I had seen you at Tentyra. I told them you were travelling as Egyptian boys, in turbans and long tunics. But when they killed that poor boy . . . I thought it was Lupus at first . . .' he turned back and looked at them with pleading eyes. 'I never dreamt they wanted you dead. I thought they would just take you back to Alexandria and put you on a boat to Rome.'

'You traitor!' cried Seth. 'I knew I should never have trusted you!'

'What about Nubia?' asked Flavia. 'What did you tell them about Nubia?'

'And Chryses,' added Seth.

'I told them . . .' Nathan hung his head. 'I told them the Nubian girl was travelling with a eunuch on camel-back and that they were a day or two—'

Without a word Seth launched himself at Nathan and began to throttle him.

'Seth! Stop it!' screamed Flavia. 'You'll kill him!'

Lupus and Jonathan tried to pull the struggling cousins apart. Finally they succeeded in pulling Seth back. Jonathan gripped one arm and Lupus the other. Seth was panting hard and the boat was rocking from their fight.

'I'm sorry,' croaked Nathan, still lying on his back beside the tiller. In the struggle his cap had fallen off. He sat up and rubbed his throat. 'I know I did wrong. But I'm going to make it up to you. I'm going to tell them you're dead, that you drowned back at Apollonospolis, and I'll take them there. That will delay them long enough for you to find Chryses and Nubia and warn them.' He ran a hand through his curls and replaced his cap.

'What will you tell them when they can't find our bodies?' asked Seth. He was still breathing hard.

Nathan shrugged. 'That crocodiles ate you?'

'They would need to believe Nubia and Chryses are dead, too,' said Seth.

'I'll tell them the Nubian girl went back to her own people, into the Nubian Desert. And that the eunuch went with her. I doubt they'll follow them all that way.'

'But what if they do follow them?' said Flavia, 'We still have to warn Nubia and Chryses. Just in case.'

'Look,' said Nathan, mopping his sweating brow, 'take the *Scarab*. I'm giving it to you. My most precious possession. My only possession. Follow them all the way to the first cataract if you have to. Don't worry about me. I'll do everything in my power to make this right.' He stepped onto the gangplank and looked back at them. 'I doubt you'll see me again.'

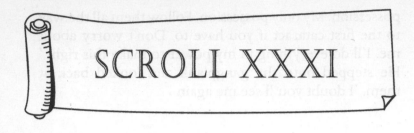

SCROLL XXXI

'Now that the governor's men know we're travelling as three Egyptian boys,' said Flavia to the others. 'We need a new disguise. Just for this place,' she added. 'In case one of their men spots us before Nathan convinces them to go back down river.'

'Do we trust Nathan now?' Jonathan asked.

'We don't have a choice,' said Seth. 'And I think he will keep his word.' He looked at Flavia and tried to smile. 'So, what's it to be? Shall we dress up as priests of Anubis? As mummies? As acrobats?'

Flavia returned his rueful smile. 'I know you hate dressing up as a woman,' she said. 'But we do still have three black wigs, plenty of eye makeup and your palla.'

'Look,' whispered Flavia. 'An inscription to Nero.'

'At a temple devoted to crocodiles,' said Jonathan. 'That's fitting.'

It was late afternoon, but a drachma slipped to a junior priest had ensured their entry. Flavia, Jonathan and Lupus were dressed as girls, and Seth pretended to be their mother. He had pulled his palla across his face, revealing only his heavily made-up eyes. He lisped that he needed to make an offering to the crocodile god to protect his three beautiful daughters against unwelcome suitors.

The walls around them were adorned with sensual figures carved in deep relief and painted in subtle colours. Slim men and beautiful goddesses in diaphanous gowns carried their eternal offerings to Sobek and Haroeris.

Their guide – a priest – was leading them through a hypostyle hall with massive pillars. Flavia fell into step beside him and whispered in Greek: 'You haven't seen two young men recently? An Egyptian travelling with a Nubian?'

'Ah!' said the priest with a knowing grin. 'Are they unwelcome suitors?'

'How pertheptive you are,' lisped Seth.

'So sorry,' said the priest. 'I have not seen the two suitors you describe. But you know, I myself have very good prospects. I would be a good husband.'

'Oh?' Seth batted his eyelashes. 'Doth one of my daughterth take your fanthy?'

The priest giggled.

Flavia felt Lupus tap her arm. Following the direction of his gaze, she saw a flash of pink then blue pass between the columns. Seth saw it, too, and turned to the priest.

'Two of your rivalth have jutht come in. Can you hide uth?'

'Hide you?' said the priest. His eyes widened, then he nodded. 'Yes, I can! This temple has a secret corridor between the two inner sanctuaries. The priests use a secret speaking hole to pass on the gods' messages to the suppliants. Quickly, follow me.'

The four of them hurried after the priest as he moved deeper into the temple. He led them into a small room painted with scenes of Sobek, through a narrow door and left along a dim inner corridor. They passed three small shrines on their right and he led them into the fourth.

'You must not tell anyone about this,' said the priest in a dramatic whisper. He pressed the figure of a bee, carved a little deeper into the limestone than the surrounding hieroglyphs and pushed a stone slab, which swung open.

'Down the stairs, then up again,' he said. 'I cannot let you have lamps but your eyes will adjust. There is a secret room between the sanctuaries, with a special speaking tube for the proclamation of Words and Oracles. You will be able to see and hear and breathe, but do not speak, or they will hear you. I ask only two things,' he added. 'First, don't tell anyone about this secret room. Second, when the suitors are gone, I would like a kiss from that one.'

He smiled at Jonathan.

Flavia stood on tiptoe to peer through a tiny hole in the thick stone wall of the secret chamber.

It had been almost too dark to see at first, but gradually their eyes had grown used to the dimness: it was illuminated by arrow-thin shafts of light which came in through the peepholes. As Flavia put her eye to the hole, a man came into view. It was Thonis, still looking like Marcus Antonius with his curly hair and greying temples. Beside him lumbered Pullo, the massive egg-headed slave of Taurus, their enemy. The two men were speaking, but she could not hear their words.

Once again, Lupus was tugging at her tunic. She turned annoyed, but saw that both he and Jonathan were staring through peepholes on the opposite wall, into the sanctuary of Haroeris. Flavia turned and looked through the peephole behind her. She gasped.

Two slim youths in white turbans and long cream tunics stood in the sanctuary. They had their backs to her and one of them was using a piece of charcoal to write something on the sanctuary wall. Flavia could not see his face or what he had written, but she saw the profile of his turbaned companion and almost cried out with joy.

It was Nubia.

SCROLL XXXII

Flavia's heart was pounding and her mind was racing. Nubia and Chryses were only a few feet away from their pursuers, men who would ruthlessly kill them.

She turned back and saw that Nathan had joined Thonis and Pullo in the sanctuary of Sobek. Nathan was speaking to Thonis, gesturing back towards the entrance, his expression urgent.

Yes, thought Flavia. *Get them out of here, quickly!*

She turned and peered through the other hole and saw to her horror that Chryses and Nubia were turning to go out of their sanctuary. If they left now, they would surely come face to face with Thonis and Pullo among the columns of the hypostyle hall. She had to do something.

But Seth was ahead of her. He had pulled off his palla and moved to a hole on the Haroeris side of their secret room. He put his mouth to this hole and stretched out his arm to block the opposite speaking hole with his balled up palla.

Lupus caught on immediately and held Seth's palla firmly over the hole.

Seth spoke softly into the speaking hole for the sanctuary of Haroeris: 'Nubia!' he said softly.

In the secret chamber, his voice was barely audible,

but Flavia saw Nubia stop at the doorway and turn in wonder.

She took her eye away and turned to peer into Sobek's sanctuary, to see if Thonis and Pullo had heard. But Lupus was making a walking motion with the fingers of his right hand, as if to say: they're leaving.

Flavia breathed a sigh of relief. Their pursuers hadn't heard Seth's disembodied voice, but Nubia had.

'Nubia,' whispered Seth again. 'Beware the Pink and the Blue. Beware the um . . . beware the Egg and the Jackal.'

Flavia put her eye to the peephole in time to see Nubia move back into the sanctuary and look for the source of the miraculous voice. The turbaned youth appeared in the doorway and went to Nubia. It must be Chryses, but Flavia couldn't see his face clearly. She could see Nubia's, however, and the look of amazement as she repeated what Seth had said. The youth shook his head, and Flavia waited for him to move, so that she could see his face. She sensed the others were waiting for her and turned to see Jonathan already at the top of the steps leading out of the secret chamber. He beckoned her and she nodded.

They had prevented an immediate disaster. But Nubia and Chryses were still in danger. They had to be warned.

Jonathan was first up the stairs from the hidden chamber. The young priest was waiting for him.

'Tell us quickly!' said Seth coming up behind Jonathan. 'How do we get to the sanctuary of Haroeris?'

'Don't I get my kiss now?'

'But we need to go urgently!'

'Back the way you came,' said the priest, and glanced

at Jonathan. 'I'll show you if your daughter lets me give her a kiss.'

Seth gave an exasperated sigh, then turned to Jonathan: 'Thweetheart,' he said, remembering to lisp this time. 'Let the kind prietht give you a kith.'

Jonathan sighed. At any other time he would have kicked the priest hard in his oxyrhynchus. But the priest had helped them save Nubia. He closed his eyes and offered his cheek.

The priest gave him a quick peck, then rushed blushing out of the sanctuary.

'Follow me, ladies!' came his voice.

But when Jonathan and his friends reached the inner sanctuary of the healing god Haroeris, Nubia and Chryses were gone.

When they emerged from the cool shadows of the temple into the bright light of late afternoon, they saw the red and gold galley already moving out into the river and turning north, back the way they had come. Beneath the shady awning at the ship's stern, Flavia saw egg-headed Pullo in pink and Thonis in his blue chlamys. Nathan, wearing his one-sleeved white tunic and pointed white cap, stood grimly between them.

They watched the governor's galley until it was out of sight, and Nathan did not turn once.

'Where to now?' said Flavia, as the wind filled the Scarab's sail and they moved out into the river.

Subdued by Nathan's betrayal and departure, they had put on their turbans and tunics again. Lupus was at the tiller and, in the bows of the ship, Jonathan was examining the map.

'To Syene,' said Jonathan, and looked up at Seth. 'Correct?'

'Yes,' said Seth.

'Why Syene?' asked Flavia and quoted the riddle that had been drawn in charcoal on the inner sanctuary of Haroeris: *'A mighty tooth am I, beneath exotic skies. In many other lands, in many shapes I rise. No strength in me remains, and yet my charms are prized.'*

From the tiller, Lupus trumpeted like an elephant.

'I know the answer is ivory,' said Flavia, 'But how does that lead to Syene?'

Jonathan tapped the map. 'Ivory comes from elephants,' he said. 'And in the nome of Syene there is an island called Elephantine. That must be our next stop.'

'I agree,' said Seth. 'There's a Roman garrison there, too. Syene and Elephantine are both on the border of Nubia.'

'So there might be Nubians there?' asked Flavia.

'I'm sure of it.'

'Lupus!' cried Jonathan suddenly. 'Watch out! We're heading straight for a hippo!'

SCROLL XXXIII

'Don't cry, Nubia,' said Chryses, 'I know they were good friends but we don't need them anymore.'

'But I loved them,' said Nubia. 'They were loyal and faithful and brave. I hope the beekeeper doesn't eat them,' she added.

'The beekeeper looked very kind,' said Chryses. 'And his little girls adored them. I'm sure Castor and Pollux will have a very happy life carrying honey and giving the girls rides. As for us,' he said. 'From now on we travel by water.'

'But are you not afraid of water?'

'Terrified. But I must be brave. You have taught me that.' He smiled at her, then pointed to the islands in the river. 'Do you see those islands?'

Nubia nodded. The islands of Syene were unlike any of the islands she had seen so far. These were not flat, marshy reed beds, but smooth grey boulders.

'That one looks like an elephant,' she said.

'Nubia! You are so clever!' Chryses laughed his strange tinkling laugh. 'That island is called Elephantine, or Elephant Island. Did you know that?'

'No.'

'Well, that is where we are going. It turns out that we both have treasure on that elephant-shaped island.'

'Your treasure is there?'

'Yes. And yours, too.'

'I have treasure?'

'I hope so.' He caught both her hands in his and gazed into her eyes. 'Nubia! The beekeeper told me that there is a Nubian Village on that island.'

'Some of my people? On the Elephantine?'

'Yes! He thinks there are members of the Jackal and Hyena clans. And also of the Leopard clan. Didn't you tell me your family is of the Leopard clan?'

'Yes!' cried Nubia. 'Oh, praise Juno! Maybe they will know if some of my family survived.'

Chryses had covered his eyes with his hands and was muttering invocations to Serapis under his breath, but Nubia gazed around with delight. The little sailboat was cutting through the mirror-bright water towards an island which might hold the answer to her dreams.

The river around her teemed with life. A purple heron watched her pass and nodded gravely, a dove cooed throatily from a smooth boulder, kingfishers plunged into the Nile and a pair of moorhens swam beside them, squeaking cheerfully and working hard to keep up.

Finally the boatman brought them gently up to the landing place and tossed the mooring rope to a waiting boy. He helped Nubia and Chryses out and accepted their coin with a beaming, toothless grin.

Nubia followed Chryses up the steps and looked around. To her left was a town with a Roman fort and an Egyptian temple. To her right was a small village of whitewashed mud huts, some roofed with palm fronds, others with domes. A palm grove made a backdrop to the village.

She heard the soft clanking and bleating of goats and a moment later a small flock emerged from among the trees, followed by a young goatherd. The breeze carried their scent, and it made her heart joyful. A movement beyond the goatherd caught Nubia's eye: some older boys were throwing a ball. Nubia scanned them and suddenly her heart thudded. One of the ballplayers was a tall, lithe Nubian youth, with a flashing smile and neat ears.

It was her cousin Kashta, to whom she had once been betrothed.

Kashta stepped forward as Nubia and Chryses approached.

'Who are you?' he said in heavily accented Greek.

'Don't you recognise me, Kashta?' said Nubia in their language. She pulled off her turban and waited for his reaction.

He studied her face for a long moment. Then his long-lashed brown eyes grew wide. 'Shepenwepet!' he cried, using her clan name. 'Can it really be you?' His face broke into a smile, then clouded over as he looked her up and down. 'But why do you wear such clothes? Like a man?'

'We have made a very long and dangerous journey. Chryses thought I would be safer dressed as a boy.'

'Chryses?' His eyes flickered towards Nubia's friend.

'Yes! Without him I could not have made this journey. The gods provided him in my hour of need.' She turned to Chryses and said in Greek, 'this is my cousin Kashta. Kashta, this is Chryses.'

The eunuch smiled shyly. 'I am honoured to meet you.'

'I honoured of meet you also,' said Kashta, in his heavily accented Greek. 'Come! Take refreshment of us. We must talk.'

'Oh, Kashta,' cried Nubia. 'How I have longed for this day!'

It took Nubia's eyes a moment to adjust to the darkness of the mud hut. There were mainly children in here, but also some women. Rush mats lined the floor, some strewn with threadbare carpets or blankets. It was cooler in here than outside, but there were flies everywhere.

'Sit.' Kashta gestured to an embroidered cloth on the floor. He clapped his hands and a thin Nubian girl appeared. 'Water,' he said. 'Bring us water. And also the good dates.' Still speaking in Nubian he said, 'You travelled alone with this person? That was not very wise.'

'I had no choice,' said Nubia, brushing away a fly. 'My friends died and I wanted to come home.'

'Our home is not safe these days,' he said grimly. 'Not with the slave-traders. That is why many of us have moved here, or closer to the border.' He spread his hands, 'but here the living is hard.'

The thin girl came in with a brass tray. On it were beakers of water and two dozen dates. The girl poured the water, smiled at Nubia, and departed.

Kashta swatted at a fly and continued. 'Some from the Hyena clan have had the idea of making beer and selling it to the Romans. There is a garrison here, you see. But selling beer is not good. We are hunters and herdsmen. We go where the animals go.'

Nubia had forgotten they were speaking their own

language until Chryses drained his glass and rose to his feet.

'Excuse me, Nubia,' he said in Greek. 'But I must see about my business. Shall I leave you to talk?'

'Oh, yes! Thank you!'

Chryses turned to Kashta. 'Thank you, sir, for the refreshment.' And to Nubia: 'I'll return in an hour or two.'

'I can see why they call it Elephant Island,' said Flavia, as they approached the island. 'It looks just like a big grey elephant!'

'Except for the town and the trees on top,' said Jonathan.

They had reached Syene at dawn and were sailing through an archipelago of rocks and islands. They were near the first cataract and there were boats everywhere. Flavia saw narrow papyrus skiffs with lone fishermen, medium-sized sailing boats like the *Scarab*, and luxury barges with reed cabins near the stern.

'Oh, look at that cedarwood barge,' said Flavia. 'It's beautiful.'

'That one's bound down river,' said Seth.

'How can you tell?'

'No sail. It will just flow with the current, so all it needs is the tiller. And when the Nile begins to flood in a week or two, it will go quickly.'

Lupus grunted and pointed excitedly towards the elephant-shaped island.

'Yes,' said Jonathan. 'I see them, too. Roman soldiers. There's a garrison here. But it's a big island. Where shall we start?'

'The landmark mentioned by Strabo,' said Seth. 'That seems to be Chryses's modus operandi.'

'Which landmark is that?' asked Flavia.

'Those stairs cut into the rock,' said Seth, pointing. 'The Nilometer.'

Nubia and Kashta were walking on a path between palm trees and the low retaining wall that ringed the island. A cool breeze had risen from the opalescent river below them.

'Kashta,' said Nubia. 'My family ... are any of them still ...'

'Alive?' He looked at her. 'Don't you remember what happened?'

'Yes,' said Nubia, and forced herself to recall. 'My mother and baby sister Seyala, they died on the road. The slave-traders killed my father and my dog. And one of my brothers died in the flames. Did the other one live?'

'I'm sorry, Nubia. Your family all perished. You are the only one left.'

'No,' said Nubia softly. 'Taharqo is alive—'

'Taharqo alive?' cried Kashta, his eyes full of joy. 'My friend Taharqo is alive?'

'Yes,' said Nubia. 'Now he fights as a gladiator for the Romans.'

'The Romans!' Kashta spat into the dust. 'The Romans say there is nothing they can do about the slave-traders. The desert is too big, they say. But even with its dangers, the desert is better than this place. Still,' he said, gazing into her face. 'I am glad I was here, because now I have found you again.'

*

I lie between sun and moon, between Egypt and Cush, between ebb and flow. Seth ben Aaron, you have reached the end of your quest. I am your treasure.

'What in Juno's name does that mean?' said Flavia. She and Lupus had climbed the stairs of the Nilometer to examine the riddle written on its wall. Now she looked down at Seth, waiting down below them in the *Scarab*. 'Any idea?'

'No,' said Seth, frowning.

Lupus pointed down, as if to say: here.

'I think Lupus is right,' Jonathan called up from the boat. 'The Nile flood will soon begin, so we're almost between ebb and flow.'

'And if the east bank is the side of the sun,' said Seth, 'and the western the side of the moon, then an island is halfway between.'

'And you said Cush is another word for the Land of Nubia!' cried Flavia. 'And that the first cataract marks the border. So this must be your final destination!'

Jonathan nodded. 'The treasure must be somewhere on this island.'

Lupus had been looking around. Now he pointed towards a palm grove near one end of the island and grunted.

'Seth!' cried Flavia. 'There's a village over there with lots of Nubians. Lupus and I are going to go and investigate. We'll be right back.'

'Come back down and sail with us!' Seth shouted up at them. 'There's a docking place at the other end. We can look together.'

'No! You sail there and we'll meet you! We haven't a moment to lose! Nubia might be there!'

She heard Seth curse and Jonathan call her name, but

she ignored them and scrambled over the low parapet. Lupus was already trotting across scrubby ground towards a village of whitewashed mud brick surrounded by a palm grove. On their left loomed the town with its Roman fort.

As they approached the village, Flavia could see children playing in the shadows cast by the huts. Village women sat nearby, chatting and preparing food. On a patch of waste ground in front of the huts, some youths were spitting a whole goat and others were preparing a large open fire. Another man had a bucket of water and was throwing handfuls of it to damp down the dust.

'They must be preparing to celebrate something,' said Flavia to Lupus.

Then she saw the Nubian couple walking together in the palm grove: a tall young man and a girl with short hair and a long cream tunic. Flavia's heart thudded. It was Nubia. She was not with the eunuch but with a tall Nubian youth.

It seemed that her friend had found her family.

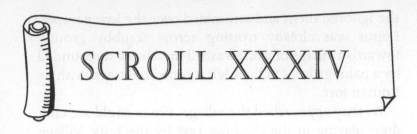

SCROLL XXXIV

The setting sun made long cool shadows of the palm trunks. Kashta stopped in one of these and turned to Nubia.

'Marry me, Shepenwepet,' he said softly. 'You will cook for me and raise my sons. I will protect you and breed many fine goats. It will not be an easy life, but we have one another, and our people. You will be free. Truly free.'

Nubia gazed up at his handsome, smiling face. Then she looked towards the others in the village: the young mothers, the men preparing her celebration goat, the grubby toddlers playing in the dust. She should have been happy, but she felt only dismay. Why? She had travelled nearly seven hundred miles to reach her own people and she had succeeded. Why did she not feel joy?

'Shepenwepet,' whispered Kashta again. 'Marry me.'

Flavia opened her mouth to call out to Nubia, but Lupus stopped her by gripping her arm with his left hand and shaking his head vehemently.

Nubia and the young man were standing very close, gazing into each other's faces.

Lupus put his right forefinger to his lips, then jerked his head forward, as if to say: Let's go closer, but quietly.

Flavia nodded and together they walked nonchalantly forward then quickly ran to hide behind a palm tree.

A hand on Flavia's shoulder made her jump. But it was only Jonathan.

'Why did you run off like that?' he scowled. 'Seth's in the boat, down there. He wants you to come back right now.'

'Jonathan!' hissed Flavia. 'We've found Nubia! There she is!'

Jonathan's eyes widened as he spotted Nubia and the youth.

'Why are we spying on her?' he asked in a whisper.

'It's a romantic moment,' said Flavia. 'Look at them!' The scene before her blurred as her eyes swam with tears. 'Look how happy she is.'

'Marry me, Shepenwepet.' Kashta pulled Nubia into his arms. 'And I will take you home.'

As he pronounced the word 'home', an image appeared in Nubia's mind: the inner garden of Flavia's house, with its bubbling fountain and the birds singing in the fig tree. Of Alma, humming in the kitchen. Of Captain Geminus working in his tablinum. Of her beloved Aristo, playing his lyre with his eyes closed. And of Nipur, her faithful dog.

Nubia felt a strange bittersweet longing. Even with Flavia, Jonathan and Lupus dead, she realised Ostia was the place she now thought of as home.

'Oh, Kashta!' she whispered. 'I came all this way to find my home. But I have seen Rome and Athens and Alexandria. I can read stories in Latin and Greek. How can a goatherd's tent be home to me now?'

His face grew dark. 'You will marry me!' he said in a

low voice. 'Otherwise I will lose face before the others. You must not think of the life you have lived these past two years. Rome is evil. Romans are evil!'

'No, Kashta. Romans are not evil. They are like us. Some are good. Some are bad. Most are a mixture of good and bad. But their world is a wonderful one.'

'What about slavery?'

Nubia nodded slowly. 'Yes, they have slaves. But I know a slave called Alma who is happier than any of the free women here. She goes only a few steps to the fountain. She chooses from a hundred types of food for dinner. She sleeps in her own little room on a bed with no fleas. She can go to the baths every day and sit in water up to her neck. She laughs at jugglers in the streets and talks with her friends at the public fountain and celebrates festivals with the family. And she is loved.'

'You have become one of them,' he said.

'Yes!' Nubia looked at him in wonder. 'I have become Roman. I am Nubian, but I am also a Roman. Thank you for showing me that.' She turned to go, but Kashta caught her wrist.

'No!' he hissed. 'You will not go.'

'Stop, Kashta. You are hurting me.'

'I will release you when you promise to stay with me.'

She stared up at him in horror. 'You will not allow me to depart?'

'No! You are betrothed to me and you must honour that. I will not allow you to return to Rome.' He brought his face very close to hers. 'My father,' he said, 'often had to beat my mother to make her obey him. Must I beat you?'

*

'Look,' whispered Flavia to Jonathan and Lupus. 'That must be the boy Nubia was betrothed to marry. They are almost kissing. Maybe we should just quietly leave and go back home.'

'What?' said Jonathan. 'After we've come all this way to find her?'

'But look at her! She's home now, with her own people. If we tell her we're alive maybe she'll feel she has to come back with us.' Flavia's voice was hardly more than a whisper. 'Maybe it's better that she thinks we're dead. It will help her fit back in to her old life.'

Lupus looked at Flavia angrily, but Jonathan nodded slowly. 'Flavia's right,' he said. 'If we suddenly appear, Nubia will be torn between her old life and us. She'll have to reject either us or them, and that will upset her.'

Lupus swallowed hard. They had travelled so far to find Nubia, but now she had found her true family. It would be selfish of them to present themselves now.

'Do you agree we should leave without telling her?' whispered Flavia.

Reluctantly, Lupus nodded.

SCROLL XXXV

As the three friends were trudging back towards the *Scarab*, they passed a youth in a white turban and cream tunic going the other way.

Something about the young man's way of walking made Lupus stop and turn. The youth had stopped too, and was looking back at them. He had catlike eyes and a small mouth.

'Come on, Lupus,' called Flavia. 'Let's go before we change our minds.'

Lupus shrugged and turned to go, too miserable to pay attention to the flicker of recognition at the back of his mind.

'I do not want to beat you, Shepenwepet,' said Kashta. 'But if you speak again of leaving, then I will.'

'Nubia!' cried Chryses's Greek-accented voice from behind her. 'Oh Nubia! I've found your family!'

Nubia turned and saw Chryses standing at the edge of the palm grove with three turbaned boys. The setting sun was behind them and at first she could not make them out. Then she recognised two of them.

'Jonathan! Lupus!' she cried in Latin. She ran to them and flung an arm around each of them. 'Oh, praise Juno! You are alive!'

'What about me,' said the third boy. 'Don't I get a hug?' He looked at her with wounded grey eyes.

'Flavia!' Nubia embraced her friend. She was laughing and crying at the same time. 'Oh, Flavia!'

Flavia laughed, too, and gave Nubia a fierce squeeze. 'We've been following you all the way! Didn't you suspect?'

'No!' Nubia shook her head. 'No! I am thinking you are dead!'

'Nubia,' said Flavia, 'you don't have to come back with us. But Chryses said we should tell you that we aren't dead, to put your mind at rest.' Flavia swallowed hard and tried not to cry.

'What Flavia is saying,' said Jonathan, 'is that we'll miss you, but we know you want to stay here with your family.'

Nubia looked over her shoulder at Kashta, whose expression was a mixture of outrage and astonishment.

'My family are all dead,' she said, softly. 'Only Taharqo remains, and he is in Rome. Her golden eyes were brimming as she looked from Flavia to Jonathan to Lupus. 'Chryses was right. You are my family. And I am so glad I have found you.'

They emerged from the palm grove into the dusty golden light of late afternoon.

'You!' cried Seth, striding forward.

'Seth?' gasped Chryses, stopping dead in his tracks. 'Seth, is that you?'

'Who else?' he growled. 'You've led me on a wild ibis chase a thousand miles up the Nile!'

'Oh, Seth!' breathed Chryses. 'You're wonderful! You

came all this way to find me.' He ran forward and threw his arms around Seth's neck.

'What are you doing?' cried Seth, recoiling. 'Get off me!'

'Oh, Seth!' exclaimed Chryses. 'Haven't you guessed by now?'

'Guessed what?'

'I'm not a eunuch!' Chryses took off his turban and shook out his silky brown hair. 'I'm a girl.'

Seth stared in open-mouthed astonishment.

'You're a what?'

'A girl. All those years I've been pretending to be a eunuch so that I could be a scribe in the Great Library.'

The two scribes stood only a handsbreadth apart, Seth a head taller than Chryses.

'Great Juno's peacock!' gasped Flavia, looking at her friends. 'Chryses is a girl! How could Seth not know that?'

'Chryses is a girl?' echoed Jonathan, in disbelief.

Nubia nodded. 'I was knowing this.'

Lupus nodded and pointed at himself.

'How did you know?' asked Flavia.

Lupus imitated a girl's graceful walk.

Nubia giggled and nodded. 'Sometimes she forgets to stomp. Also, she does not have the bump here at front of her throat. And,' concluded Nubia. 'I peeked one day when she was doing latrine.'

'How could he not have known?' repeated Jonathan. 'She's beautiful.'

Lupus elbowed Jonathan in the ribs and gave him a grin.

Jonathan scowled down at his friend. 'I'm just stating a fact,' he said defensively.

Seth was gazing at Chryses. A look of wonder had spread across his face. 'Then my dreams . . .? You weren't trying to bewitch me?'

'Dreams? You had dreams about me?'

Seth nodded, dumbly.

'You should have trusted them, you silly fool.'

'But I thought you were . . .'

'Idiot!' she rebuked him gently.

'Cat worshipper!' growled Seth.

'Seth animal!' hissed Chryses.

'Mosquito!'

'Spouter of water!'

Suddenly they were in each other's arms, kissing passionately.

The four friends stared in open-mouthed astonishment.

Presently, Seth and Chryses drew apart.

'Disgraceful!' grumbled Seth. 'Such a public display of affection!'

'I'm surprised your god didn't strike you down!'

'Why did you kiss me?'

'Why did I kiss *you*? You kissed me!'

'I did not!'

'You did, too!'

And suddenly they were kissing again.

Lupus mimed being sick.

Jonathan raised an eyebrow and grinned. 'These Egyptians are crazy.' After a while he added, 'This could go on for some time.'

Flavia laughed and caught Nubia's hand. 'Let's go back to the boat. We have lots to tell you,' she added, as they started towards the riverbank.

'And I have much to tell you,' said Nubia.

'Where's our boat?' exclaimed Jonathan. 'Where's the *Scarab?*'

Lupus grunted and pointed.

'It's in the shadow of that huge barge,' said Jonathan, 'which will probably crush it in a moment.'

'Oh, isn't it beautiful!' exclaimed Flavia. 'It's painted with lotus blossoms and papyrus and it has a cabin with latticework windows and a palm leaf top where you could rest in the shade.'

'And look!' said Jonathan, pointing. 'There's a man at the very back cooking a meal.' His stomach rumbled. 'It smells delicious.'

'That's the way to travel,' said Flavia with a sigh. Lupus nodded his agreement.

'And that's the way we shall travel,' said a voice behind them.

The four friends turned to look at Chryses in amazement. She was holding hands with Seth.

'That barge is yours?' said Seth, staring.

'Yes, it belongs to me,' she said. 'And in a week or so, when the Nile begins to flood, we shall all travel back to Alexandria in style.'

'That barge belongs to you?' repeated Seth.

'Yes! My grandfather said all I had to do to claim it was to turn up with the papers.' She reached into the neck of her tunic and a moment later brought forth a folded piece of papyrus.

'The treasure map!' cried Jonathan.

'It's actually a map of how to get here with a deed for the barge on the back,' said Chryses.

'Does that mean there is no fabulous treasure?' said Flavia. 'No countless gold of Ophir and of Cush?'

'My name is Chrysis,' said the girl with a shrug and a smile. 'Chrysis means "a vessel of gold".'

'Then you're the treasure?' breathed Flavia.

'If Seth wants me, I'm his.'

Nubia frowned. 'You were not being rich lady's slave?' she asked. 'Rich lady who is eaten by crocodiles?'

Chrysis laughed and shook her head. 'I'm quite a good storyteller, aren't I?'

'And you are not afraid of crocodiles?' said Nubia.

'Of course I am. I'd be a fool if I wasn't!'

'And you're rich?' said Jonathan.

'Yes,' purred Chrysis. 'Grandfather has built me a little house in Rhakotis with an inner garden and balcony overlooking the canal and a shop front. I will copy and sell scrolls. It will be my own bookshop.'

'But if you're rich, then why did you lead us on this wild-ibis chase?' asked Jonathan.

'For a wager.'

'For a wager?' croaked Seth.

Chrysis smiled up at him. 'Grandfather said he didn't think you had the backbone to be my husband. I thought you did. He said that although you were eighteen, you had never set foot outside the walls of Alexandria. So I said: If I can get Seth to travel seven hundred miles up the Nile to claim me, then can I marry him?'

Jonathan raised his eyebrows. 'And he said yes?'

'He said yes.'

'But who in Hades is your grandfather?' said Seth.

'Oh!' cried Flavia, and began to jump up and down. 'I know! I know!'

Lupus nodded, too, and winked at Flavia.

'Oh,' said Jonathan. 'Of course!'

'Who?' yelped Seth, looking from one to the other. 'Who's her grandfather?'

'Philologus!' cried Flavia and Jonathan together, as Lupus mimed the chief scribe hobbling along on his walking stick.

Chrysis grinned at Seth. 'You have some very clever friends,' she said, and kissed him on the cheek. 'Grandfather even helped me make up some of the riddles and puzzles for the journey.'

'Of course!' cried Seth, hitting his forehead with the heel of his hand. 'That's what he meant when he said there were no rules to the game. I thought at the time it was a strange thing to say.' He stared at Chrysis. 'But you could have been killed!' he said. 'Hippos, crocodiles, scorpions, desert heat, ducks . . .'

Chrysis laughed. 'And you can't die in the city? Fevers, brigands, slipping on the stairs and breaking your neck . . .'

'Yes,' said Seth. 'I've been meaning to ask you about Onesimus. Did he really slip or was he pushed?'

'Of course he slipped!' cried Chrysis. 'I would never hurt him. If anything, his death was your fault!'

'*My* fault?'

'Yes. I told Onesimus I loved *you*, and not him. He ran away in tears. That's when he slipped and fell.'

'Did he know you were a girl?'

'Does it matter?'

'No, I suppose it doesn't. You told him you loved me?'

'Of course I do, you fool!' Chrysis laughed and stroked his slim brown cheek. 'I loved you when you were pink and pudgy, and I love you even more now that you are brown and muscular. I knew you could do it.'

They kissed.

Seth pulled back and cleared his throat. 'You said something about marriage?'

Chrysis nodded. 'Don't you want to be a bookseller with me and raise lots of little scribes?'

Seth gave her his slow grin, then nodded. 'Yes,' he said huskily. 'I do.'

They kissed again.

Jonathan cleared his throat and gestured towards Nubia. 'What about her? Why did you take Nubia with you?'

Chrysis pulled back from Seth. 'I was walking on the beach of the eastern necropolis one morning and there she was, dripping with salt water and tears. *The daughter of mighty Proteus, Old Man of the Sea, met me as I walked alone along the strand . . .*' quoted Chrysis. 'When I found out she wanted to return to the Land of Nubia and that she had skill with camels, I decided to put my plan into action immediately. It was as if the gods had brought us together.'

'God,' said Seth. 'Not gods. *Hear O Israel, the Lord our God is one.* If we are to marry you must convert to my religion.'

Chrysis gazed tenderly up at him. 'Of course I will,' she said, and whispered: 'Speak my name, and I shall live forever.'

'Chrysis,' he whispered. 'My golden one.'

Jonathan looked at his friends and grinned. 'These Egyptians are crazy.'

SCROLL XXXVI

The annual flood of the Nile had begun and was carrying the painted barge away from the island of Elephantine, towards Alexandria.

Nubia waved goodbye to the Nubians from the village. Kashta was not among them. It made her heart sad, but she understood. She had changed so much.

'Look!' said Flavia beside her. 'There on the right bank. That strange bird with the long curved beak.'

'That's an ibis,' said Chrysis, who stood on the other side of Nubia. She looked cool and elegant in a green silk shift. Golden bangles clinked on her arms and her straight silky brown hair just brushed her smooth shoulders. 'The ibis comes with the flood.'

'It looks as if it's writing something in the water,' said Flavia.

'Yes,' agreed Jonathan, 'using its beak as a pen.'

Lupus held up his bronze stylus.

'Or stylus,' added Nubia.

Chrysis laughed and turned to the four friends. 'Now you know why the Egyptians gave the scribe god Thoth the head of an ibis.'

'Of course!' breathed Flavia.

'That ibis looks so scholarly,' said Chrysis, and sighed. 'He reminds me of my dear old grandfather. I wouldn't

232

have been able to stay in the Library for five years without his help,' she said. 'But binding my chest became such a chore and we both knew I couldn't keep up the pretence much longer.'

Nubia looked at Chrysis. 'How long do you think it will take us to get to Alexandria?'

'Three weeks if the gods favour us,' said Chrysis, then corrected herself as two young men came to stand beside them at the rail. 'If *the Lord* favours us.'

Nubia glanced at Seth and Nathan. Nathan had arrived back from Apollonospolis subdued but happy, his mission accomplished. He had convinced the authorities they were dead and no longer a threat. It meant they would have to return to Italia incognito, but at least they were safe for the time being.

Standing beside his cousin, Seth looked handsome in a dark blue linen tunic and a black turban. 'You know,' he said, 'I'm glad I came on this wild-ibis chase. I learned something important.'

'What?' asked Chrysis, gazing up at him adoringly.

'God's instruction, his Torah, is not only written in scrolls. It is also written in the world around us.'

'And a wonderful world it is,' sighed Chrysis, catching his hand.

'You, my cousin,' said Nathan, 'are a very lucky man. You have found something much better than all the gold in Ophir.'

'I know,' said Seth, and kissed the top of Chrysis's head.

'I have a big question for you, Chrysis,' said Flavia. 'And because it's my birthday today, I'm going to ask it.'

'Flavia!' cried Seth. 'Is today your birthday?'

'Ooops!' said Jonathan. Lupus gave a comical grimace.

'Oh, why didn't you tell me?' Chrysis gave Seth a mock slap on the wrist. 'Bad Seth-dog!'

'Bad pussycat!' he growled back.

'*I* remember today is your birthday,' said Nubia. She reached into her belt-pouch. 'It is just something very little.'

'Oh, Nubia!' cried Flavia. 'You remembered!' She looked at the boys. 'THAT is friendship,' she said. 'THAT is why I came seven hundred miles to find her.'

'So did we!' said Jonathan, in an injured tone, and added, 'What is it?'

'It's a little faience scarab beetle,' said Flavia. 'It's lovely.'

'When we get back to Alexandria,' said Nubia. 'I will buy you chain for it.'

'No!' cried Jonathan. 'Lupus and I will buy the chain, won't we Lupus?'

Lupus shrugged; then he gave Flavia a mischievous grin.

'What was your question?' Chrysis asked Flavia.

'Excuse me if this is rude,' said Flavia. 'But I wanted to know why you pretended to be a eunuch.'

'I've been wondering that, too,' said Nathan.

'Ever since I was little,' said Chrysis, 'I wanted to be a scribe in the Great Library like my grandfather. I nagged Grandfather from the age of seven. Finally, on my thirteenth birthday, he said I could become a scribe, but that I had to pretend to be a eunuch.'

'Hmmph!' said Seth. 'It's an abomination.'

Chrysis stared at him in mock horror. 'You enormous hypocrite! I hear YOU dressed up as a Greek matron!'

'Twice,' said Nathan. 'He pretended to be a woman twice.'

Seth shrugged and gave her a sheepish grin.

'And he also pretended to be an Egyptian boatman,' said Jonathan. 'He was so funny! Listen: *I've come from vithiting my thick thithter in Diothpolith!*'

Nubia giggled and Lupus guffawed.

Flavia pointed at Jonathan. '*A thcorpion thtung your ear!*'

All four friends laughed, Seth and Nathan, too.

'*I'm going to Theebth!*' added Jonathan. Lupus fell laughing onto the polished deck and kicked his feet in the air.

'Master of the Universe,' exclaimed Chrysis, rolling her eyes. She turned to Nubia. 'Stop this silliness and play us your new song. Come, let us sit on the divan.'

'A new song?' cried Flavia, clapping her hands. 'Oh, Nubia! Play it for us.'

'Yes, play it,' said Seth with a wink at Chrysis.

They all moved to sit on the striped silk divan which formed a semi-circle at the prow of the barge.

'Wait!' cried Flavia, when they were all seated. 'What's your song called?'

Nubia smiled and lifted her Egyptian reed flute to her lips. 'My song is called *Going Home*.'

And she began to play.

FINIS

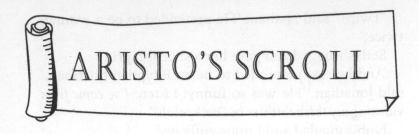
ARISTO'S SCROLL

Acanthus (uh-*kan*-thuss)
(modern Dahshur) ancient city with pyramids on the west bank of the Nile; it got its name from a sacred enclosure of acanthus plants

Achilles (uh-*kill*-eez)
Greek hero: a fast runner and the greatest warrior of the Trojan War

Aesculapius (eye-*skew*-lape-ee-uss)
Greek Asklepios: he was the god of healing with a large sanctuary at Epidauros in Greece and another on the Tiber Island in Rome

Aethiopia (eye-thee-*oh*-pee-uh)
not modern Ethiopia, but the Roman term for the extreme southeastern region of the world; this included the Land of Nubia

Africa
the Roman term for the coastal strip of North Africa, divided into five Roman provinces; from west to east: Mauretania Tingitana, Mauretania Caesariensis, Africa Proconsularis, Cyrenaica and Egypt

Alexander the Great
(356–323 BC) Greek ruler from Macedonia in Northern Greece who conquered most of the known world by

the age of thirty-two and founded the city of Alexandria

Alexandria (al-ex-*an*-dree-uh)
Egypt's great port, at the mouth of the Nile Delta, founded by Alexander the Great circa 331 BC; by the first century AD it was second only to Rome in wealth, fame and importance

alpha (*al*-fuh)
first letter of the Greek alphabet; also the name of one of the districts of Alexandria; N.B. I have guessed the location of this district for the map

Ammon (*am*-on)
sometimes spelled Amun: Egyptian god of air who later merged with Zeus to become an oracle god; often shown bearded and with rams' horns, his main sanctuary in the Ptolemaic and Roman times was at the oasis of Siwa

amphitheatre (*am*-fee-theatre)
oval-shaped stadium for watching gladiator shows, beast fights and the execution of criminals

ankh (onckh)
famous Egyptian symbol for 'life'; it resembles a cross with a loop at the top

Antirrhodos (an-tee-*ro*-doce)
small island in the Great Harbour of Alexandria

Antonius (see Marcus Antonius)

Anubis (an-*oo*-bis)
jackal-headed Egyptian god, he is associated with death and mummification

Apis (*ap*-iss)
important Egyptian bull-god, usually pictured as bull with sun disc between horns

Apollonospolis (apollo-*noss*-po-liss)
(modern Edfu), a site on the west bank of the Nile with a famous Ptolemaic temple to Horus

Aramaic (air-uh-*may*-ik)
closely related to Hebrew, it was the common language of first century Jews

Arsinoe (ar-*sin*-oh-eh)
name of a city and nome (regional district) in ancient Egypt; Arsinoe was a popular Ptolemaic girl's name, like Berenice and Cleopatra

atrium (*eh*-tree-um)
the reception room in larger Roman homes, often with skylight and pool

Augustus (awe-*guss*-tuss) AKA Octavian Augustus
(63 BC–AD 14) Julius Caesar's adopted grand-nephew and first emperor of Rome; he defeated Marcus Antonius and Cleopatra

beta (*bay*-tuh)
second letter of the Greek alphabet and name of one of the districts of Alexandria; N.B. I have guessed the location of this district for the map

bows (rhymes with 'cows')
the front end of a boat or ship

brazier (*bray*-zyur)
coal-filled metal bowl on legs

Brucheion (broo-*kay*-on)
the Royal district of Alexandria, where most of the Greeks lived, possibly another name for the Beta District

Caene (*kai*-nay)
Greek name for Qena, the great bend in the river Nile just north of Thebes (Luxor)

Caesarium (kie-*zar*-ee-um)

a magnificent monument in Alexandria; it was begun by Cleopatra in honour of Marcus Antonius, then finished by Octavian in honour of himself

Canopic Way (kan-*oh*-pik way)

road from Canopus to Alexandria and the main east-west thoroughfare in that city

Canopus (kan-*oh*-puss)

town to the east of Alexandria; it was notorious among Romans for its corruption, especially in the first century AD (when this story is set)

Capitolium (kap-it-*toll*-ee-um)

temple of Jupiter, Juno and Minerva, usually located in the forum of a town

carnelian (kar-*neel*-yun)

semi-precious stone; very popular in Roman times for signet-rings; ranges in colour from orange to reddish brown, most often apricot coloured

Castor (*kas*-tor)

one of the famous twins of Greek mythology (Pollux being the other)

cataract (*kat*-uh-rakt)

from Greek 'down rushing', the part of a river where it changes level; Egypt's so-called first cataract was located at Syene (Aswan)

cella (*sell*-uh)

innermost room of a temple, where the statue of the god usually stands

Cheops (*kee*-ops)

Greek version of the name Khufu; a pharaoh from Egypt's Old Kingdom and builder of the Great pyramid at Giza

chlamys (*khlam*-iss)

rectangular Greek cloak, usually pinned on the right shoulder

chryselephantine (kris-el-uh-*fan*-teen)

Greek word meaning 'made of gold and ivory'

Chryses (*kry*-sayz)

Greek name meaning 'golden'; it was the name of a priest of Apollo in Homer's *Iliad*

Chrysis (kry-*seess*)

Greek girl's name meaning 'golden'; it was the name of the daughter of a priest of Apollo in Homer's *Iliad*

Cibotus (kib-*oh*-tuss)

Greek for 'box' or 'ark'; name of the man-made harbour which was part of Alexandria's larger western harbour, Eunostus

Circus Maximus

famous racecourse for chariots, located in Rome near the imperial palace

Cleopatra (klee-oh-*pat*-ra)

(69–30 BC) Cleopatra VII was the Greek ruler of Egypt during part of the first century BC; her royal palace was in Alexandria

codex (*koh*-dex)

the ancient version of a book, usually made with papyrus or parchment pages; plural is 'codices'

colonnade (kall-a-*nade*)

a covered walkway lined with columns

Colossi of Memnon (ko-*loss*-ee of *mem*-non)

twin seated statues of Amenhotep III at Luxor; in Roman times they were thought to represent Memnon, a mythical hero of the Trojan War

Corinth (*kore*-inth)

prosperous Greek port and capital of the Roman province of Achaea

cornucopia (kor-noo-*ko*-pee-uh)

Latin for 'horn of plenty', a cone-shaped basket with fruit tumbling out; it represented bounty

Crocodilopolis (krok-oh-di-*lop*-oh-liss)

literally 'City of Crocodiles'; at least two cities on the Nile had this name

cuirass (*kweer*-ass)

from the Latin *corium* 'leather'; a breastplate worn by ancient soldiers

Cush (kush)

also spelled 'Kush'; one of the ancient names for Nubia, modern Sudan

Cynopolis (kine-*op*-oh-liss)

literally 'City of Dogs'; a city on the west bank of the Nile with a sanctuary to Anubis

dactylic hexameter (dak-*til*-ik hecks-*am*-it-ur)

a form of meter in poetry, used in the epics of Homer and Virgil

delta (*del*-tuh)

fourth letter of the Greek alphabet; it is the name given to the Jewish Quarter of Alexandria; N.B. unlike the other districts, we think we know its location

The Delta

name given to Lower Egypt because the mouth of the Nile resembles the capital Greek letter delta

Demotic (d'-*ma*-tik)

Egyptian language and also the script which developed from hieroglyphic scripts

Dido (*die*-doh)

Mythical Queen of Carthage who features in Virgil's *Aeneid*

Dinocrates (die-*nok*-ra-teez)

architect from Rhodes who helped Alexander the Great design Alexandria circa 331 BC

Dionysus (dye-oh-*nie*-suss)

Greek god of vineyards and wine; he was a favourite of Marcus Antonius

Diospolis (dee-*oss*-po-liss)

literally 'City of Zeus'; another name for Thebes (modern Luxor)

Diospolis Parva (dee-*oss*-po-liss *par*-vuh)

(modern Hiw), a site on the west bank of the Nile on the Caene Bend; it was called parva (little) to distinguish it from Diospolis (Thebes)

dom-fruit

fruit from the dom palm, a type of palm that used to grow in Upper Egypt and Nubia

Domitian (duh-*mish*-un)

the Emperor Titus's younger brother, and officially his co-regent

drachma (*drak*-ma)

(plural: drachmae) a silver coin roughly equal in value to a sestertius, it was the main unit of currency in Roman Egypt

ehem! (eh-*hem*)

Latin exclamation, meaning 'Well, well!'

Elephantine (el-uh-fan-*tee*-nay)

island in the River Nile at Syene (Aswan) just before the first cataract

Ephesus (*eff*-ess-iss)
important town in the Roman province of Asia (modern Turkey)
Epidauros (ep-id-*ow*-ross)
Greek site of a sanctuary to Aesculapius, the healing god
epsilon (*ep*-sill-on)
fifth letter of the Greek alphabet and name of one of Alexandria's districts; N.B. we do not know the location of this district
Etesian (ee-*tee*-zhyun)
Greek for 'yearly': the name of a strong dry trade wind in the Mediterranean; blowing in summer from the northwest, it cooled the streets of Alexandria and enabled boats to sail up the Nile
euge! (*oh*-gay)
Latin exclamation: 'hurray!'
Eunostus (yoo-*noss*-tuss)
Greek for 'safe return' and the name of Alexandria's natural western harbour
eunuch (*yoo*-nuk)
a boy or man whose physical development has been halted by castration
exedra (ek-*zeed*-ra)
semicircular seating area, like a small theatre, usually for talks and lectures
Fayum (*fie*-yoom)
fertile lakeside region in Egypt which had a thriving population in ancient times; many famous Roman 'mummy portraits' come from this region
festina lente (fess-*tee*-nuh *lent*-eh)
a famous Latin saying: 'hurry slowly', in other words 'quickly but carefully'

Flavia (*flay*-vee-uh)
>a name, meaning 'fair-haired'; Flavius is the masculine form of this name

gamma (*gam*-uh)
>third letter of the Greek alphabet and name of one of Alexandria's districts; N.B. I have guessed the location of this district for the map

Geb (geb)
>Egyptian god of the Earth; his hieroglyph was the goose and he was sometimes called the Great Cackler

gladiator (*glad*-ee-ate-or)
>man trained to fight other men in the arena, sometimes to the death

gratis (*grat*-iss)
>Latin for 'free' or 'no charge'

Hades (*hay*-deez)
>Greek word for the land of the dead; also the name of the god of the dead

hallelujah (hal-eh-*loo*-ya)
>Hebrew for 'praise the lord'

Haroeris (har-oh-*air*-iss)
>Egyptian god Horus in the aspect of a wise god who heals

Helios (*heel*-ee-oss)
>Greek for 'sun'

Heptastadium (hep-ta-*stade*-ee-um)
>Greek for 'seven stades'; the causeway and aqueduct leading from mainland Alexandria to the island called Pharos; it divided Alexandria's two great harbours, but ships could pass beneath it

Hercules (*her*-kyoo-leez)
>very popular Roman demi-god, the equivalent of Greek Herakles

Hermes (*her*-meez)

Greek god of travel, commerce and messages; he is the equivalent to the Roman god Mercury and shares characteristics with the Egyptian god Thoth

Hermonthis (her-*mon*-thiss)

(modern Armant) a town on the west bank of the Nile about 12 miles south of Thebes (Luxor)

Hermopolis (her-*mop*-oh-liss)

literally 'City of Hermes'; an Egyptian town on the west bank of the Nile with a Roman garrison and toll station, as well as a sanctuary to Thoth

Hero (*here*-oh)

Hero of Alexandria was a Greek mathematician who studied in the Museum in the first century AD; he invented the first recorded steam engine and other things

herpestes (her-*pest*-teez)

herpestes ichneumon is the Latin term for Egyptian mongoose

hieroglyph (*high*-ro-glif)

Greek for 'sacred carving'; the famous Egyptian 'picture writing'

Homer (*ho*-mer)

Greek poet who is credited with composing the *Iliad*; he lived about eight centuries before Christ

Horus (*hore*-uss)

Egyptian god of the sky, son of Isis and the resurrected Osiris; he is often shown as a baby in Isis' arms, a falcon, or a man with a falcon head

hypostyle (*high*-po-stile)

a space with a flat roof supported by pillars, usually in multiple rows

ichneumon (*ik*-noo-mon)

herpestes ichneumon is the Latin term for Egyptian mongoose

Ides (eyedz)

thirteenth day of most months in the Roman calendar; in March, May, July and October the Ides occur on the fifteenth day of the month

inundation (in-un-*day*-shun)

the yearly flood of the Nile (in the days before the Aswan dam)

Isis (*eye*-siss)

Egyptian goddess often shown with her baby son Horus and a sacred rattle, or sistrum; she was the sister of Osiris, Seth and Nephthys

Italia (it-*al*-ya)

Latin word for Italy, the famous boot-shaped peninsula

Juno (*joo*-no)

queen of the Roman gods and wife of the god Jupiter

Jupiter (*joo*-pit-er)

king of the Roman gods, husband of Juno and brother of Pluto and Neptune

Kalends

the Kalends mark the first day of the month in the Roman calendar

Khufu (*koo*-foo)

pharaoh credited with building the Great Pyramid of Giza; in Greek his name is Cheops

kohl (coal)

dark powder used to darken eyelids or outline eyes

kyria (*kir*-ya)

Greek for 'lady' or 'madam', the polite form of addressing a married woman

lapis lazuli (*lap*-iss *laz*-oo-lee)

a dark blue semi-precious stone much prized by the ancient Egyptians; this was what the ancient Romans called 'sapphire'

Library

the great library of Alexandria was probably part of the Museum

Lochias (*low*-kee-ass)

A promontory on the far east of Alexandria's Great Harbour, this is where the Ptolemaic royal palaces were located

Lower Egypt

the Delta and northern part of Egypt; its symbol was the bee

Lycopolis (lie-*kop*-oh-liss)

literally 'City of Wolves'; city on the west bank of the Nile which held the Egyptian jackal sacred

Macedonian (mass-uh-*doe*-nee-un)

anyone from the part of Northern Greece called Macedonia; Cleopatra's ancestors were from Macedonia, so she was Macedonian not Egyptian

mammon (*mam*-on)

Aramaic word for 'wealth'

Marcus Antonius (*mar*-kuss an-*tone*-ee-uss)

(82–30 BC) AKA Mark Anthony, a soldier and statesman who lived during the time of Julius Caesar; he was an enemy of Augustus and a lover of Cleopatra

Mareotis (merry-*oh*-tiss)

a huge lake just south of Alexandria

Mauretania Tingitana (more-uh-*tane*-ya tin-gee-*tah*-nah)

(modern Morocco) was the westernmost Roman

province of North Africa; one of its capitals was Volubilis

megillot (m'-*gill*-ot)
Hebrew for 'scrolls'; usually refers to five books of the Hebrew Bible which were grouped together: Song of Songs, Ruth, Lamentations, Ecclesiastes, Esther

Memnon (*mem*-non)
Mythological African warrior whose mother was the goddess of the dawn; the Colossi of Memnon did not depict him, but rather an Egyptian pharaoh

Memnonium (mem-*non*-ee-um)
term applied by the Greeks to the whole Theban necropolis in the Valley of the Kings: the so-called Colossi of Memnon were nearby

Menelaus (men-uh-*lay*-uss)
Mythical king of Sparta who fought with the Greeks against Troy; his sojourn in Egypt is related by Homer in the *Iliad* IV:351–397

modius (*mo*-dee-uss)
basket used for measuring grain

modus operandi (*mo*-duss op-er-*an*-dee)
Latin for 'way of operating' or 'method of doing something'

Moeris (mo-*eer*-is)
lake in the Fayum oasis, it was much bigger in Roman times than it is today

mulsum (*mull*-some)
wine sweetened with honey, often drunk before meals

Museum (myoo-*zee*-um)
shrine to the Muses in Alexandria; it had courtyards, lecture theatres, gardens, zoos, living quarters and half a million scrolls which comprised the Library

Naucratis (now-*kra*-tiss)

town on the Canopic branch of the Nile

Nephthys (*nef*-thiss)

goddess in Egyptian mythology, she was the sister of Isis, Osiris and Seth

Neptune (*nep*-tyoon)

god of the sea; his Greek equivalent is Poseidon

Nero (*near*-oh)

Emperor who ruled Rome from AD 54–AD 68

Nicopolis (nik-*op*-oh-liss)

town on the Egyptian coast between Canopus and Alexandria; it was founded to commemorate Octavian's victory over Marcus Antonius

Nile

The great river of Egypt, flowing 750 miles without obstruction from Syene (Aswan) to Alexandria; in ancient times it flooded every summer, bringing the silt and irrigation needed for the following year's harvest

nilometer (nile-*om*-it-ur)

a device for measuring the rise and fall of the waters of the Nile; on the island of Elephantine at Syene (Aswan) the nilometer was a flight of stairs with markings on the wall beside it but other nilometers were marked pillars

nome (nome)

administrative district of Egypt; there were twenty-two nomes in Upper Eygpt and twenty in Lower Egypt

Nones (nonz)

Seventh day of March, May, July, October; fifth day of all the other months

Nubia (*noo*-bee-uh)

Roman term for the area beyond the first cataract at Syene (Aswan); now known as Sudan, in Roman times it was also known as Cush or Aethiopia

Nut (noot)

Egyptian goddess of the sky and mother of Osiris, Isis, Seth and Nephthys

Octavian (see Augustus)

Oedipus (*ed*-ip-uss)

mythical Greek hero who successfully answered the Sphinx's riddle

ohe! (*oh*-hay)

Latin for 'whoa!'

Ombos (*om*-boss)

(modern Kom Ombo) town on the east bank of the Nile near Syene (Aswan); it was a stop on trade routes from Nubia and the east and had a famous temple dedicated to Sobek the crocodile god

Ophir (*oh*-feer)

a rich port mentioned in the Bible; scholars do not know its location

Osiris (oh-*sire*-iss)

Egyptian god of fertility and the underworld, after being murdered by his brother Seth, his sister/wife Isis resurrected him

Ostia (*oss*-tee-uh)

port about 16 miles southwest of Rome; Ostia is Flavia's home town

Oxyrhynchus (ocks-ee-*rink*-uss)

town in middle Egypt famous for a huge find of papyrus documents dating back to Ptolemaic and Roman times; its inhabitants worshipped the 'sharp-nosed' pike

palla (*pal*-uh)

a woman's cloak, could also be wrapped round the waist or worn over the head

Pan (pan)

Greek god of shepherds and wild places; he is half man, half goat

Paneum (pan-*nay*-um)

a conical hill in the centre of Alexandria; it was a shrine to the god Pan

pantomime (*pan*-toe-mime)

Roman theatrical performance in which a man (or sometimes woman) illustrated a sung story through dance; the dancer could also be called a 'pantomime'

papyrus (puh-*pie*-russ)

the cheapest writing material, made from pounded sedge of the same name

Paridis (pa-*ree*-deess)

Latin for 'of Paris' (genitive of the name Paris)

pater (*pa*-tare)

Latin for 'father'

patrician (pa-*trish*-un)

a person from the highest Roman social class

pavo (*pa*-vo)

Latin for 'peacock'

pedis (ped-iss)

Latin for 'louse' (singular of 'lice')

Pharos (*far*-oss)

Name of an island off the coast of Alexandria on which a massive lighthouse was built; people began to call the lighthouse 'pharos' too

Phoenician (fuh-*neesh*-un)

Semitic sea-people who established trading posts in

coastal positions all over the Mediterranean; they are described by the word Punic

Pillars of Hercules

(modern Straits of Gibraltar) the two rocky promontories which flank the entrance to the Mediterranean sea from the Atlantic Ocean

Plato (*play*-to)

(427–347 BC) famous Greek philosopher who wrote many dialogues including one called *The Republic*

Pliny (the Elder) (*plin*-ee)

(AD 23–79) Gaius Plinius Caecilius Secundus was a famous Roman author, admiral and naturalist; he died in the eruption of Vesuvius in AD 79

Pollux (*pol*-luks)

one of the famous twins of Greek mythology (Castor being the other)

Portus (*por*-tuss)

a large harbour a few miles north of Ostia's river mouth harbour; built by the Emperor Claudius, it was relatively new in Flavia's day

Poseidium (po-*side*-ee-um)

a temple to Neptune (Greek Poseidon) overlooking Alexandria's Great Harbour

province (*pra*-vince)

a division of the Roman Empire; in the first century AD senatorial provinces were governed by a proconsul appointed by the senate, imperial provinces were governed by a propraetor appointed by the Emperor

Ptolemaic (tall-eh-*may*-ik)

referring to the Greeks who ruled Egypt for three centuries after the death of Alexander the Great; they were mostly called Ptolemy

Ptolemy Soter (*tall*-eh-mee *so*-tare)

(367–283 BC) one of Alexander the Great's generals, he became the first Greek ruler of Egypt and the first of the Ptolemaic dynasty

pylon (*pie*-lon)

Greek for 'gateway'; this term is often applied to the entrances of Egyptian temples

Rhakotis (rah-*ko*-tiss)

a suburb of Alexandria; may have been the original fishing settlement

Rhodes (roads)

large island in the Aegean Sea and capital of the Roman province of Asia

Rhodopis (ro-*do*-piss)

an Egyptian princess from Naucratis, mentioned by Strabo

Sabbath (*sab*-uth)

the Jewish day of rest, counted from Friday evening to Saturday evening

Sabratha (sah-*brah*-tah)

town in the North African province of Africa Proconsularis (modern Libya)

scroll (skrole)

papyrus or parchment 'book', unrolled from side to side as it was read

Sedge (sej)

a large family of plants which usually grow in rivers or wetlands; papyrus is a type of sedge

Septuagint (*sept*-oo-uh-jint)

The Greek translation of the Hebrew Bible, composed in Alexandria sometime during the Ptolemaic period (first three centuries BC)

Serapeum (sir-a-*pay*-um)

Famous monumental temple in Alexandria to the god Serapis, there was an annex of the Library there; one of its columns still stands (confusingly called Pompey's Pillar)

Serapis (sir-*ap*-iss)

A made-up Graeco-Egyptian god; he had characteristics of the Egyptian bull-god Apis and of Osiris, and also of Hades, the Greek god of the underworld

sesterces (sess-*tur*-seez)

more than one sestertius, a brass coin; four sesterces equal a denarius

Seth AKA **Seti**

Egyptian god of chaos, confusion and the desert, sometimes shown as a man with the head of a Seth animal.

Seth animal

a made up hieroglyphic animal that represents chaos and confusion

signet-ring (*sig*-net ring)

ring with an image carved in it to be pressed into wax and used as a personal seal

Siwa (*see*-wa)

date palm oasis in the 'Libyan' desert: there was a sanctuary to the god Ammon there

Sobek (*so*-bek)

Egyptian god of crocodiles, sometimes shown as a man with the head of a Crocodile

sol (sole)

Latin for 'sun'

Soma (*so*-ma)

Greek for 'body', also the name of the building where Alexander's body was entombed

stade (*stayed*)

a measurement of distance: a stade is about 200 metres, making roughly eight to a mile

stern (rhymes with 'turn')

back of a ship; Roman ships often had a swan's neck ornament here

stola (*stole*-uh)

a long tunic worn by Roman matrons and respectable women

Strabo (*strah*-bow)

(c. 64 BC – c. AD 24) a Greek historian from Asia minor who is known for his *Geography*, which includes sections on Egypt and North Africa

stylus (*stile*-us)

metal, wood or ivory tool for writing on wax tablets

sun-bread

sourdough oven-baked bread

Syene (sigh-*ee*-nee)

(modern Aswan) city on the border of Egypt and Nubia, just downriver from the first cataract; there were granite quarries and Roman garrison here

tablinum (tab-*leen*-um)

room used as a study or office

tegula (*teg*-yoo-la)

Latin for 'roof-tile'

Tentyra (ten-*teer*-uh)

(modern Dendera) town on the west bank of the Nile whose inhabitants hated the crocodile

Tentyrites (ten-*teer*-rites)
men from Tyntyra; according to Strabo they were skilled crocodile hunters
terebinth (*tare*-uh-binth)
small tree of the cashew family which produces turpentine: in Roman times it was valued for its perfumed resin
testudo (tes-*too*-do)
Latin for 'tortoise'
tetradrachm (tet-ra-*drak*-m)
an Alexandrian tetradrachm was equal to four drachmae or one denarius
Thebes (theebz)
(modern Luxor) a major city on the east bank of the Nile and site of two important temples: Karnak and Luxor
Thoth (thoth)
Egyptian god of wisdom and scribes, sometimes shown as a man with an ibis head
tinea (*tin*-nay-uh)
Latin for 'bookworm'
Titus (*tie*-tuss)
Titus Flavius Vespasianus has been Emperor of Rome for almost two full years when this story takes place
Torah (*tor*-uh)
Hebrew word meaning 'law' or 'instruction'. It can refer to the first five books of the Bible or to the entire Hebrew Scriptures (Old Testament).
Tralles (*trah*-layz)
(modern Ayin) a town in Asia Minor (modern Turkey) east of Ephesus

tunic (*tew*-nic)
   piece of clothing like a big T-shirt; children often wore a long-sleeved one
tyche (*tie*-kee)
   Greek word for 'luck' or 'fortune'
Upper Egypt
   the southern part of Egypt; its symbol is the sedge plant
Venus (*vee*-nuss)
   Roman goddess of love, Aphrodite is her Greek equivalent
vigiles (*vij*-il-layz)
   watchmen – usually soldiers – who guarded the town against robbery and fire
Volubilis (vo-*loo*-bill-iss)
   town in the Roman province of Mauretania (modern Morocco)
votive (*vo*-tiv)
   an object offered to mark a vow, prayer or thanksgiving to some god
wax tablet
   wax-coated rectangular piece of wood used for making notes
Zeus (*zyooss*)
   king and greatest of the Greek gods; his Roman equivalent is Jupiter

THE LAST SCROLL

When most people think of ancient Egypt, they think of pyramids, mummies and pharaohs. But the dynasties of the pharaohs are only one part of that country's history. Alexander the Great founded the capital of his empire there shortly before his death. His Greek successors, the Ptolemies, ruled Egypt for 300 years. After the fall of Cleopatra in 30 BC, the Romans made Egypt a province.

Roman Egypt became the main supplier of the grain for Italy, and as grain ships traveled back and forth, so did people. Some Romans began to worship Egyptian gods and goddesses like Serapis and Isis, and in the Flavian period there was a vogue for Egyptian songs and dances in Rome. However, even under Roman rule, Greek rather than Latin remained the language of Alexandria and Egypt.

In the first century AD, Alexandria was one of the most important cities in the Roman Empire, second only to Rome. Whereas Rome had grown up as a collection of crooked streets around seven small hills, Alexandria was planned from the start. Its wide streets were laid out on a grid pattern designed to catch the cooling Etesian breeze. It boasted one of the Seven Sights of the ancient world, the great lighthouse, but also had world-famous buildings such as the Museum, the Serapeum, the Caesarium and the Soma, where Alexander's body was on show in a clear sarcophagus. Alexandria had a freshwater lake and five sea harbours to cope with the huge volume of trade that passed through it. Impressive underground cisterns supplied water to almost every house in the ancient city.

A visitor to Roman Alexandria would have seen people from all nations and genders, including eunuchs. A eunuch is a man who has had his genitals partly cut or completely removed. This was often done to boys so that they never developed as men but remained 'a third sex', something between a man and a woman. Such men were usually slaves, and were employed in various different capacities in the ancient world. Like gladiators, eunuchs were often desired and despised at the same time. Some men even castrated themselves in a religious frenzy, especially those who worshipped the Eastern goddess Cybele.

Towns along the River Nile really did worship particular animals. The town of Oxyrhynchus, named after the 'sharp-nosed' pike, was one of them. So was Cynopolis, a city which venerated dogs. History records bitter rivalries between the citizens of different animal-worshipping towns, sometimes leading to riots and death. At Crocodilopolis near Fayum there was a bejewelled crocodile, and boy acrobats did handstands on its back.

Ancient Greek and Roman tourists went to Egypt, just as we do today. They marvelled at the great Pharos, visited the pyramids and turned up at dawn to hear the Colossi of Memnon 'sing'. And, just like many modern tourists, they left graffiti on the monuments they visited.

CAROLINE LAWRENCE

Caroline Lawrence is American. She grew up in California and came to England when she won a scholarship to Cambridge to study Classical Archaeology. She lives by the river in London with her husband, a writer and graphic designer. In 2009, Caroline was awarded the Classics Association Prize for 'a significant contribution to the public understanding of Classics'.

She also writes *The Roman Mystery Scrolls* – a hilarious and action-packed series of shorter mysteries featuring Threptus, a former beggar boy turned apprentice to a Roman soothsayer.

And don't miss Caroline's whip-cracking new series, *The P.K. Pinkerton Mysteries*, set in America's Wild West and starring Virginia City's newest detective, P.K. Pinkerton, as he fights crime against a backdrop of gamblers, gun-slingers and deadly desperados!

Choose one of the twin portals on Caroline's website www.carolinelawrence.com to enter
Ancient Rome www.romanmysteries.com
The Wild West www.pkpinkerton.com